BOMBYX BIOGRAPHIES

MICHELLE MANNISTO

BOOK 1

BookJourney

Book Journey Publishing

TABLE OF CONTENTS

PROLOGUE

Running as fast as she possibly could, the twelve-year-old girl panted as she raced down the road. With a stolen sword in her blood-speckled hand, she looked back, her brown bangs partially blocking her view.

The man was right behind her. His face was contorted with pain as he grasped his gashed arm, spreading the hot liquid that had turned his black, long-sleeve shirt into a deep crimson.

She looked down at the sword in her grasp, saw the red liquid still dripping off, and smiled in remembrance of how she had stolen the man's sword, cut his arm with it, and escaped when his triumphant victory was evident, and her escape was nigh to impossible. All she needed to do to complete her escape was get to the old, burned-out building, which was only two blocks ahead. The world was a blur around her as she hastened her sprint, but, as she turned right at the end of the street, she quickly remembered that she had to turn left instead of right at the old brick building with the graffiti words "Old School" on its side for to the right was a dead end.

She turned on her heel and sped toward the entrance, but in her way stood the man.

He was dressed completely in black with 'D-A-M-L' plastered on the front of his bulletproof vest. The man raised his long, slender knife and snarled. His arm bled heavier with each passing second for, as his emotions rose, his heart rate quickened.

Thunder boomed above them, and a lightning bolt streaked across the darkening sky, threatening to start a downpour.

Raising her knife, she charged first, letting out a battle cry. The clang of steel-hitting-steel echoed through the narrow alley.

The man's breath heaved hot and heavy, and his brow wrinkled with pain and frustration, undoubtedly because he hadn't been able to complete his mission in killing a pathetic twelve-year-old. Determined, the man pushed hard against her blade, forcing it back toward her already scarred throat.

Remembering the cold steel cutting into her delicate skin, she shoved her heel into his knee.

He let out a stifled cry as he collapsed on the ground.

She held her sword to the side of his neck.

If she sliced his jugular artery, the man's chances of survival would be slim.

The girl hesitated in cutting the bristled skin of the strange man who tried to kill her, and the man took advantage of her hesitation and thrust at her heart.

The blow knocked her sword away, but the girl unsheathed her knife and took the final thrust.

The man struggled on the ground for a bit, grasping his neck, but quickly expired.

The girl wiped her blade clean of the mix of sticky, red

liquid and salty tears. She was a killer, and she could not deny it. Nevertheless, she knew this would keep her enemies at bay for a while. After taking a scrap of paper and a pencil from her school bag, she scribbled down a message and stuck it in the body's black shirt. Shaking her head with grief, she ran back down the alleyway.

———◆———

Later that day, a man in a black suit walked up to the body and noticed the white notebook paper sticking out of the back of the shirt. He picked it up and read, "It has begun." The suited man crumpled up the paper and threw it on the ground. "Yes, it has."

CHAPTER 1

Mr. Hyle the Anaconda

I ran my hand over the rotted, charred doorway of the burned-out building that I once knew as home. The enormous wooden doors were splintered and burned into black ashes. Five windows that once brightened the smoky, dark building lay shattered in hundreds of dulled shards on the ground beneath. Still, the smell of smoke wafted through the breeze as well as the smell of death and freshly spilled blood; the blood of those I cared about... and my own.

Memories of pain flooded in: the look of horror on a twelve-year-old boy's face; the pain of cold, hard metal entering my stomach; and the tears of sadness, agony, and—worst of all—heartbreak. *I will see you again, Dĭcărĕ, I will keep my Promise. I will help you escape.* The tears welled up in my eyes as I thought of that Promise. For a long while, I had prepared for the day I would set out to keep that accursed oath, but that day had not yet come. That, I had to admit, was mostly of my conscience's doing, since the task ahead of me wasn't exactly good.

Every single day since that ill-fated evening, I thought about Dīcărĕ, his older brother Frŏns, and his father, whom he insisted we call Pătĕr. They were so important to me that it almost killed me to recall that the latter two had been dead and the foremost had been gone for at least two years. Whenever I thought of Dīcărĕ, all kinds of things popped into my head, including him spending those two years in a detainment cell, in serious pain, in worry and loneliness, or all the above! I hoped that maybe one day I'd see him again.

When I'm strong enough, when I know enough, and when I'm skilled enough, I'll get him back. I promise. "You hear that you evil, kidnapping, murdering, lying, deserving-of-a-stab Damsels? I'll get him back, and by the time he's recovered, you'll all be dead! Dead! You hear me!" I yelled, and a nearby Wetly Pigeon startled, flying into the overcast, lavender sky. I let the tears fall as I collapsed onto my knees. "I'll get you all, every last one of you. I promise… I promise."

Wiping tears away, I stood and walked back down the dirty, sewage-filled road to my school, the Wetly Kindergarten through High School for Needy Children. My dad had thought I was needy enough for that school full of weirdoes but not needy enough to remain in his care, since he abandoned me on the side of the road after enrolling me. Nice dad, huh?

The November breeze blew down from the mountain, chilling my face and turning my cheeks rosy pink. Within seconds, a torrential downpour soaked me to the bone, and I quickened my pace. As I passed by the worn, graffiti-covered brick buildings, men in black jackets and loose jeans stared at me from their filthy doorways with the look of mutual respect I had earned years before mixed with a look of pity. Being caught out in the open in a Wetly storm is a cause of pity for all who are native to the town.

At the end of the street, I heard a woman scream from inside the corner house. It was the lair of Breaker, a trigger-happy drug dealer. I shook my head with disgust and carried on. The first rule you learn in the streets of Wetly: never stick your nose in someone else's business unless you want it blown off by a bullet the size of your pinky, along with the rest of your head. Let's just say that if you looksee, you're dead, see?

As I came to the entrance of the school and entered, I sighed with contempt at the cursed place. Trotting down the hallway, I heard a familiar, somewhat-masculine voice calling me.

"Yeah?" I turned around and recognized him. "Oh, hey Bartholomew. How's it goin'?" I asked drolly. He was my best and only friend, and every time we'd see each other, we'd say the same thing. I'd ask him how he's doing, and he'd say, "Fine."

"I should be the one asking that!" he exclaimed to my surprise. "I heard that your dad showed up and asked you to live with him and his girlfriend." His little-bit-shorter-than-shoulder-length, dark brown hair was flattened to the point on which he couldn't see out of his wide eyes.

"Yeah, well, I don't believe in a boyfriend living with a girlfriend, so I don't want to get involved with that." I shrugged my shoulders and poked a lock of his hair. "Can you see out of that wet seaweed you call hair?"

He waved me off and grunted. "Yes, I can, actually, but that's beside the point. My mom and I wanted to know if you agreed."

I rolled my eyes. "Well, since you got no answer out of my previous reply, it would be a definite *no*."

Bartholomew shook his head. "Come on, Alaĕna, you could

die of the cold in that box. You know I would ask my mom if you could live with us, but, since my dad… well… you know…"

"…left," I blankly finished.

"Yeah… *that*," he crankily replied, crossing his arms over his narrow chest. "Well, money's been tight, *and* it would be awkward having an unrelated girl who's my age living with my mom and me."

We shivered at the grotesqueness of the thought.

He put a hand on my shoulder. I brushed him off and gave him a quick jab with my fist. "No touchy the arm-uh-y,"

He rolled his eyes, at least I think he did since the brown mop on his head didn't help much, and said in a sub-par facsimile of my voice, "Yeah, yeah, I know. No touchy my arm-y or you will pop my personal space bubble-y!"

"I don't seriously sound like that. Do I? It's hard for the owner of the voice to know what they actually sound like. Come on, Bartholomew, or we'll be late. You know what Mrs. Hyle will do to us if we're late." I shivered.

The boy sighed and brushed back his kelp-like hair. "Yeah, I guess you're right. I don't want to end up like Psycho Sarah or Perplexed Peppy, ooh, or even Bizarre Betsy. But this conversation is not over!"

I ignored him and pulled him toward our musty old classroom.

That classroom, which was one of only three rooms—a principal's office, a broom closet, and that school room—in that school, was the pride and joy of those brave enough to handle us kids. Those valiant souls rounded up to a whopping number of three:

Mrs. Hyle, our math, science, and society teacher. I did not like her. She was snooty and smelled like rotten fish tacos. Trust me when I say that since I've eaten them before. I was on the edge of death in the middle of winter, and that was the only thing available to eat.

Then, there's Mr. Hyle, or Principal Melancholy as the students called him. Yes, my principal and my teacher were married. That meant that I couldn't complain about Mrs. Hyle's behavior and get her fired. Well, possibly, if he was a good principal, but since he wasn't, I was out of luck.

Last, but not least, was Mr. Cĕtĕră. His full name was a practical joke: "Măgīstĕr Ĕt Cĕtĕră," which means "teacher and the rest". It explained him perfectly since he was my Latin and history teacher. Sometimes, he would bring me a cake on my birthday, but then Psycho Sarah would smash it into little pieces if I wasn't careful.

Lots of weird things happened at that school, such as the time that I accidentally turned Mrs. Hyle's worst student into a Wetly Pigeon since they're well known for being the most idiotic fowl in the world. I thought it was pretty funny. Luckily, the pigeon *mysteriously* changed back when he was sent home.

Other than those things, the school was just a place for weirdo kids to be dumped. Bartholomew and I were the only normal kids. Well, as normal as I knew of.

After Mrs. Hyle's class, we explored the mountains behind us, at least, until… the *fence*. To be precise, a ten-foot-tall stone wall. They weren't allowed to put barbed wire at the top because it was a hazard to us "precious darlings". Ha! Those impru-dent… um… I'll change the subject. Anyways, they, excluding Mr. Cĕtĕră, didn't care a wink about a single student at that school.

Almost every day, the kids dreamed of climbing the wall to freedom, and that day was not one of those days. After Mr. Cĕtĕră's class, we were unwillingly guided, or forced if you prefer, outside into the freezing rain by—you guessed it—Mrs.

Hyle! Too bad nobody could get her arrested for child abuse, because that would have totally made my day. Fortunately, there were canopy trees scattered everywhere, otherwise there would have been a lot of kid-popsicles that day, as well as many other days.

The ten-foot-tall canopy tree we sat under covered and sheltered us to a certain extent, but the cold, sharp icicles that dangled above our heads occasionally came screaming down from the heights, nearly impaling us.

"It is freezing!" Bartholomew declared, shivering at the cold and curling up into a tighter ball. "Are you trying to kill us?" he yelled at the school, shaking his fist. "I have to take care of my mom, you kid-killing monsters!"

Tragically for him, the principal heard him.

"Mr. Healdton, come here!" Mr. Hyle roared from his warm office on the left side of the old, cracked, brick building that was our pitiful school.

"Why don't you come out here and get him!" I snapped.

The response wasn't pretty and included a lot of swearing. So, I'll shorten his message to: "Ms. Bombyx, come here! And bring that"—I'll skip that word for, though he might enjoy using it, I certainly don't—"Mr. Healdton!" His voice boomed like thunder.

I wished to my lucky stars that it was just thunder, but my luck wasn't all that great that day, or any other day, for that matter.

"Sīs, Sīstă Plūī," I mumbled under my breath.

Bartholomew stepped out from underneath the tree and offered his hand to help me out of the mud pit I was sitting in. I took it, and he pulled me up. Expecting the hard, cold pellets of rain to begin hitting my head, I flinched but, when no watery bullets came, glanced up and realized that it wasn't raining.

"That's weird. Didn't you just say 'please, stop raining' in Latin?" Bartholomew stared at me a lot like Perplexed Peppy.

I nodded slowly. "Yes, um, that's weird." I scolded myself for the slip-up. *I have got to stop doing things like that; otherwise, it will be the Pigeon squabble all over again. Heh, Pigeon squabble.* "Uh, let's go." I pointed toward the building and started walking.

"Yeah, good idea!" He trotted briskly behind me, trying to keep up.

When we arrived in his mold-smelling office, the man waved off his wife. The room was about ten feet long and eleven feet wide with a window whose height was nigh to that of the walls, which were seven feet in height. Leaning forward in his swiveling plastic chair and placing his hands upon the seemingly ancient oak desk in front of him, he sternly commanded, "Come here." The dark-gray-haired man motioned for us to sit down on the two metal chairs.

I sat on the left since that was the seat that I sat on a lot. I wasn't an exemplary student with picking one too many fights, and the thing I did to that kid the one time—Pigeon Person— yeah, I got detention for a month because I was always the one to blame in that school.

"Yes, Principal Hyle, what is it this time? Detention for a year for me?" I asked, mockingly.

"Ms. Bombyx…" he began.

I abruptly cut him off. "Miss Alaĕna, if you would, Mr. Hyle. I don't let my father have the pleasure of having a descendant with his last name."

"Ms. Bombyx, Mr. Healdton," he said, ignoring my last comment, "you directly insulted the school and me. We do not harm you children in any way. This school has been kind to you, and so, for your disgrace and vile tongue, next term you will not be welcome here. I will inform your parents."

Ha, vile tongue. Look who's talking, Mr. Potty Mouth. "No parents for me, Principal Melancholy," I bluntly stated, "or Mr. Hyle." I smiled sweetly.

"I will call your father," he motioned to me, then to Bartholomew with his pale, skinny hand. "And your mother."

Bartholomew's eyes widened. "My mom?" His voice sounded shaky.

"Leave Bartholomew out of this!" I snapped defensively, trying to save Bartholomew from the heartache of telling his mom that he was expelled from the only free school in the area. His mother never finished school after having him at fifteen. All she wanted was for her son to have a chance for a good life outside of Wetly where he had enough sense to not be like his father or like herself. "I said it, not him. He has a life ahead of him and his mom to take care of, but I have nothing! Nothing! Expel me right now. Don't take this out on him." I rose from my chair and knocked it over with a loud clang.

"Ms. Bombyx, Mr. Healdton did a crime and must pay for it," Mr. Hyle replied unsympathetically.

My eyes narrowed, and I reached over to my right side where my knife was nestled.

The motion drew the attention of Mr. Hyle.

"He did not do a 'crime'. He stated the facts. And it's Miss Alaěna, Mr. Hyle, not Ms. Bombyx. You sent us out there to freeze to death! You're the one who did a crime! Ěs Sěrpěns! You are a dirty, rotten snake!" I cried, putting my whole heart into those Latin words. I squeezed my eyes shut and shook my head. *Oh great, not again.*

At that moment, the principal's body began to change. His torso lengthened, his arms melted into his sides, and his legs fused to make a tail. Scales grew all over his trunk-like body, his canine teeth grew into long fangs, and the rest of his teeth grew into backward-slanted, serrated points. The man's tongue turned red, shrinking in width and growing in length. The end split to create a fork. His head shrank and flattened, his eyes moved to the sides of his head, and his pupils turned to slits. He had become a full-grown, twelve-and-a-half-foot-long anaconda.

"Oh my… wow. He just turned into a snake! And you just said he was a snake!" Bartholomew cried.

Mrs. Hyle and Mr. Cĕtĕră came running into the room.

"Honey-kin!" the woman screamed, sprinting over to him.

He slithered through his empty shirt and jacket and over to her, his forked tongue flicking in and out.

Are you serious, honey-kin? I had to try really hard not to laugh.

Mr. Hyle the Anaconda turned to me, bared his fangs, and loudly hissed.

I slowly backed away.

Bartholomew stared at me. "Alaĕna, what did you just do?"

"I'm sorry. I didn't mean to Mrs. Hyle. I'm sorry." I pled, close to tears. *It's an improvement.*

She yelled and pointed her crooked finger at me. "You're a witch! One of those horrible *things.* You turned my husband into a snake! Please, somebody, call the police! *Help!*"

I spun around, looking for a way out.

Mrs. Hyle grabbed my arm and pulled me, screaming, "Police, help! She's a monster! She's going to kill me!"

I struggled to get free.

"Alaĕna, over here!"

I looked around to see Bartholomew standing next to Mr. Cĕtĕră. I punched Mrs. Hyle in the gut, and she released me, allowing me to sprint over to them.

"Mr. Cĕtĕră?" I said as we hastily ran from the musty room.

"I know you must be scared, but just know that you are a

Măgūs Lătīnūs, a Latin Magician. I will explain later. You're in danger. We must hurry!" Mr. Cĕtĕră urged us on.

"How on earth did you know that?"

He didn't respond.

We came to the entrance and crashed through. He guided us to his red '68 Chevy and told us to get in.

Bartholomew was the monkey-in-the-middle, and I got shotgun.

The man drove us half of a mile up the badly paved road and sighed. "I'm sorry I didn't tell you sooner, Alaĕna. I thought you could remain hidden until you were older, but your rambunctious attitude didn't help much."

"Well, sorry, he was asking for it," I blankly replied, shifting uncomfortably in my seat and tugging at my seatbelt. "And you didn't answer my question! How do you know so much?"

"Alaĕna, please, I can't explain it right now. We have to get you farther away. You are in danger here, and so is Bartholomew. All I can say is that you are… different. People don't understand your unique gift, and they want to exterminate anyone who has this gift."

I snorted a laughing sigh. "Oh great… how positively wonderful. I might as well go knock on Banana Bear's door."

Mr. Cĕtĕră sighed but remained silent.

Turning my head to the mud-covered window, I looked out at my rapidly changing surroundings. From my home of garbage-filled motor homes, graffiti-covered brick buildings, and brown grass to perfectly manicured mansions, painted wooden buildings, and perfectly cut grass, we traveled. Still, the rain poured down in a merciless torrent, hitting the roof of the truck like tiny bullets. *Tink, tink, tink, tink, tink, THUD!*

Suddenly, softball-sized hail fell from the sky, smashing cars into unrecognizable metal heaps.

Foreigners. I huffed.

The huge chunks of ice bounced off Mr. Cĕtĕră's truck. All Wetly natives had anything they held of value shatter and dent proof.

Mr. Cĕtĕră sighed. "Look, Alaëna, let's start this over. I'll tell you this: you are a very special girl with a very special ability. You can use Magic."

Rolling my eyes, I said, "Well, duh! Of course, I can. Mr. Hyle wouldn't be a snake if I wasn't able to use Magic. Another thing, why won't you answer my question?" My hands were in fists by this point.

The man sighed a bit more heftily. "Alaĕna, please. Wait until we're at least off the mountain road."

I grumbled but conceded. My chest burned hot, and my cheeks flushed. Thoughts raced through my head as the road began to incline into a portion of the road, which had a sheer drop-off to the right and a vertical rock wall to the left. *Why won't he answer the dumbfounded question? It seems easy enough. Maybe I should drop the subject. But, wait… What if something happened to him? What if he was threatened? What if it's a conspiracy? Everything's a conspiracy these days. My life is a conspiracy, for that matter.*

"Um, sorry to interrupt your, uh, anyways… What on earth happened back there! Mr. Hyle is a snake, and the police are going to catch us sooner or later, ask us questions, and probably arrest us! So, Mr. Cĕtĕră, what's going on?" Bartholomew asked, waving his arms around in what little space he had.

"Bartholomew, it's really complicated, and I didn't want you to get caught up in all of this… I truly didn't." A sadness filled Mr. Cĕtĕră's face as he said that, but it quickly disappeared when he swerved to the right to avoid a semitruck driver who was unknowingly switching lanes due to some severely cracked windows.

My stomach leaped into my throat as the driver accidentally floored the gas-filled semi off the side of the road and over the cliff. Bartholomew and I stared back and saw a huge explosion engulfing several large pine trees in a fiery inferno. We could feel the heat from inside the cab.

We sighed with relief when we saw that the semi driver had seen the cliff just in time to jump out of the vehicle, grab onto the railing, and then pull himself back onto the slick road. Unfortunately for the guy, he was forced to sprint across the dangerous highway to get to the safety of a lone pine tree anchored to the side of the road.

Mr. Cĕtĕră was oblivious to all of this.

After getting over the shock of the event that had unfolded behind us, Bartholomew exclaimed, "Well, I'm involved, now, so you might as well tell me! What is Alaĕna—no offense to the *what*, Alaĕna—and who is she? How did she do those things back there? How did she make the rain stop using Latin? You said she's Măgūs Lătīnūs, which means absolutely nothing to me and probably to her!"

Well, Bartholomew, it actually does, I thought. But I see where you're going. Let's see how much it takes to make him sing like a Wetly Pigeon on hunting day!

"I…" Mr. Cĕtĕră tried to say, but I interrupted him.

"I agree, what is a Măgūs Lătīnūs?" I put my hands on my hips and glared at him.

"Lūctūs Bōnūs," Mr. Cĕtĕră grumbled. "A Măgūs Lătīnūs is someone who can use the Latin language to make certain things happen, like turning Mr. Hyle into a snake and stopping the rain for a moment. Oh, and turning students into pigeons." He added blankly. I glowered at him, but he continued, "There, happy?"

Bartholomew and I looked at each other and grinned. We

secretly did a fist bump, knowing that our devious and irritating plan worked.

I smiled. "Yes, Mr. Cĕtĕră, was that so hard?"

Mr. Cĕtĕră rolled his eyes, giving up on hiding anything else. "You two are too conspiratorial for your own good."

In reply, I bombarded him with questions. "So, is there anything else we should know, Mr. Cĕtĕră, or is that even your real name? Why wouldn't you tell us before? Did somebody threaten you? Is it a conspiracy? Everything these days is a conspiracy. Our mayor is chock full of conspiracies, you know." I knew if I kept going like that, then he would eventually get annoyed to the point of spilling out answers.

"Yeah, didn't he use a fake name?" Bartholomew asked. "Ow!" He exclaimed as I jabbed him with my elbow.

"He used a fake passport to fly in from Saudi Arabia, Bartholomew. He's a terrorist! It's been proven. Everybody, except you, knows that!" I nodded positively.

"How come it's okay when you touch me but not when I touch you? What about my personal space bubble, huh, Alaĕna?"

"You're a guy, duh! Guys don't have personal space bubbles. Girls have to have space bubbles to protect themselves from boy cooties!" I crossed my arms and scrunched up my nose.

Mr. Cĕtĕră rolled his eyes.

"There is no such thing as boy cooties. Everybody knows that! Girls have cooties, not boys!" Bartholomew pointed at me accusingly.

"No, boys!"

"Girls!"

"Boys!"

Bartholomew gave one final allegation about my gender before Mr. Cĕtĕră exclaimed, "Enough! How old are you, anyways?"

"Thirteen and one day," Bartholomew and I stated in unison.

He blushed.

I frowned.

"I'm older, though," I proudly stated.

"By only twenty minutes." Bartholomew stuck out his tongue.

I stuck out my tongue in reply. "That's twenty minutes I've been in the air and you haven't."

"Well…" Bartholomew started.

Mr. Cĕtĕră quickly intervened. "Oh, please, don't start that again. How 'bout I tell you where we're going?"

"Yes, please!" We said in unison. I scrunched up my nose at Bartholomew. In response, he crossed his eyes and stuck his tongue out of the side of his mouth.

Mr. Cĕtĕră sighed and shook his head. A look of sadness appeared once more on his gently wrinkled face.

"Well?" I motioned him to continue.

"We're going to your dad's house, Alaĕna." Mr. Cĕtĕră replied as he turned right down a newly paved road. He drove down and into an overpopulated neighborhood that lay in the valley where the semi exploded.

"My dad? Are you crazy?! Turn us around! I would rather be pelted with peanuts than go to his house!"

Bartholomew gasped. "Wow, peanuts! You would swell up and look like puffer fish, minus the quills…"

"Spines," I corrected.

"Yeah, sure, whatever." He waved his hand dismissively.

"But, Mr. Cĕtĕră," I asked, "why would you even think about driving me to my dad's house, especially after what he did to me? Aren't you afraid I'm going to assault him or something?"

"Well, you should know better than to assault someone… and look, we're here!" Mr. Cĕtĕră said, dropping the subject.

The man was hiding something, but what?

After parking the Chevy in the slick driveway, Mr. Cĕtĕră retrieved an umbrella from underneath the bench seat, put it up so he wouldn't get completely soaked, got out, and closed the door. He walked to the house, rang the doorbell, and entered the two-story mansion when the door opened. The large, white door promptly shut once my Latin teacher disappeared from view.

The house was new and modern-looking, which wasn't my style. No, I was a log-cabin-in-the-woods kind of girl, though I hadn't been in the woods because there was so much dangerous wildlife living in the Wetly Forest. Not to mention there were many strange and unexplainable creatures.

It was said that if you were to go too close to the edge of the forest, you would never be seen again. Well, never be seen alive, that is. Once, a Wetlian walked up to the side of the forest and disappeared, only to be found torn to pieces, half-disintegrated, and half-eaten. In addition, three clutches of eggs the size of chicken eggs were found in the stomach of the Wetlian. No one dared to retrieve the body for proper burial because they feared the wrath of the creature that had done the injustice to the man. Since then, none had dared to go within a mile of the forest, and the city even put an electrified barbed wire fence around the sides of the forest that faced the city. But, to the mayor's displeasure, I jumped over the marker and gained fifty bucks from all the criminals who bet I couldn't do it.

Sighing at the memory, I tried to get out of the vehicle, but the door wouldn't budge. "Wonderful. My door's stuck." I groaned, wiggling the offending handle. "How's yours, Bartholomew?"

He climbed to the driver's seat, pulled the latch, and

pushed. Nothing. Frustrated, Bart replied, "Stuck like Pigeon Peter trying to coo an answer to a pop-quiz question." The boy pushed again, and still nothing happened.

I joggled and jiggled my door and, eventually, I called to Mr. Cětěră, who was, of course, inside. "Oh, why… the explosion must have fused them. Oh, wait, we would've been baked alive. I think a more logical and probable reason would be that the door handles broke, just got stuck, or had something of that sort happen to them due to the hail. Oh, this is just my luck. My stinky, awful, pitiful luck."

"Yeah, good conclusion. Too bad we don't have any hammers or plasma cutters or…" Bartholomew looked at me and smiled his classic *I have a brilliant idea that will either crash and burn or work splendidly*. It usually crashed and burned. "You could use Magic to open it!"

"Oh no, no, no, and *no*! Mr. Cětěră, please get us out of here!" I shook the door handle repeatedly and violently banged on it. "How 'bout the windows?"

"He took the keys. No power. I can't open it." He tapped the window.

"But it's an old truck. It should be manual." I looked around for the lever used to roll up the window.

Bartholomew rolled his eyes. "He upgraded it, remember? It's automatic, er, electronic."

I put my head in my hands and mumbled, "Ugh, great, I'm stuck in a truck with a boy, a boy! How positively wonderful!" *A boy… why did it have to be a boy? They are so, ugh. Yes, ugh is the perfect way to describe them.* "Well, he should be wondering what happens to us. So, maybe he'll come for us when that happens."

We waited a little while, about three minutes, for him to come outside. However, he was a no-show.

"What's taking him so long?" I sighed, tapping my fingernails on the door.

Bartholomew shrugged and then hesitantly asked, "I don't know… Alaĕna, what's so bad about being in the truck with a boy?"

I glared at him. "Because boys are always trying to…" Pain crossed my face, and I tried quickly to hide it. "I can't explain."

"Oh," he looked down sadly and then said softly, "that kind of thing. I understand. I know you're used to a certain type of guy, but you know I'm not like them."

"I know you aren't." I sighed and then absentmindedly punched him in the shoulder, grinning as he glared.

We had reached the five-minute mark of our waiting game when it hit me like a bug being squashed on a car windshield— sorry to those who like bugs.

"Duh," I exclaimed as I climbed over Bartholomew to the other side. I unlocked the door and opened it. "Man Alive, are you so dumb—and possibly me—for not thinking of it sooner? Come on, Bartholomew!" I jumped out the door and into a puddle, becoming instantly re-drenched. It was raining harder than when we first ran into the truck. Thankfully, the hail had stopped.

"Wow, I guess we are dumb, though the words…" Bartholomew started to recite as he climbed out, "idiotic, foolish, unintelligent, dim-witted, brainless…"

"I get the point, Bartholomew. You don't need to recite the whole thesaurus, even though they explain you perfectly sometimes."

He nodded, looked shocked, and then glared at me with a vengeance.

I ignored him and trotted to the front porch of the square house. Once I reached the door, I entered. Ugly as it was, I was glad to get out of the rain.

When Bartholomew followed me inside and stood beside me, I declared, "Does anyone get that modern, or at least this kind of modern, is ugly beyond all reason?" I looked around the living room, which had bleach-white furniture scattered about, lime-green walls and accents, and weird neon squares overlapping to make a bizarre work of art on the far wall.

It was a dark-colored-wood-lover's nightmare.

"Did someone bleach this place, or am I in a hospital bed looking at the ceiling?"

Bartholomew smirked and began to search for Mr. Cĕtĕră.

"There you are!" Mr. Cĕtĕră boomed, causing Bartholomew to jump with surprise and me to reach toward the knife hanging from the leather scabbard underneath my jacket. "What took you so long?"

I put my hand over my heart, leaned over, and said, "We got stuck in the truck. My door was unable to open. Bartholomew was an unintelligent boy because he forgot to unlock the other door." I straightened up, leaned my weight over to one leg, and put a hand on my hip. My long bangs blocked the view from my left eye, and I squeezed my braid out, letting a cascade of rainwater fall onto the white tile entryway behind me.

A nauseating hag, or beautiful woman in some people's eyes, entered the room and pled, "Oh, please, dear, don't just stand there! You're getting the carpet wet *and* dirty!"

"Sălvĕ, Ms. Peterson," I said half-heartedly and stepped onto the tile.

"Oh, please, call me 'Alilah'," she corrected, obviously not hearing my exasperated tone, and started pushing me toward the equally bleached kitchen where I could move around more freely.

"Are you a clean freak?" I asked bluntly. "Salina Parkinson's a clean freak. She screams whenever she sees my school. Did you attend my school when you were younger?" I pestered her, expecting her to crack.

She just smiled and called her boyfriend, or my—ugh—dad, on the phone, telling him it was an emergency.

Emergency… I grumbled to myself before tapping Bartholomew on the shoulder and whispering to him, "Does she have some sort of mental illness or is she just plain ignorant?"

He shrugged his shoulders.

It took about three or four minutes, but, sorry to say, he arrived back from work. The sight of him made me want to throw up, but that was breakfast, which I rarely had and couldn't afford to lose. So, nevertheless, I saw that extraordinarily, extremely, repulsively, abhorrently, idiotic, puerile, immature troglodyte—sorry, I couldn't help it.

CHAPTER 2

Old Foes

There stood the demon of my life: my father. He was six-and-a-half feet tall and had cropped brown hair, an athletic build, a good tan, emerald eyes, and straight white teeth. Overall, he was—how can I bear to say it—handsome.

"Hello, father," I spitefully spat as I glared at him. "Or should I call you 'it'?"

"Alaĕna…" he started, but I cut him off.

"How's it been? Clean, warm, safe, and loved, unlike me who's been stuck in a cardboard box. Cold, dirty, unloved, not knowing if somebody's going to jump me and beat me to death! Where were you? Where were you when I was cornered by one of those muggers and almost kidnapped? Where were you when I almost died?!" I cringed because a partially healed wound in my stomach shot streams of pain all over me. *Too close, that was way too close.*

"A—Alaĕna," he stuttered, but I ignored him, just as he had done to me.

"Oh, right, you were pretending I didn't exist while gallivanting around with your girlfriend. What about me? Did you ever care?" I was wired. In the deepest depth of the blackest pit of my heart, I held my memories of him.

"Alaĕna…"

"Did you ever visit? No! Did you ever try to bring me back? No! Did you ever send me some money to help me out? No! Did you ever wish me Merry Christmas or Happy Valentine's Day or Happy Birthday or Happy Thanksgiving? No! You didn't even name me!"

He seemed hurt by my last comment.

"Why didn't you name me? Why? Just tell me why? You had no idea what I was going through while you were living in your luxurious house. I've seen people die while you sit here in comfort." Tears came to my eyes. "Why didn't you come back for me?" My father was shaking, and I was about to say something else when Bartholomew put a hand on my shoulder. I flinched then sighed.

"I know it's been rough for you. I am truly sorry for the way I acted. I'm sorry for the things you've been through." A tear fell from his eye as he said these words. "I knew that you were different from the rest of the children your age and, when your mother left, I didn't know what to do because I was young, very, very young, and scared. So, I got rid of you. And now, I am so sorry." My father's shoulders slumped, and his tall frame shrunk pitifully.

Part of me wanted to forgive him, and the other part wanted me to punch him in the gut. *But wait, my mother left?* "She didn't die, my mom, she left?"

"Yes, she left, took your twin, and left. Your twin was normal, and you were special." He smiled, obviously trying to make me feel better, but…

"I have a twin!" I yelled in astonishment. "Who's my twin? Is my twin a boy or a girl? What's the name of my twin?" I was dumbfounded. *I have a twin out there with my mom!*

"I don't know. She left right, I mean *right* after your twin was born. She left me to care for you. I'm not sure what had happened, but she's gone, and so is your twin. He, or she, probably thinks you don't exist." He eventually got out with a great bit of anxiety. "Oh, this is not how I wanted this to go," he muttered to himself.

I sighed and glanced at my friend. "Bartholomew, you can let go now."

"Oh… what… oh, yeah," Bartholomew blushed and let go of my shoulder. After a moment, he thoughtfully said, "Sorry, Alaĕna. I think I just might have figured out who your twin is. Not really that hard to figure out, especially since…" Bartholomew was about to continue when… BANG!

"Get down on the floor and put your hands in the air! Alaĕna Bombyx, step forward!" Thirty men in dripping-wet, black uniforms and bulletproof vests burst through the door. Swords were at their left sides, and a long knife was at their right. As an attempt to scare me, they were pointing puny handguns at me. The uniforms read, "D-A-M-L", which stood for "Defense-Against-Măgī-Latīnī".

Oh no, not again. Look, I have to keep my cool and act like this is just another day in Wetly, messing with Banana Bear and Cheeky Monkey, I said to myself. Besides, after what I did, they should be terrified of me. "Oh wow, I have a defense force against me. I feel so important now." I sarcastically stated, putting a hand on my hip and one near the opening of my jacket. *Good, now, keep on going like this. They'll never suspect a thing.* As another man entered the room, my thoughts trailed off into one word: *No.*

There stood the man I hated most.

Memories flooded in. Flashes of light, clangs of metal, and pain… such pain. He, unlike the others, had a sword in his hand, which I knew he could use. "Who are you to say what I have to do?"

The man smirked. "Well, girlie, isn't it nice te see ya again? Ye 'aven't been behavin' like ya should've. Ye've been misbehavin'."

I ran at him, drawing my knife, and pushed him out the door.

He tumbled to the ground and groaned.

Hastily, I jumped on top of him, put my knife to his throat, and said, "I'm no *girlie!*"

"Alaĕna, what are you doing?! You know him?" Bartholomew asked, flabbergasted.

"No," I replied, keeping my gaze on the man. "All I know is that he and the rest of his kind want to kill me."

The man used his brute strength to get my hand away and throw me off. He quickly got up and, when he had regained his balance and composure, said, "No use lyin', girlie. I don't want te kill ya, not yet. I'll leave 'at decision up te 'im. An', o' course, ye know me! I almost killed ya. Don't ya remember?"

I shook my head and lied. "No, I don't."

He sighed sadly. "Oh, girlie, ye've kept yer oath a little too well."

"What oath? And who's the '*im*?" Bartholomew asked, mimicking the man's voice with the "'im" as he looked frantically for a way to escape.

The man laughed. "Why, lad, the '*im* is 'er boyfriend, if I'm correct."

I simply looked away, trying to control my rising anger.

He continued, "An' 'e knows somethin', somethin' 'at'll change everythin'."

I shook my head. "That makes no sense."

He heartily laughed. "Oh, I'm sure it makes none te ye, but not te yer teacher over 'ere.' 'E knows more 'an 'e lets out." The man glanced at Mr. Cĕtĕră, and they shared the look for a moment.

Huffing to disguise my confusion, I said, "I'm still trying to figure him out, so I don't expect too much."

"O' course ya know nothin' of 'im, 'e just revealed 'imself today as an Agent o' the Rats." I glared at him, and he grinned. "Why don't ya turn on yer pretty toothpick an' show 'em 'oo ya really are."

I sneered and tried to make my way back to Bartholomew. I needed to protect him. "And who am I? You know nothing about me."

"Oh, girlie, yer o' so very wrong. I know everythin' 'bout ye. I know oo' ya are, oo' ye'll be, an' I know what ya are, what ya really are. An' I know what ya mean te yer Rat kin, so no sense lyin' 'bout it." He swung his sword, and I jumped back, bumping into Bartholomew and causing him to fall over with a loud *oof*.

I laughed. "Oh, of course you do. It's not that hard to figure out. I…" He swung his sword, and I dodged. "…am…" He sliced vertically, and I stepped to the side. "…a…" He thrust at my stomach, and I jumped back. "…Măgūs Lătīnūs!"

He took a basic stance and said, "No girlie, I know yer a Rat, but I know yer mer 'an 'at. By the way the lad acted 'round ye, I could 'ell 'at yer so much mer 'an a regular Rat."

Shaking my head, I said, "I don't know who you're talking about, and I'm not a Rat in the first place!"

"Oh, girlie, my per girlie, ye remember what the lad did fer ya, an' ye be feelin' bad fer it. Ye 'ink 'bout it an' dream 'bout it every night. 'Ink 'bout 'is weapon an' what it did te ya!" He swung his sword at my head, and I ducked. "What ya duckin' fer girlie, I've seen what ye can do. Now, show 'em." He motioned with his head to my counterparts.

"Why do you want them to know?" I quietly inquired.

"So 'ey will want te kill ya."

"Who, since it's certainly not them?" I motioned to my companions.

"Oh, per girlie don't know 'oo 'e 'as put 'er faith in."

I tilted my head. "What do you mean, snake?"

He just grinned as he swung his sword, again and again, forcing me into drastic measures.

Swiftly, I sprinted inside and rolled over to one of the men, who had moved into position so that they could keep the others back and gag Mr. Cĕtĕră. I held my knife to his throat. The man in my grip didn't struggle because my blade was pressed against the jugular artery on the side of his neck. He merely sighed in resignation.

"Drop your weapons or he dies," I commanded, and Ms. Peterson screamed with surprise.

The Damsel, as we not-so-affectionately called D-A-M-L Agents, with the weird accent grinned as he stepped inside the threshold. "Well, well, well… 'twas ye 'oo did it."

I pressed the knife harder, splitting skin, and the man in my grasp grunted.

"Alaĕna, what are you doing?" Bartholomew asked, horrified.

Ignoring Bartholomew and keeping my gaze on the man in front of me, I asked, "This is what you wanted, isn't it?"

His sly smirk answered my question.

I rammed the pommel of my knife into the skull of my Damsel hostage, knocking him unconscious, and pulled his sword out of its sheath. Now, I had a knife and a sword which gave me the advantage.

"Nice work, girlie, now ye can show 'em what yer really made o'. 'At yer made o' the stuff 'at surrounds ya." He cut horizontally, and I blocked.

Bartholomew's eyes widened.

The Damsel vertically sliced, and I blocked. He frowned and pushed harder.

He's trying to get me on the offensive, but why? Isn't it enough that he exposed my skills with a sword and that I'm willing to take a hostage? A scream interrupted my thoughts, and I turned around to see Bartholomew being held with a knife at his throat by one of the other Damsels.

I almost let a curse loose but held my tongue. Instead of reacting violently, I decided that I would give the Damsel the offensive but not in the way that he wanted. "Ĕxīstō Mŭrĕs, Ētĕnĭm Qŭŏd Ĕst Qŭĭd Tū Ĕs!" I commanded as I stared the man straight in the eye and smiled. "Ah, the irony—the sweet, sweet irony—of this moment is o' so satisfactory."

He growled with anger.

Ms. Peterson squealed with fright as the D-A-M-L became the R-D-A-M-L, the Rat-Defense-Against-Măgī-Latīnī.

Sluggishly, the men shrank into little rodents, rats to be exact, and scampered around the room. The Damsel with the weird accent quickly joined the ranks in rat-hood.

Then, just seconds later, rats started pouring into the house. The walls and floors became a living mass of brown fur, squeaks, whiskers, and hairless tails. The room was soon filled with the rank smell of wet rats.

"Eek!" Ms. Peterson shrieked, and I plugged my ears because the high pitch was too much for me. "Rats!" She, apparently forgetting all sense of dignity, jumped into my father's arms.

I snorted, holding back a laugh. I walked toward the door, stopped, and snapped my fingers.

The rats squealed and stopped moving, but they quickly continued to scamper about, looking for the kitchen, no doubt.

"This is for what you did. I am not a Rat. You are. I deserve to run away, and you *don't*." I said quietly to the former men who had become rats, particularly to the red-eyed one who seemed to be gathering a group of rats to assault me. I walked toward the red-eyed one and raised my new sword in preparation for turning him into rat stew.

Hastily, Mr. Cĕtĕră popped my bubble of joy by yelling, "Alaĕna, they are still to be considered men!"

Groaning, I thought, *Like I care?* Then, with an exasperated tone, I said, "But they weren't men in the first place! I think of them as Rats and, therefore, I turned them into Rats." I paused but then sighed. "But I suppose you're right. I need that red-eyed one alive." I reached down and grabbed him by the middle.

He struggled, kicked, snapped, and squealed, but my hold on him was firm.

"Oh, stop squirming! You're going to be fine as long as you do as I say," I grumbled.

He glowered at me with his beady, red eyes.

I stuck him in my pocket and partially zipped it so that he would be trapped but wouldn't suffocate. Glancing to my right, I saw Bartholomew standing still as a railroad tie, my father's jaw dropped like a croaking toad, and Mr. Cĕtĕră turned as green as a seasick frog. Ms. Peterson, on the other hand…

"Please, get them out of here!" Ms. Peterson screamed.

Bartholomew nodded in agreement, slowly lifting his feet one at a time out of the ankle-deep swarm of rats.

"I don't know. This seems like an improvement to me," I

said.

Ms. Peterson glared at me.

"Okay, okay, fine, let's see…" I looked at Mr. Cĕtĕră. His face was red with the strain of holding his breath. After pondering for a moment, I commanded, "Mŭrĕs, Dīgrĕdī Ĕt Vīrī Quī Fūĕrūnt Mūtăvĕrūnt Īn Mŭrĕm, Mūtă Īn Sĕ Sūŏs Prīmŏs Hūmănŏs! Praĕtĕr Prō Mūrĕm Cūm Ŏcūlŏs Mălŏs Părvŏs Rūbĕrŏs."

Immediately, the rats ran outside, to the delight of Ms. Peterson and the horror of her neighbors, who were standing outside, wondering what all the screaming was about. Also, the man-rats turned back into men, and——thankfully——were fully dressed in their black, SWAT-team-looking uniforms. Conversely, the rat in my pocket remained the same.

"Whoopee! It worked! The rats disappeared, the lesser D-A-M-Ls turned back into men, and the greater D-A-M-L stayed a rat! I didn't know if it would work because a lot of these rats have red eyes. Of course, that's why I added evil. I didn't know for sure that he was the only evil, red-eyed rat, but it worked, nevertheless! Whoopee!" I jumped once for joy.

"My house is free of vermin!" Ms. Peterson exclaimed, jumping down from her boyfriend's arms.

I looked at her with a 'seriously-you-think-that' expression on my face. "Well, almost," I said, motioning to my pocket.

Ms. Peterson seemed to ignore my statement and said, "Now that it's all over… Eek!" She shrieked, again.

I covered my ears and earnestly pled, "Please, Sīstă, no more shrieking!"

"Eek! Look at my floor! Just look at it!" she shrieked, ignoring my heart-filled plea and pointing at the rat-poop-covered floor.

My dad stepped over to her and put a hand on her shoulder.

"Dear, it'll be fine. I agree with my daughter. So please, calm down."

For once, we agree, I thought.

Abruptly, my father clasped his hands together and declared, "Now, we should be glad that Bartholomew and Alaĕna are safe."

"When did you start caring?" I snapped, picking up where I left off in an earlier conversation. "You never did. Why now?"

"Alaĕna, just give it a rest." Bartholomew groaned, being careful not to step in any rat droppings as he made his way over to me. "He dumped you on the side of the road and enrolled you in a school for psychopaths and the like. You have suffered serious trauma throughout your life and have both abandonment and anger management issues. You somehow learned how to sword fight and had no problem threatening to kill somebody—which I will ask you about later. I get it, to a certain extent, just please stop picking on your dad! He's sorry, so just forgive him." As soon as he said that, he regretted it.

I glared at him. "So you're defending him now. Is that how it is?" Stepping on a pile of rat poop without an undignified *yuck*, I twirled the sword in my hand and smiled. "Ah, what a beautiful weapon. Glad it's found a better owner."

He glared at me but got the message: stop defending Mr. Bombyx.

Mr. Cĕtĕră shook his head at our interaction and changed the subject. "So, Alaĕna, you know that man in your pocket?"

"I don't know him," I said plainly, which was true since I didn't know his name or anything about him, other than the fact that he wanted to kill me.

Mr. Cĕtĕră pushed harder. "The man, he said it was you? What does that mean?"

"He was lying." I bluntly replied. "And, as for the meaning,

I haven't a clue."

"What was the oath?" He inquired.

Is he trying to make me fall in pain? Wait, is he? That's preposterous. How on earth would he know? But I have to tell somebody… let's see… yep, this is really going to hurt! Slowly, I said, "The oath was his doing. He made me do it, and, if I hadn't, I would've died." The pain was so great that I collapsed on the ground, clutching my stomach.

"What's wrong with her? I didn't see the man stab her or anything," Bartholomew asked, kneeling at my side with concern written all over his face.

"I believe it was the oath. If she said anything about it, it would cause her pain, but why?" Mr. Cĕtĕră replied.

I breathed hard. The pain would eventually subside, but it would seriously suck in the meantime.

"Isn't there anything you can do to help her?" Bartholomew asked.

Mr. Cĕtĕră shrugged his shoulders. "I don't know. I don't major in this sort of Magic."

"Well, there has to be something!" Bartholomew exclaimed.

"Bart," I weakly said, "the pain will end. This has happened before and, before saying anything, I figured out the severity of pain I would go through after telling Mr. Cĕtĕră what I told him." Crossly, I added. "I just hope that it helped."

Mr. Cĕtĕră seemed surprised at the anger in my voice.

"Now," I began, "help me to my feet."

Mr. Cĕtĕră helped me up along with Bartholomew and said, "It will help in the future."

"Though it still doesn't explain why you can use a sword. Was that included in the oath?" Mr. Cĕtĕră asked, stepping away from me.

"No, that wasn't included." I cringed, and a spark of pain

flew through my body. "Really, that shouldn't be counted as saying anything. Accursed words, accursed oath, o' how I wish there was no D-A-M-L."

The rat in my pocket squealed.

"Yes, I'm talking about you, vermin," I spat.

The rat squealed, trying his hardest to bite me.

"You know, rat, all of this is your fault. Maybe I should turn you into rat stew?" I suggested, and, as the rat had stopped squeaking, I smirked.

"I, too, wish that there was no D-A-M-L, but, alas, we must live with it. It seems you have been given the brunt of the battle between us," my Latin teacher stated.

"Yup, that's me, the punching bag of the battle." I swayed, and Bartholomew steadied me.

"Wait," Bartholomew said. "I thought I was the punching bag."

I softly punched him on the shoulder. "There, are you happy now?"

He rubbed his shoulder. "Yep, I'm happy."

I quietly chuckled and asked, my face contorting with pain, "Want to know any more, Mr. Cĕtĕră?"

"No, I'll wait until you've recovered. Because of your condition, I'll have to inform our ride that he'll have to pick us up here. I'll be right back." He walked outside to be out of earshot and out of sight.

My father shook his head as if to clear it and stood on my left side to steady me. "That was something I shall never forget," he stated.

"And you'll never forget if I turn you into a mongoose, either. Why didn't you help me?" I demanded.

"I'm sorry. I was in shock," he stuttered.

I sneered. "Why were you in shock? You didn't get a scratch

or even a bruise. You just stood there and watched like the coward I know you are."

The rat in my pocket squealed again.

"You see? Even the evil man-rat in my pocket knows that you are a coward," I pointed out.

My father shook his head defiantly, and said, with a bit of anger in his voice, "Daughter, I am many things, but I am not a coward."

"Then why did you leave me?" I asked, looking at him with eyes wet with unshed tears. "Why didn't you come back for me that day seven years ago? Why did you leave me?"

"But I did come back for you, don't you remember?" I could see he was trying to compensate for everything that had happened.

"Why did you leave me?" I had always wanted to know why he had left me on that particular day.

"I…" he started, but didn't continue.

I sniffled, and a tear fell from my eye. Hastily, I brushed it away. "That's what I thought. I risk my life to give you answers, and yet you have nothing to lose and give me no answers." I began to walk away, but he caught my shoulder.

With fear glimmering in his eyes, he explained, "Alaĕna, it's complicated. They threatened me that if I let you stay with me another day, they would kill me."

Before I could respond, Mr. Cĕtĕrǎ came in and said, "Well, our ride is going to be here in about ten minutes." As he saw my face, he seemed to notice that something was amiss. "Is everything all right?"

"Sure, if you count the fact that my father abandoned me because he was threatened okay," I said.

"So, he told you that?" he said, looking at my father.

By the look on the older man's face, I assumed that my

father wasn't supposed to tell me.

My father gulped and said, "She was pressuring me. I had no choice. You saw what she can do!"

"You always have a choice, Mr. Bombyx. You should know that." He stepped closer.

I was feeling rather uncomfortable with the situation, and based on his fidgeting, so was Bartholomew.

My father glared at my Latin teacher. "Mr. Cĕtĕră, if you are telling me my decision to…" I blocked out the rest of their conversation and motioned to Bartholomew to follow me to the other room.

Once we had seated ourselves on the bright white table in the lime-green kitchen adorned with stainless steel appliances, I noticed their conversation was about me. How I was born and some of the following events.

Ms. Peterson even added a comment here and there.

Then, I thought of it. I was a… a… I don't even like to think about it now. No sir, nope-uh-dee-nope-nope-nope!

Bartholomew quietly sat there and tried to pretend that he wasn't listening but ended up saying, "Wow, I guess we're more alike than we thought. Don't wanna be like your dad—or my dad, for that matter—when I grow up!"

I nodded in agreement.

The conversation took up about five of those ten minutes. Finally, they got to a rather interesting discussion that I thought was intriguing, but, unfortunately, Ms. Peterson intervened. "Boys, I don't need to hear this discussion again."

Mr. Cĕtĕră frowned, and my father sighed, saying, "Yes, dear."

I groaned with disappointment and walked back into the room with Bartholomew.

Ms. Peterson nodded. "Good, now, don't do anything insensible while I'm gone. I'm going upstairs to go get some cleaning supplies." She walked upstairs and left Mr. Cĕtĕrǎ and my father to glare at each other.

I looked at Mr. Cĕtĕrǎ, then at my father. *This is awkward.* I thought.

"Oh, look, the rain has stopped, and the sun has come out," Bartholomew stated, breaking the uncomfortable silence. "So… what do we do now?"

"We take you to the M-L-P-A." Mr. Cĕtĕrǎ replied. A stray rat scurried past him and out the door, causing him to jump. "Vīvūm," he mumbled, bending down and putting a hand over his chest.

Lucky, I thought. *I can't speak Latin like that. Otherwise, I might raise somebody from the dead! Oh, bad picture in my head. Scary picture in my head!* I shuddered and, turning to my Latin teacher, inquired, "What does M-L-P-A stand for?"

He took a deep breath, still recovering from the rat, and explained, "The Măgī-Latīnī-Protection-Agency."

"Huh, that begs the question: how many Măgī Latīnī are out there?" I looked quizzically at Mr. Cĕtĕrǎ.

"Not very many. By the time we get to them, the D-A-M-L has already been there, and, most of the time, it's not a pretty sight, if there's a sight at all. They enjoy kidnapping, torturing, and murdering Măgī Latīnī." Mr. Cĕtĕrǎ shook his head, seemingly shaking the memories out of his head.

Well, at least, he's not thinking about my dad and, ugh, that, I thought. "How do you know all these things? Are you really who you say you are?" I picked up and dusted off my new sword. Once I had inspected the blade thoroughly for any marks, I cut a hole in my jacket and slid the blade in so that it hung by its leather hilt.

"Well, I am a Latin teacher. I do teach some history.

However, I work for the Măgī-Latīnī-Protection-Agency. They knew you were one from the very beginning. They tried to get the school to let us rescue you, but they wouldn't agree. So, the M-L-P-A sent me in to watch over you and help train you until legal matters could be settled. We usually try to do these things legally, but, in your case, we were forced to enforce an E-E-P, which stands for Emergency-Evacuation-Protocol." He looked at me for some sort of response, and I couldn't help but laugh.

"What?" he asked.

"E-E-P., eep." I laughed.

Bartholomew looked at Mr. Cĕtĕră and made the coo-coo sign with his hand to his head.

Grouchily, I countered the young teen, "I'm not coo-coo, Bartholomew. Heh, rhyme. Sorry, continuing… But you could say that I have an articulate sense of humor."

"Sure," he said sarcastically.

"Well, anywho… Mr. Cĕtĕră, is Măgīstĕr Ĕt Cĕtĕră your real name?" I asked.

"Yes and no, my real name is something I will not say, but I only changed it when I joined the M-L-P-A."

"Okay… I think I know why you changed it." I lifted my chin and narrowed my eyes, looking very learned. "Firstly, because you had to protect your identity from possibly killing any outside family or friends. Secondly, you probably hated it."

He gave me a blank look, but then smiled. "Ah yes, the little detective is back," he laughed.

I felt insulted. "Who are you calling little? I'm five-foot-five if you haven't noticed."

"I noticed," my dad stated as he entered the conversation.

I gave him the evil eye and ignored him.

Bartholomew glared at me in return. "Alaĕna, quit treating your dad like that!"

"He abandoned me!" I exclaimed. "I'll treat him however I please."

"But he was threatened!"

"So what? He still abandoned me, just like my mom abandoned…" It hit me like a bug hitting a car windshield—sorry once more to those who love bugs. It just keeps coming up. "Bartholomew, how could I have been so blind? I know who my twin is."

CHAPTER 3

Dragonfly

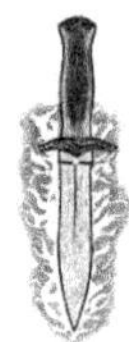

My father, Bartholomew, and I were in shock.

"I don't believe it. All of this time, and we never figured it out." I said after telling everyone of my eureka moment.

"I figured it out before you did, but I forgot after the infestation, the scene when you fainted, and the time when I learned about, uh, that." Bartholomew sighed. Walking over to me, he said, "But, the ironic thing is that I see a resemblance you would've thought someone would have noticed."

I shrugged. "I just can't believe my twin is you."

"Yeah, me neither. Talk about a movie-like story. I can hear it now: 'Twins separated at birth, find each other thirteen years and one day later.' Wait, don't they already have a show like that on TV? It looked really cheesy to me, and not even close to realistic. We're realistic."

"Bartholomew, off point," I reminded him.

"Sorry," my brother apologized. "So, Mr. Bombyx, I guess you're my dad then." He gave my dad a quick smile, which was a kind of an awkward please-tell-me-why-it-had-to-be-you smile.

Looking quizzically at his newly found son, my dad said, "I suppose, Bartholomew, but what is your mother's name?"

"Eleanor Healdton, spelled capital H-e-a-l-d-t-o-n."

"Sounds familiar. It might be possible, but some part of me just doesn't seem to recognize it. It's been so long, maybe…" He stopped mid-sentence. We looked at him to continue, but he was lost in the ocean of memories.

"It's only been thirteen years. That's not that long," Bartholomew argued.

"I know, but I did try to forget about her, mostly because I was heartbroken," he countered.

I… understand, I lugubriously thought before looking at Mr. Cĕtĕră, who had been standing quietly in the background. "Mr. Cĕtĕră, did you know Bartholomew was my twin?"

Mr. Cĕtĕră sighed. "It's complicated."

I was about to go on another question-filled rant, but Bartholomew cleared his throat and motioned negatively. I crossed my arms and reluctantly changed subjects. "So, we're going to the M-L-P-A? Is that so I can train with other kids like me? Is the majority my age, younger, or older?"

"Yes. We are going to M-L-P-A, and, to make it easier for ourselves, we call it Mulpa. Most of the kids are around your age, although their abilities most often don't show up until they are fourteen to sixteen years old. On occasion, some are over twenty years old, as in the case of Mr. Vŏx, who you will meet. So, you, Alaĕna, are an anomaly.

"Although there was this one girl. She received her abilities when she was only four. However, the D-A-M-L got to her first. She turned them into sunflowers without her parents noticing and planted them. She ended up being accused of intentional murder—the nerve of accusing a *four*-year-old of murder, humph—and the court found her guilty. The judge, by the way, was a top agent of the Damsels. They killed her. That poor, poor girl."

"Anyways," he continued, "many Latin Magicians share her fate because the Damsels have taken over most of the government. The president is one of them. Teachers, students, parents, therapists, and gym guys in shorts and tank tops are all agents."

"Now, that's a conspiracy. But Damsels, that's just funny!" I laughed, and Mr. Cĕtĕră shook his head.

"I've heard of the D-A-M-L. Something about them being involved with Russia in World War II? Didn't realize they were taking over the world," Bartholomew said, tapping his cheek thoughtfully.

"Yes, there are very few countries not under their control. They are determined to exterminate the Măgī Latīnī." He grimaced. "They have already taken over a hundred million lives. They don't realize that the Măgī Latīnī can help improve the world. They just think that they're a dangerous infestation of vermin that need to be… dealt with."

"But, during the process, they get turned into sunflowers and rats…" I pondered for a moment then said, "And pigeons, my apology to Peter. Also, snakes, anacondas, to be precise." I let out a sly grin. "By the way, Mr. Hyle didn't happen to be one—a Damsel, that is? Because if he was, I would feel so much better about it."

Mr. Cĕtĕră snorted, holding back a laugh. "Unfortunately, no. He was not one of them. Though, by the way he treated you kids, one would think so."

I smiled and elbowed Bartholomew.

"Oh, yeah, he treated us like Alaĕna treats her dad,

ooh, even worse? Nah, Alaĕna's even worse when it comes to her—ouch!"

I punched my best buddy in the side.

"You…" wheeze "…know…" wheeze "…that does…" wheeze "…hurt!" Bartholomew looked like he was going to pass out.

"Cowboy Up, Bartholomew! You'll be fine. I'm sure you don't want me to use my new sword to show you real hurt, do you?" I slapped him on the back, causing him to lose his balance and do a face-plant into a pile of poop.

"Ah, nasty," Bartholomew sputtered, spitting and rubbing his sleeve over his face trying to get the dung off. "Where's Ms. Peterson anyways? You would think she would be back by now with her brooms and vacuum cleaners." Little did we know that upstairs, where the cleaning supplies were held, Ms. Peterson had fainted due to a mix of hyperventilating and stepping on a dead, trampled rat.

"Ms. Peterson? Ms. Peterson!" I called and, quickly, I heard groaning, a loud thump, and then, at last, the familiar "Eek!" How I hated that screech.

"Alilah, sweetheart, are you all right?" My dad asked as he raced up the stairs.

Sweetheart! I thought, nearly growling to myself. *Oh, that traitorous…*

"Oh my," Ms. Peterson gasped, as she walked down the stairs, holding on to her boyfriend's arm, "This place looks awful! I better go get my vacuum." She walked back upstairs again.

My dad followed her, looking back at us. "She whacked her head on the way down, forgot everything that happened," he tittered nervously.

"Isn't that her nature?" I asked.

Although looking quite peeved, he jumped as if he had just remembered something important, a bit like how Alilah remembered the Damsels. "Alilah, don't step on the rat again!"

I whistled. "Wow, does she need to get some medical attention? Does anybody know a good doctor?" I shook my head.

Mr. Cĕtĕră cut into the conversation by asking, "Alaĕna, swing that sword, would you?"

I was puzzled, but I did as he said. I grabbed the hilt of the sword with my right hand, pulled it out, and swung it.

Mr. Cĕtĕră studied my every move.

"What's wrong, Mr. Cĕtĕră?"

"Nothing's wrong… it's just that I'm amazed. Not a single ML has been able to hold, let alone swing, a sword in over four thousand years. You see, the Măgūs Lătīnūs kind have a curse that prevents them from using weapons. So, this is incredible. I, personally, have never held a weapon, being a Măgūs Lătīnūs myself. For the sake of it, may I try holding it?" Mr. Cĕtĕră asked.

I nodded. "So, you are a Latin Magician. I was wondering why they were trying to gag you. Only Măgī Latīnī are gagged, or people who are being kidnapped."

I switched my hand from the hilt to the side of the blade beneath the hilt and placed the palm of my left hand underneath the middle of the blade. "Here." I held the sword out to him.

He grabbed the hilt, but immediately jerked his limp hand back, cringing with pain.

"What's wrong, Mr. Cĕtĕră?" I inquired.

He shook his hand, trying to lessen the pain. "Oh, this happened last time as well! Whenever I try to take up a sword, a gun, a knife, anything like that, my hand goes limp and numb, and it takes about three minutes for me to be able to use it again."

"Ow. Well, I've held all three of those things and nothing happened."

He looked a bit surprised but quickly hid it.

I noticed that his supposedly limp hand twitched a bit. *Odd*, I thought.

"You've held all those things? Are you serious? I haven't held one of those things, let alone all three," Bartholomew exclaimed.

"Yeah, and I just might have used them as well."

"What?!" Bartholomew seemed more than surprised. He seemed appalled and flabbergasted.

I beamed. "Yep, no big-y."

"No big-y? No big-y! Are you kidding me? Wait, no, you never kid. You are always so serious, but I suppose it's good that you're serious since you're holding a sword in your hand."

"I suppose," I said solemnly but quickly lightened up. "But, what about the time that I laughed at you when your…"

Bartholomew blushed and waved his hands in front of him. "Oh, please don't bring that up! Man, was that humiliating."

"I saw London. I saw France. I saw Bart's underpants," I chanted.

"Oh, now that's mature."

"Says the boy."

He stepped closer. "What's that supposed to mean?"

"It means what you think it means," I said, also moving nearer.

"Why you…" He looked like he was going to try to tackle me or do something similar to that, but Mr. Cĕtĕră interrupted by sternly saying his name.

"But… she said…"

"I know what she said, but trust me, she's holding the sword," he whispered to him.

Bartholomew glared at me and crossed his arms.

I rolled my eyes. "Boys."

He stuck out his tongue and spat, "Girls."

After a slight pause, I asked, "I was wondering, Mr. Cĕtĕră, when exactly are we going to leave this dump?"

Mr. Cĕtĕră seemed frustrated with the two of us but smiled. "In a couple of minutes."

Curious, Bartholomew asked, "What kind of ride is it?"

Mr. Cĕtĕră's smile grew larger. "You'll see when it arrives. However, I might tell you what it is sooner if you two stop bickering like a couple of siblings."

"Au contraire, Mr. Cĕtĕră, we are siblings," I said with a bad French accent.

Mr. Cĕtĕră was going to say more, but Ms. Peterson caught our attention when she ran down the stairs, carrying a vacuum, with my dad, who was following in tow and carrying a broom and dustpan. The reason they had retrieved the broom and dustpan was that they knew that it was a pain to vacuum up rodent poop. She offered me the vacuum, and my dad presented me with the broom and dustpan.

"Ugh, are you kidding me? You clean it up. I did this in self-defense. However, when putting it in perspective, I'm sure you're glad that I didn't use this sword in the offensive like the Major Damsel wanted me to do. Trust me when I say that sword fights are very, very messy." I pushed them away. As they didn't move an inch, I rolled my eyes and said, "Nŭnqūăm, Bărcălă!" I know that it was vindictive. I lost my cool with her. I should've apologized, but I didn't.

Alilah flinched, and a tear fell from her eye. She might not have been able to understand what I said, but she understood the meaning.

Bartholomew gasped, and Mr. Cĕtĕră seemed shocked.

I crossed my arms and marched outside.

"What did you just call her?" My father angrily demanded.

"I could have called her a sunflower, and you wouldn't have known. Learn Latin. It'll be good for you."

He seemed stunned by my words and was speechless.

Bartholomew quickly followed me outside and irately whispered, "Alaĕna, that was uncalled for!"

I didn't say anything else, just stood, looking into the gray, cloudy sky. Something within me wanted to be up there, free in the clouds. But that was just ridiculous, since I hated heights *and* airplanes. "Oh well, then," I replied and sloshed my way over to the sidewalk since the downpour had created a giant puddle that had taken the place of the lawn. Looking up at the sky, I noticed a whooshing chop-chop-chop sound. "Qūĭd Īn Tĕrră?" I mumbled. When Mr. Cĕtĕră rushed outside, I asked if it was a helicopter.

"Correct, but what kind?" Mr. Cĕtĕră asked, trying to see what I knew.

"Osprey?" I guessed.

"No, the noise is different, more like a mix of helicopters. It sounds very strange," Bartholomew corrected.

I looked at him as if he had two heads. "How on earth did you know that?"

He grinned. "Because I love aircraft."

I was surprised to say the least.

"Well, Bartholomew, you were close. Let's go see what it really is." He walked to the middle of the street.

We looked at each other and then followed him.

When we had gotten to the sidewalk, I looked up and gazed upon the weirdest thing I had ever seen. "Qūĭd Īn Tĕrră Ĭd Ĕst?" I gazed up at the bizarre helicopter. It had twenty-foot-long wings on each side, each with two large propellers. Along with a couple of small propellers in the front, it had another propeller on each side and two more small propellers on the tail. It was completely black save for some red runes in a language unfamiliar to me.

"So awesome…" Bartholomew's smile was as wide as the Mississippi.

"The Drăcōmūscă, the DM. Its name means Dragonfly," Mr. Cĕtĕră proudly announced. "One of the MLs thought of it. It's genius, pure genius. A team of Magicians built it using Magic and technology. One of the many ways Magic can help to improve the world."

"Hmm, it's cool that the Măgī Latīnī built this," I said as the DM circled, preparing to land in the street.

"Most of the MLs major in certain areas, such as engineering, biology, archeology, geology, physics, and marine biology. Some very special MLs major in Magology which is the study of Magic and its creatures, such as the Sĕpīa Vōlătīcă."

"Sĕpīa Vōlătīcă, Flying Cuttlefish, really?" I shook my head and laughed.

Mr. Cĕtĕră looked around nervously, glaring at me. "The Sĕpīa Vōlătīcă is no laughing matter. Trust me."

I put my hands up in surrender as the Dragonfly landed. "So, we just get in and take off?" I yelled over the noise.

The neighbors stood in their doorways with their jaws dropped. One was on the phone.

"Yep," he yelled in reply. "This is where you and your father part! Bartholomew can come along if he wants. We'll contact his mother to let her know what happened to him!" Mr. Cĕtĕră seemed relieved about leaving my dad, though he did speak with him for about a minute about something that I couldn't hear over the extremely loud noise.

When Mr. Cĕtĕră returned, he asked Bartholomew if he

wanted to come, and the boy yelled, beaming, "Uh, duh! Of course, I wanna come."

My dad walked up to me and apologized once again for his actions in the past.

I brushed him off and told him he had many more apologies to go.

He nodded his head, seeming to understand.

Finished with my father, I jumped in the black helicopter and adjusted my sword so that I could sit down. The rat squealed and squeaked uncontrollably as I tried to make myself comfortable.

Bartholomew hopped in and sat next to me.

Mr. Cĕtĕră closed the door and sprung into the copilot's seat. The man then handed each of us a headset, which had a microphone attached to it and allowed us to converse freely with one another.

"Welcome, passengers!" The pilot announced through the headsets that we just put on.

I jumped when I saw that the pilot was just fifteen years old.

"I'm Jacob Tĕrră, your faithful pilot. I'm a Măgūs Lătīnūs, just like you. You're Alaĕna, right? And wow, is that a sword? And what is that noise?"

"Yeah, I'm Alaĕna, and, yes, this is a sword. That noise is a rat." I pulled out the man-rat from my pocket and enlightened, "It's a long story."

"That is one evil-looking rat," he declared, eyeing the rodent carefully.

"He's a former Damsel," Bartholomew explained.

"Ah." Jacob Tĕrră nodded.

I stuck the man-rat back in my pocket, which he was none too pleased about, and asked, "You're fifteen?"

"Well, actually I'm fourteen-and-a-three-quarters. I've been flying since I was five. My dad was a pilot for the Marines. He died in action because of a complete helicopter engine failure. So, I'm determined to make the helicopter engine un-failable, and I have. This engine has been proved to be un-failable." He smiled, and I knew he was proud of his dad—and his helicopter engine. "I just hope that one day the government will accept my research and mass produce these babies." He patted the door of the helicopter. "Well, Mr. C, looks like we're ready to fly. Hold on to your lunch."

Jacob started pushing a bunch of buttons, flipping switches, and pulling a couple of levers. "Here we go!" The helicopter jerked as it lifted off the ground.

I peered out the window and saw my dad and Ms. Peterson waving. She looked like she was crying, which was weird since I barely even knew her and vice versa. Maybe she was just happy the last of the living rats was gone.

As the helicopter bounced around even more, I felt around for something to grab onto and ended up grabbing Bartholomew's arm.

He grunted and showed me a handle to hold on to.

I took that instead.

We rose a hundred feet, two thousand feet, five thousand feet, and then seven thousand feet into the air and then sped forward at 235 knots, according to Jacob.

I heard some sounds on the headset. "Wahoo! Yeah! This is so awesome!" I figured out that it was Bartholomew shouting into his headset.

Jacob Tĕrră smiled. "Maybe you'll be an engineer and pilot, like me."

"Oh, that would be awesome. This is so cool! Whoa, oh yeah, this is fun!" my brother joyously cried as he tossed up his hands.

I chuckled because I had never seen Bartholomew like that. I hated heights, but I loved seeing Bartholomew having fun.

We flew for about five hours before Jacob pushed a button and spoke. "Five-eight-seven-one asking for permission to land."

A voice conveyed through the radio replied, "Permission granted. What took you so long, Jake?"

Jacob grinned. "I had to pick up a couple of recruits: a thirteen-year-old girl and her friend, and also a former Damsel who is now a rat, apparently."

We heard laughing. "A rat, you say? That's the first time anyone actually hung onto a Damsel-turned-animal. Now, to look on the bright side of things, it looks like we might have found you a girlfriend. We haven't had a thirteen-year-old around here in what? Thirty years? Much less a girl. Is she pretty?"

"Oh, quit it, Goober. Ya know, she is listening to this conversation," Jacob stated.

I assuredly cleared my throat. "That's right. I'm listening."

Bartholomew wholeheartedly chuckled, and Mr. Cĕtĕră joined him in his merriment.

"Uh, gotta go. See you in a couple minutes. Oh, goodness, dude, why didn't you tell me it was on?" We heard a loud laugh and then a bunch of static.

Jacob sighed. "Poor Goober. Vŏx always playing jokes like that on him. One time he recorded this line of Goober singing in the shower and played it on the speakers. Ha, it was funny, though you have to feel kinda bad for the guy."

Just as I shook my head and smiled, the Drăcōmūscă jolted upward.

Jacob groaned. "Sorry, updraft. This is going to be a rough landing. So, hold on tight and tighten your seat belts." We tilted at a horizontal and then a sub-vertical angle. He was talking while he pushed some buttons and flipped some switches, causing the propellers to rotate and making a smoother ride for us, although it was still pretty jarring. The landing was hard, but, with the excellent design and amazing pilot, the Drăcōmūscă made it safely onto the black helicopter pad, which resided inside the side of a rocky mountain. The opening closed above our heads as soon as we landed. Our pilot turned off the engine and opened his door.

Mr. Cĕtĕră got out, walked off into a hallway, and vanished from sight.

Bartholomew and I jumped out of the aircraft with an audible *clang*.

"Phew," I whistled, looking around me. All around me were parts sprawled about. Sparks were flying everywhere, and the banging of hammers and whirring of drills rang through the gigantic room. Also, people were yelling in… Latin?

"This place is cool, isn't it?"

I jumped and placed a hand on my sword. Because I had been so engrossed in absorbing the magnitude of the place around me, I hadn't noticed that Jacob had walked up next to me.

"Whoa, sorry I scared you! So, please don't hurt me! But… amazing, isn't it?" he inquired, motioning to everything.

I nodded, relaxing. "Indeed, very." As he was out in the open, I was able to get a decent look at him.

He had really short, black hair and was beginning to grow a little mustache, though it might have been a grease smudge. He had broad shoulders and was two inches taller than me. What really stood out to me were his friendly eyes and warm smile with straight, white teeth, which contrasted boldly against his dark brown skin.

Jacob looked to Bartholomew, who had joined us, and me, proudly announcing, "Welcome, Alaĕna and Bartholomew, to the home base of the M-L-P-A!"

CHAPTER 4

What's a Chocolate Bar?

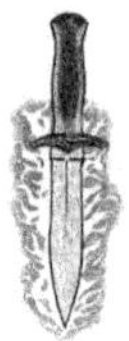

With jaw dropped, my brother's eyes widened. "Wow, this place is radical."

Studying the room, I saw only metal walls and titanium floors. I didn't know how he could like all of that so much. So I stared at him critically and slapped my forehead with my hand, groaning. "Really? Radical? How about these: out-of-this-world, breathtaking, awe-inspiring, amazing, unreal, awesome." I paused for a moment, then scrunched my nose and waved my hand in front of my face. "But also smelly!"

"Oh, so rats don't bother you, but this does? This is paradise for me." Bartholomew sighed.

Jacob laughed. "Looks like I have an engineer-in-training." He slapped Bartholomew on the back, knocking him off balance. The fourteen-year-old laughed even harder.

I smirked. "Until now, I didn't know you liked anything of

this sort, Bartholomew."

"Well, if you spent ten seconds in my room, you would know. I have so many helicopter and airplane drawings, you would be overwhelmed," Bartholomew huffed.

"How would I know? You never invited me over. You always came up with some sort of excuse," I said.

He sheepishly looked down, playing with a bolt on the floor, and sighed. "Well, the truth is… my mom has lost it."

"Lost it?" I asked. "What do you mean, your mom has lost it? As in our mom has gone insane?"

Bartholomew continued to gaze at the helipad. "Oh, um, yeah. She cracked when she got a phone call one day. She had yelled into the phone and then started crying. She's never been the same." He frowned.

Jacob thought for a moment and then smiled. "Maybe she heard that she had been elected president."

I raised an eyebrow. *Pūĕr, was that a bad joke. I could think of something way better.* I thought. "Or," I suggested, "maybe she heard that her daughter was alive and best friends with her son and felt guilty for leaving her daughter with her father who thought that she had abandoned him and then found out that her daughter was consequently abandoned by the man she knew as her lover. Makes sense to me."

Jacob looked puzzled.

Bartholomew blinked. "That first one, I don't get. Second, better, but very confusing! Although, if you're trying to make me feel better, you're doing horribly."

"Eh, true." I did a quick smile, trying to be warm and friendly, but not very well. Jacob covered for me and beamed his now-famous ear-to-ear-smile. Footsteps approached from the left side.

"Is this the girl I need to run away from?" A fifteen to

sixteen—I think since I learned early on that I was terrible with guessing ages—year old boy came into view. He had the same stature as Jacob, but he had very light blond hair and light tan skin.

Jacob nodded to me. "Uh, yeah, you might want to start running."

The boy laughed and held out his hand for me to shake. "So, does she bite?"

"She does," I said, shaking his hand. "If you're edible, but, evidently, you're not," I smirked.

He nervously tittered and looked at Jacob, who was trying not to laugh. Pointing to the thing in my jacket, he asked, "Whoa, is that a sword?"

I sighed. "Yes, it is a sword, otherwise that would be one large toothpick."

"I do know what a sword is, but never mind. So, he's the ML?" the young man asked.

"No, I am," I said plainly.

He blinked and looked at Jacob, who just shrugged his shoulders.

Bartholomew held out his hand and introduced himself. "Name's Bartholomew, and you?"

The young man, still seeming a bit shocked, shook my brother's hand and replied, "Gūběrnătŏr Ăssistěntěs Vălětě. My friends call me Goober."

Bartholomew chortled, and Goober glared at him, which then caused my brother to stop and look around, whistling innocently.

Goober shook his head and continued, "Anyways, I'm the master when it comes to radio controls and flight assistance unless my treacherous coworker interferes."

"But not girls," Jacob whispered in my ear, smirking.

Goober frowned. "I heard that."

"Yeah, you can't even talk to a girl without turning red, especially her," he said teasingly as he pointed to me.

"When you say her, do you mean me? Is it because I'm the girl you embarrassed yourself over while speaking into a headset?"

He blushed.

I concluded that it meant yes.

"I tell ya," Jacob began, "he's never messed up that bad before. I mean, he's messed up really, I mean *really* bad before, but that's the worst so far!"

Goober glared at him.

Jacob shrugged him off and continued, "But it seems as if you're fine with him."

I smiled. "I have a 'don't pay any attention to your punching bag' policy." *And,* I thought, *teenage boys are idiots. Even teenage boys say teenage boys are idiots. The old guys talking about their teenage years say that they were idiots. Hmm, though, so are most teenage girls. Oh well, lucky for me I just have parent abandonment issues and not being-an-idiot issues.*

"Yeah," Bartholomew sighed, "punching bag." He rubbed his arm.

I huffed, "Come on, Cowboy Up, it was just a soft jab."

"Cowboy Up, humph, you try having bruises the size of a hedgehog, and what does 'Cowboy Up' mean, anyway?"

Jacob and Goober looked at Bartholomew then me.

"Suck it up; be a man—though I don't think I would want to be one anyway, blech—get a backbone; harden your hide… you get the point. Be like me when I was writhing on the ground with pain and don't whine."

"I do have a backbone. It's called a spine. Ever heard of it?"

"Well, I actually have, you…"

"Alaĕna," Jacob and Goober said in unison, attracting the attention of all the kids, who subsequently stopped working to listen. Goober took it from there. "Control your anger. When we get angry, we spout off Latin, and you might end up turning somebody," he motioned to Bartholomew, "into a pig. Trust me… it's happened before to basically all of us." Jacob nodded.

Unexpectedly, all the teens around us began to tell stories of people whom they had turned into animals.

One girl said, "I got in a fight with my mom and, unknowingly, turned her into a cow."

Another kid nodded. "Yeah, I remember that."

A boy with curly, red hair said, "I turned my grandpa into a dung beetle." Everybody looked at him weirdly. "What? Some of us have more active imaginations than others, and I happen to be one of them."

I blinked and shook my head. "Okay, so, Măgī Latīnī have anger management issues?" All the kids said "Yep", "Yes", "Ītă", or just nodded their heads. "Luckily, I have learned to control my temper over the years," I pompously declared. Bart rolled his eyes.

A deeper voice boomed throughout the room, capturing the attention of everyone present at the moment.

I turned my head to see Mr. Cĕtĕră. In his hand was a cup of coffee that had what looked like a hand-painted '#1 Măgīstĕr' on its side. However, the writing looked as if someone had used a typewriter. *It must have been made using Magic or a master painter's hand,* I thought.

Another man, who was wearing a faded orange jumpsuit, stood next to him.

Mr. Cĕtĕră commanded loudly, "Who wants to show those Damsels they're completely wrong?"

"We do!" All of the teens shouted.

Mr. Cĕtĕră smiled and asked, "How do we show them they're wrong?"

"We can show them that they're wrong by making useful inventions with our Magic," they responded.

Mr. Cĕtĕră's beam broadened. "Good." Turning to the man next to him, he said, "Mr. Vŏx, would you please show Goober how to control the headphones? We don't want any more… embarrassing moments."

Goober turned red with discomfort.

"Come on, Goober, let's go. And try not to make a fool of yourself again," Mr. Vŏx said.

Goober glowered at him. "But you're the one who did it! Besides, she hasn't killed me yet, so it wasn't like Bella. Beauty and war, yep, that's her. But no matter what, she's the girl for me."

"Oh, yes, Bella. She still hates you," Jacob said.

Sighing, Goober replied, "I know, and I'm not surprised either."

I was tempted to ask what happened, but I decided against it. Thankfully, Jacob partially filled me in.

Jacob snorted. "That's what happens when you assume an ML is out of earshot. Măgī Latīnī have more acute senses than regular people."

I nodded affirmatively.

Mr. Vŏx let out a stifled laugh. "When they want to, that is. I tell Goober to clean his station and, nope! He thinks that I said, 'Go get a chocolate bar'. Vīvūm." He started walking away with Goober when I asked, "What's a chocolate bar?" Once more, silence filled the room. The gaze of every single pair of eyes was planted on me. Every jaw was dropped.

Jacob, Goober, Bartholomew, Mr. Vŏx, and Mr. Cĕtĕră all looked at me in awe.

"You don't know what a chocolate bar is?" Bartholomew gasped.

I huffed. "I barely know what an apple is, how would I know what a chocolate bar is? Does it have peanuts in it? I'm deathly allergic to peanuts."

"No, well, depends on what kind of chocolate. If it's just plain chocolate, you're fine. Although, some chocolate is processed in a facility that processes peanuts…" Jacob said, trailing off in thought.

Bart seemed quite stunned. "No apples, no chocolate, no peanuts… what do you eat?

"I eat whatever I can get my hands on. I'm not exactly a millionaire. I can't afford a stick of gum since the only way to get money in Wetly included things that weren't exactly… uh… legal. Although, you can get a bit of cash off of dares. Heh, they're all suckers." I sighed as I began to feel very different again. Nervously, I studied the holes in the floor. They were a couple inches across and had a rod in them which cut them in half. *What are those for?* I learned only later that those holes were used to hold down aircraft. Due to the lack of schooling I received, I barely knew anything about anything, including the holes in the ground.

"Now, look what you guys did!" A tall, brown-skinned girl walked onto the helipad. "You hurt her feelings. Why don't you all either apologize or get back to work? The more you work, the less you get in trouble. Wait, is that a…"

"Yes, it is a sword, and I am the Măgūs Lătīnūs, not my brother—ugh, that's weird—Bartholomew," I answered. "And that thing squealing his little head off in my pocket is a Damsel who is now a rat. Long story, which I will explain one of these days."

She appeared to be startled but simply nodded, not saying

a word.

All of the teens' eyes were lowered, except for Bartholomew's and my eyes, that is.

"Yes, ma'am," they all replied before beginning their work once more.

I gazed at the girl for a moment.

She looked to be about eighteen years old and had black, frizzy hair with a couple of red streaks. I could hear what I thought was a hint of an Italian accent.

I wish I could have that look, even that accent, I thought. *She seems so confident, so sure of herself, must've had a great childhood, unlike me,* I thought, feeling sad with the memories of my past. Sleeping in the snow, frostbite, wounds that could have—should have— killed me, and then… I hardened myself, steeled my resolve, looked straight into her eyes, and asked, "Who are you?"

She grandly introduced herself. "I'm Isabella Walsh, or Medici, on my mother's side. I'm from Italy. You must be Alaĕna. Sălvĕ, Amīca Parvă Mĕă!"

I looked at Bartholomew, who seemed entranced by her. *Teenage boys are idiots. They are all idiots, especially when it comes to girls. Well, except for Dīcărĕ. He was great, well, after I taught him a lesson or two, that is.* To snap him out of his stupor, I slid to his side and punched him in the shoulder.

"Ow! Why must you be so violent?" Bartholomew ex- claimed, rubbing his arm.

"I grew up in a violent environment?"

"Well, so did I, remember? Hello? Fellow Wetlian here!"

"Oh, please. We had completely different childhoods. You were safe, loved, and…"

Bart groaned and yelled, "Would you shut up about that? Not everything is about you!"

My arms trembled, and my cheeks heated up. I was about

to go at him when Mr. Cĕtĕră pulled me back.

"Alaĕna, that's enough!" Mr. Cĕtĕră declared. "Do we need to detain you?"

"No, do I need to detain you? If you don't want to be detained—which you really wouldn't like—then let go of me!" I shook him off, and the man-rat began squealing louder and shriller than before. I glowered at Mr. Cĕtĕră.

Mr. Cĕtĕră put up his hands. "Alaĕna, I was trying to help you."

"I'm not the one who needs help," I said.

He seemed confused by my tone of voice, which was not accusing, but sad. So, he asked, "If not you, then whom?"

"My family," I answered. This has nothing to do with my oath, since they were my family long before that dreadful evening.

"I thought you didn't have a family," Bartholomew stated.

I sighed and shut my eyes tightly. "Look, I had someone taking care of me. Someone I actually might have cared about. But that's over and dead now, with nothing to be done about it. So, can we move on to another subject?"

Bartholomew and Mr. Cĕtĕră nodded. The man said, "Of course, Alaĕna, that's fine. Well, Mr. Vŏx, Goober, continue on your journey, and Isabella, why don't you show Alaĕna around and tell her the basics of being a Măgūs Lătīnūs? Jacob, why don't you show Bartholomew our aircraft?" Bartholomew's eyes lit up, and I guessed that he was trying not to jump up and down with anticipation.

"Aw, sweet!" my brother joyously exclaimed.

I looked at Bartholomew and rolled my eyes. *Who is he listening to? The average surfer dude on TV?*

Bartholomew eagerly followed Jacob to a hallway with a sign that said "Air Craft" on it in neon lights.

Neon, why is it always neon, why not just a sign that says "Air Craft" in just plain lights? I asked myself. Before he disappeared, I called, "Vălĕ, Bartholomew!"

"Vălĕ, Germăna Mĕă!" he replied.

My Sister, what a weird thing to think about. I looked at Isabella, who was motioning for me to follow her. Before I did, I looked back at Bartholomew and thought, *We are lifelong friends but now brother and sister. And what about my father being threatened? What does that have to do with anything? Pūĕr, my life is a mystery; a mystery I hope will one day be solved. Hopefully, it will be by me and not some bad guy.*

———◆———

About two hours later, we had almost finished our tour which included a Construction Center, a life-size model of a weird guy with a scroll in his hand who was the founder of Mulpa who looked suspiciously like Mr. Cĕtĕră, a Biology Center, an Archaeology Center, and the rest of the things Mr. Cĕtĕră mentioned earlier, save one.

"Where's the Magology Center?" I asked Isabella as we walked down a dark hallway. Every once in a while, a door would appear with a glowing sign above it.

Hesitantly, she replied, "Uh, I don't think Mr. Cĕtĕră would want me to show you that place, since it's for top personnel only."

I looked down, disappointed. "Oh, okay. So, where do I sleep?"

She beamed. "I think you'll like your room."

I looked at her in amazement and gasped. "I have a room?"

She scrunched her eyebrows in confusion and stated, "You look surprised."

"I've never had a room unless you call a box a room," I

responded.

She stopped walking, and her jaw dropped about half an inch. "I didn't know that. I thought your dad had taken care of you," she assumed.

"Ha! He was a wimp! As soon as I was old enough, which was when I was about six, he dumped me on the side of the road. He only came back for me last week. Ms. Alilah Peterson, his girlfriend, almost screamed when she saw who I was with." I chuckled as I remembered her horrified face.

Isabella looked concerned. "Who were you hanging out with that day?"

"A couple of people who owed me a buck fifty each from a dare I made them. I said that the mayor would scream like a little girl if I put a rat on his chest in the middle of the night, and they said he would scream like a little boy. I won to the complete humiliation of the mayor. For being a terrorist, he sure is a wimp."

Shaking her head, she asked, "What did they look like? Did they tell you their names?"

"Oh, them, hmm, they looked kind of like me with black clothes. They dressed warmly, and both carried guns that weren't loaded but were just for show. I've learned that they can't resist a dare. There's a bunch of people like them in Wetly. I always outsmart them. And they wouldn't dare tell anyone their names. They usually make up nicknames. My Wetlian nickname is Sharp Hand."

"Sharp Hand?" she asked.

"Yeah, it's kind of a long story," I said. "Same with Banana Bear, Cheeky Monkey, and Apple Arm. Apple Arm is how, for the most part, I got my fake name. Yeah, what I did to him is not exactly something to be proud of."

She seemed a bit frightened as she asked me what I had

done to him.

I responded in rather a casual tone, "Cut his arm when he had tried to, um, do things to me. The doctors ended up having to amputate it because of a serious infection that was spreading to the rest of his body."

"Wow," she looked surprised, maybe a little bit frightened. "So, did you hurt him with a knife or that sword?"

"Oh, this sword? No, of course not. I got this today. Nah, I used this knife." I unsheathed my knife and held it out for her to inspect. "I carry it around for protection. I know it's a bit more conspicuous than a gun, but guns are way too loud. Knives are much quieter, except for the part when you cut somebody, and they scream really loudly."

Isabella blinked and shook her head before cocking it and pointing to my throat. "What's that?"

I felt the familiar ridge, which was the faint scar on the front of my neck. "A scar," I replied.

"How would you get a scar like that on your neck?"

"I was attacked by a dog," I fibbed.

She frowned but didn't ask anything more.

Zipping up my jacket further, I continued our previous conversation. "Now, back to the subject. Can I please see the Magology Center? It seems that I would be useful there."

"And why?"

"They could study me and try to figure out why I can use weapons."

"Yes, that is a bit of a puzzle, isn't it?" She acknowledged. "Well... I can't take you there since it's against the rules. So, let's just go to your room."

I heaved an annoyed sigh but reluctantly agreed.

Down an elevator and through three hallways was my room. Its door was made of titanium, which seemed a bit excessive to me. Looking at the doorknob, I saw that it had a card-swipe security system. After Isabella swiped a key, a little light on the lock turned green, and I heard the solid 'clunk' of the door unlocking. As I stepped inside the pitch black room, I felt for the light switch and, when I found it, flipped it up. Gazing in awe and wonder, I said, "Wow. This room is huge!"

Isabella looked around and muttered, "It isn't that large."

A twin-sized bed sat beside the wall on my left; a large, dark brown maple desk which was complete with a comfy, swiveling chair hanging beside it on my right; and a mini fridge-and-freezer was beside the desk. I opened the fridge and noticed that it was stocked with A&W Root Beer, fresh fruits and veggies, sliced turkey, and homemade cheese. There were also a couple of packages of generically branded milk chocolate bars and... "What are 'buttery fingers'?" I inquired.

Isabella answered, "They are peanuts..."

I quickly shook my head and waved my hands. "Oh no, can you please get this out of here? I am deathly allergic to peanuts."

Isabella seemed surprised but quickly grabbed the candy from the fridge. "You are? Sorry, I'll get that away from you. We don't need you dying because of a bite of Butterfingers."

"I think I would rather die at the hands of the enemy than that pathetic death," I said, and the man-rat started squealing again as if he was saying *I can arrange that for you.* "Not today ratty."

"By the way, how did you come by him?" Isabella asked, pointing at my pocket.

Reluctantly, I explained to her a brief story of how I turned him into a rat.

Once I was finished, she said, "So, you have a Damsel higher-up in your pocket?" I nodded, and she held out her hand. "Hmm... I'll take him if that's all right with you. I assume my father will want him interrogated."

I put up a finger. "First, I want to know if I can ask him some questions as well."

"What questions…" she began, but I cut her off.

"That's something between *it* and me. Do I have your promise?" I held out my hand.

She reluctantly took it and responded, "Yes."

I grabbed Mr. Ratty out of my pocket and handed him to her.

He was not very happy about it and struggled the whole time.

She took him, and he almost dropped to the floor, but she got a good hold on him eventually. She opened the 'buttery fingers' bag, stuck him in there, and carried the bag and the man-rat out the door. Speedily, she tossed me the room key and inquired, "Have you met him before now, truthfully?"

I mimicked his tone of voice and accent as I replied, "Yes, girlie."

The woman left with a surprised look on her face.

After she had closed the door, I walked over to the bed. Soft, tan sheets covered it. Three puffy, soft pillows covered the head of the bed, which was also made of maple wood. A wood—I'm guessing that you're beginning to see a pattern—two-drawer nightstand was placed beside the bed. Atop the nightstand was a hand-carved wooden lamp with a curlicue light bulb. Also, an electric clock faced the mattress which said eight o'clock p.m.

Inside the top drawer, someone had put a Latin Dictionary. I flipped it open. The first page was signed by Mr. Cĕtĕră, and it read as follows:

To my dear Alaĕna,

Things might be hard for you now and in your future. But you will find being a Măgūs Lătīnūs is not so hard. I have watched you grow up to be a beautiful young lady with a fiery temper but great compassion and intelligence. You have been as a daughter to me, and I hope that I have been as a father to you. Know that whatever happens, I have and will always love you.

Sincerely,

Măgīstĕr Ĕt Cĕtĕră, Teacher and the Rest

Smiling, I thought, *He always did seem like a father to me, more than my biological but less than Pătĕr.*

I set the book back into the drawer and closed it. At the wall near the foot of my bed were two doors, which I opened one at a time. First, I unlocked the one to the right. It was a three-piece bathroom. The second door opened to reveal a large walk-in closet adorned with my style of clothes and, at the end, a shelf holding a complete set of black leather armor. I wondered why there was armor there but didn't bother myself with it.

Seeing a space next to it, I slipped the knife out of my jacket, placed it on the shelf, and put my sword next to it so that its hilt rested against the shelf. After two steps toward the door, I sprinted back and grabbed my knife from the shelf. Sighing with contentment, I walked out the door and ventured to the middle of the room where the table and matching chairs sat, waiting to be used. The walls were covered with huge half logs, and the floors were dark brown—oh, you get the point. The place was made to look like a log cabin, which was my dream home.

I ran to my bed and jumped on it. There was neither the thud of my back hitting concrete nor the pain that soon followed, just my sigh of complete and utter relief. After turning on my lamp, I set my knife on the nightstand and switched off the main light. It took me a little while, but I was eventually able to convince myself to get up, take a shower, and then put some PJs on. That shower was like heaven since I hadn't touched hot water in over two years. Twenty or so minutes passed, and I got out of the shower, dried off, and put on a pair of PJs. Once that was done, I galloped to the bed and flopped down on the soft sheets. As soon as my head hit the pillow, I fell asleep.

CHAPTER 5

The Voice

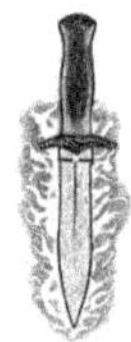

After three hours of deep, peaceful slumber, I heard a voice. It was soft, yet strong. It was young, yet ancient. It was alien, yet familiar. It, in summary, puzzled me.

"Who is it?" I asked, wiping the grogginess from my eyes.

The voice spoke to me again, *Show them.*

I sat straight up, grabbed my knife, and jumped out of my bed. "Who's there?"

Show them, it stated, and the voice spoke no more.

"Oh, great." I put my head in my hands. "I'm losing my mind." I sighed and fell backward onto my bed with a whooshing thump and a slight bounce. *Wait, I know that voice. It's the one that gave Dīcărě my name! But what does it mean by 'show them', anyway? Show who? And what am I supposed to show?* I thought as I crawled under the covers. Weariness overruling my curiosity, I pulled the blankets over my head and soon conked out.

Later that night, I had an odd dream where I was walking down the hallway toward an old wooden door whose hinges were rusted and whose wood was rotted and infested with termites. I put my hands on the door and realized that it was locked. For some reason, I began to chant, "Păx Ăd Tĕrrăm Per Măgōs Latīnōs Ĕt Ūnīcornĕs Vōlătīcĕs." The door slowly opened. I stepped in, and a light showed before me. I thought I saw feathers and heard the clip-clop of hooves.

The time has come, dear one, and now you must show them. Show them a glimpse of who you are, it said in a loud and glorious yet soft and supple voice that seemed to echo throughout the room.

The dream ended.

Groggily, I rubbed my eyes and stretched. The dream trickled back into my memory. "What did that door lead to and why did I chant, 'Peace to the earth through the Latin Magicians and' what was it? 'Ūnīcornĕs Vōlătīcĕs'. Flying Unicorns? They must be creatures of Magic. But what does it have to do with me?" Before I could give it any more thought, a grainy voice wailed through the halls.

"Goooood Morniiiiiing Măgī Latīnī, this is Mr. Cĕtĕră, your Vice President speaking. This is today's schedule: seven o'clock to eight o'clock is breakfast; eight o'clock to nine o'clock is the meeting at the Biology Center; nine o'clock to nine-thirty is the usual. However, if you are not assigned to a center, then please come see me in my office, and I will assign a center to you. Nine-thirty to six o'clock you will do-what-you-do in your assigned Centers. Also, a special announcement for all of you wannabe Magologists: the Magology Center has a spot available after an unfortunate accident. To the young, puerile BOY Galen, that joke you played on Hal was not funny, and,

Miss Lyn, could you please repair the door to the Center? It's rusted, rotted, *and* termite-infested due to Galen," Mr. Cĕtĕră said, exasperated. "That is all."

After he finished, it hit me. "That's it!" I exclaimed as I sat up.

"What's it?"

I jumped as I noticed Bartholomew standing in the doorway. "Whoa!" I fell off my bed and turned red with embarrassment and anger. "You are a buffoonish, foolhardy, imprudent idiot!" His eyes widened he began to say something, but I jumped out and marched right up to him. "I have never met a more brainless boy in my entire life." I punched him in the gut and shoved him out the door.

He wheezed, "Alaĕna… Mr. Cĕtĕră… wanted… to meet… with you…" and almost collapsed.

I put my hands on my hips. "Cowboy Up. Any guy should be able to take a punch from a girl."

He glared at me and steadied himself using the door.

I took a deep breath and apologized, "I'm sorry, Bartholomew. You just need to knock before you come into a girl's room."

He nodded. "Don't know any other girls except you. I'm kind of new when it comes to girls. I know my mom, but she…" My brother squeezed his eyes shut with pain, although he eventually continued. "I have to feed her and things like that. She really is out of it. The only time she talked was when she asked if you were going to move back in with your dad." He looked down and shook his head, his hair bouncing a bit.

I continued in a quieter and softer voice, "Where does he want me to meet him?"

"Didn't you hear?" He snapped out of his saddened state. "His office. Mr. Cĕtĕră himself said it in the announcement right before you said, 'That's it'. By the way, what were you talking about?" He tilted his head a bit to the left, as a dog does while trying to hear a sound better.

Should I tell him? No, it isn't the right time… and he would think I'm going insane. Pūĕr, are my secrets adding up. I grinned. "I finally figured out that math question we were dared to solve. Ya know, the one from last week?"

Bartholomew thought about it for a moment then smiled. "Oh, *yeah*, that one. Oh man, you're lucky. I could never have figured out that one. What was the answer?"

"Why would I tell you since it would ruin the whole point, wouldn't it?"

Bartholomew shrugged. "Yeah, I guess so. We better get going. Never know how long it's going to take to get anywhere around here. I have to wonder if they tried to make this place unbelievably confusing," he grumbled.

"That's what I thought! But, anyways, let's go." I suddenly realized a very important detail. "Whoops. Got to get dressed first! Shoo, Bartholomew! Out you go! Meet you in Mr. Cĕtĕră's office!"

Before he was completely out, he handed me a map and said, "Trust me, you'll need it. As I've said before, this place is more bewildering than the mind of Psycho Sarah."

"Ha, that's bad." I smiled. "Thanks, Bart." As he had abruptly stopped, I frowned and skewed my head a little bit.

He looked a bit bashful as he said, "Alaĕna, I just wanted to say that I'm glad we're family. I had a hunch that one day we would be family, one way or another." I was about to ask him what he meant, but he closed the door.

What does he mean by 'one way or another'? I pondered. *Ugh! He is completely and utterly annoying. Now, what he said is going to haunt me for eternity. If boys ever say anything halfway competent, they go and do something like that. I suppose I'm getting a taste of my own medicine.*

I walked over to my closet, put a pair of black pants on, slipped on a turquoise shirt, buckled a belt around my waist, and put on my rugged black jacket.

Bumping onto the shelf, I grunted with pain and slid my sword into the belt, along with the knife that I had retrieved from my nightstand. My jacket was long enough to hide the eleven-inch-long blade of the knife, but the sword stuck out very conspicuously.

On the way out, I grabbed an apple, locked the door, and ran down the hallway.

Looking at Bartholomew's map, I took the elevator up three levels. The music was Beethoven and Mozart. *I hate elevator music. It usually has cheesy songs, at least, so I've heard since this is only the second time I've been in an elevator. But, at least, the music's classic instead of the modern, weird, teenybopper*—yes, that's an actual word—*music they have these days.* After the elevator, I sprinted down the dark hallway and took a left at a 'T' turn, then a right at a 'Y' turn. Two wrong turns and three right turns later, I met Bartholomew at the door.

He crossed his arms across his chest and gave me a questioning look. "What took you so long?"

Instead of dignifying his question with an answer, I embarrassed the poor boy whom I could call brother by asking, "What did you mean by 'we would be family, one way or another'? Hmm, my rather confused-looking Bartholomew, what did you mean?"

"Uh… um…" He swallowed hard then said, "We better get inside. We're already late."

"I suppose, but you may procrastinate now, but mark my words: I will get my answer one day one way," I clenched my hand into a fist and shoved it near his face, causing him to flinch, "or another." And with that, I marched through the door, leaving him red as a ripe tomato.

In the stainless-steel-walled room sat Mr. Cĕtĕră, who was lounging in a brown, leathery chair behind a metal desk piled high with stacks of papers and folders. "Ah, Alaĕna," my Latin teacher said, clasping his hands together. "I hope you like your room. Where's Bartholomew?"

I pointed with my thumb toward the open doorway.

"What did you do to him?" he asked, eyeing me and then the doorway.

I placed a hand on my chest and concocted an innocent look to put on my face. "Me, Mr. Cĕtĕră?"

"Bartholomew!" Clearing my throat, I gave it my best shot to have an English accent as I yelled, "Come on lad, the hunt is afoot, and you are keeping the king from his white stag!" I waited for a response, and, when I did get it, it wasn't the response I had hoped for.

As Bartholomew screamed, we ran immediately outside.

"Bartholomew?" I looked around, but he was nowhere to be seen. "Bartholomew!" I called.

Without delay, Mr. Cĕtĕră joined me.

"Where is he?" I asked.

Bartholomew cried out again.

"This way," I yelled as I ran off down the left hall.

"No… get off me… help me!" Bartholomew shouted.

Though I knew the dangers might be great, I ran to my best friend and brother.

"Wait, Alaĕna, wait!" Mr. Cĕtĕră yelled, but I ignored him and continued.

I came to a huge room and gasped at the struggle before me. "Qūĭd Īn Tĕrră?"

In a panic, Bartholomew cried, "Help me!"

I watched helplessly as Bartholomew was lifted into the air by the slimy arms of a... what?

"Alaĕna, that's a Sĕpīa Vōlătīcă, a Flying Cuttlefish!" Mr. Cĕtĕră exclaimed as he sprinted over to me.

"Well, that doesn't help me save Bartholomew, does it now?" I snapped.

He grunted and yelled to Bartholomew, "Stay away from the mouth! It has a beak that will crush through a man and teeth that can slice through flesh."

"I'm trying to stay away from all of it!" Bartholomew yanked one of the tentacles off of his torso, which left a few nice-sized, smoking holes in his side. The creature dropped him, and he tried to crawl away but it grabbed him by the legs and pulled him back into the air.

I cringed and started to make a dash toward it, but Mr. Cĕtĕră caught my arm. "No, don't, Alaĕna. That won't work."

I wrenched my arm free and queried, "Well, what can we do to rescue him?"

He looked me in the eye and said, "Alaĕna, we can do nothing. When someone is chosen by the creatures to be its prey, there is nothing you or any Măgūs Lătīnūs can do. He's dead unless he can save himself."

I shook my head and defiantly declared, "No, you're wrong. I can and will do something. Hold on Bartholomew!" I turned on my heel and sprinted to the Sĕpīa Vōlătīcă. A tentacle appeared in front of me, and I jumped over it, softening my landing with a shoulder roll.

"I'm holding!" cried Bartholomew.

I rolled again to get closer. *This creature is of Magic, and I'm assuming that only a weapon of Magic can kill it,* I thought. Taking a deep breath, I reached into my jacket and slid the knife from its sheath. Holding it with both hands I yelled with all my heart, "Căpĕrĕ Flămmaĕ, Ăccĕndī!" And the blade became as clear as glass, showing the inside where there appeared to be dozens of individual flames flickering like a midsummer's bonfire.

Running beneath the Flying Cuttlefish, I slashed the arm that was holding Bartholomew.

The creature shrieked as its slimy, white limb fell to the floor with a thump, and Bartholomew cried out with pain as his head hit the hard cement floor, knocking him unconscious. The white flesh of the arm was smoking where I had cut it and was slowly disintegrating.

I had to distract it so that it wouldn't bother Mr. Cĕtĕră as he tried to get to Bartholomew and drag him to safety. So, I yelled, "Hĕūs! Măssă Măgnă Cībă Mărīs, Vīdĕ Hīc!"

Its huge black eye glared at me, and the beast turned upon me.

I ducked as an arm reached to grab my head, causing it to miss by just inches. "Hă! Sī Īllūd Ĕst Optīmūs Tūūs, Quăm Ĕs Dēdēcūs Ăd Spēcīĕ Tūō!" I taunted.

The creature let out a low rumble and clacked its enormous beak.

I jumped backward into a back handspring when it tried to knock me off my feet by hitting my legs. During my move, I glanced over in the direction that I had last seen Mr. Cĕtĕră. He was there helping Bartholomew up along with a few other adults and teens who I didn't recognize.

As the heel of my right foot touched the wall when I finished my back handspring, the Sĕpīa Vōlătīcă rushed at me.

Expecting this, I rolled forward and underneath it, but one of the tentacle's suction cups stuck to my left arm, and I screamed with agony. Though my vision had been blurred due to the pain, I could see that it had left a red hole in my arm the exact shape of the suction cup. It burned as though someone had poured rubbing alcohol on the open wound. I pressed my arm against my stomach and squeezed the hilt of my knife to the point at which my knuckles were completely white. *Well, at least it's not bleeding,* I thought.

The creature charged me again, and I dropped to the ground. My arm screamed with pain, but at least it passed over me without getting me once more. In front of me was my right hand, stretched out to avoid stabbing myself which would be a horribly painful way to die since I would disintegrate one atom at a time and feel every atom burn.

Using my outstretched hand and the hand beneath me, I pushed myself up to a kneeling position and stood. The pain was so great that I thought I was going to be sick, but I held on. Glancing behind, I saw the snapping beak of the Sĕpīa Vōlătīcă not five feet from my face. That moment was one of those 'one-second life or death decisions', and I recognized that I wouldn't be able to move out of the way in time or even fall to the ground. Therefore, I did the most logical thing and jumped towards and over the hideous, shrieking beast, knife in hand. It felt like I was in slow motion as the creature passed underneath me and while I twisted in mid-air. Its pupil dilated as my shadow passed over it. With one quick motion, I thrust my knife into its eye and let go. The beast shrieked, and I fell to the ground.

Tears came to my eyes as I landed on my shoulder, fracturing or breaking it. Either way, it hurt like crazy. Following that, I banged my head on the floor which was made of perfectly smooth and hard cement.

I tried to get up but to no avail, because my arms would no longer obey my command. As I shifted my weary gaze over to the Sĕpīa Vōlătīcă, I saw that it was closer to the ground than before, and the eye that I had stabbed, much to my delight, was completely gone. My knife had done its work and was slowly burrowing its way through the beast's body. The Flying Cuttlefish was experiencing the blade's heat at its maximum. *Cooked calamari, don't people eat that?* I thought.

The creature was but a foot from the ground when the ringing sound of metal hitting cement echoed through the room. The being shrieked one last time, then began vibrating. Before you could say Bob's your Uncle, I was covered in steaming hot cuttlefish meat. Every patch of skin on me burned as if someone had covered it in hot coals. The good thing was that the experience allowed me to move my limbs again.

"Y-ouch!" I exclaimed as I jumped up, flinging cuttlefish everywhere. By that time, I was wondering if anybody was going to help me, since, of course, I was missing part of my arm, I was covered in second-degree burns, and, to top that off, I had a broken or fractured shoulder. "Stătīs Ībī Ĕt Spĕctătīs Ăpūd Mē, Cŭr?" Then, I noticed they weren't staring at me but at my knife, which was firmly lodged in the floor. So, I limped over there, yanked the knife out, and commanded, "Căpĕrĕ Flămmaĕ, Exstīngūī!"

The flames acknowledged my voice, and the heat dissipated.

Sheathing my magnificent weapon, I turned to the thirty or so spectators that had gathered and asked, "Are you cowards? You must be, since you didn't help me! You could have at least distracted it or something!" The question was barely audible, so nobody seemed to notice it.

Bartholomew had finally regained consciousness and was repeatedly yelling, "Alaĕna! You have to help Alaĕna!"

I glanced at him one last time, fell to my knees, and then finally collapsed. The world began to spin around me and slowly fade into darkness.

The last thing I saw were two sets of hands, one dark and

one light, reaching toward me, and then… nothing.

My last thought was, *I hope this doesn't become a regularity!* And the cold grip of unconsciousness pulled me into a comforting embrace, cutting me off from the world.

———◆———

I awoke to the sight I hated as much as I hated my father. *Great, white, I feel like I'm trapped in a snowdrift.* I attempted to sit up, but a hand gently pushed me back down.

"Nice to see you awake. It's been about four days since you came here. A few of the MLs have been taking turns watching you." The face was blurred, but I guessed it was Jacob. I tried to say something about how Bartholomew was doing, but he cut me off. "Bartholomew's fine, a bit, well, *a lot* beat up, but alive." He smiled and leaned back in his metal chair. The creaking noise that the chair made caused my head to throb at an even higher scale.

"What you did was amazing," Jacob said, oblivious to my pain. "I arrived right after Bartholomew was rescued. Watching you take down the VS was spectacular, just incredible! And that knife… no one has ever seen anything like it. Because you see, Măgī Latīnī cannot forge weapons or even hold them. They can't even prick a Damsel with a needle! Where did you get it? And how in the world were you able to fight with it?"

"Uh…" I began, but Isabella Medici, who was standing in front of my bed wearing a nurse's uniform, interrupted me by saying, "Jacob, don't bother my patient with questions that can be answered later."

Jacob sighed, stood, and began to walk out of the room but, before that, stopped right next to Isabella and held his hand out to her.

The woman placed what might have been a five-dollar bill in it.

The young man closed his hand, put the cash in his pocket, and continued on his way.

"Sălvĕ, Alaĕna, are you feeling better?" Isabella asked.

I noticed that she phrased it so that it was a "yes or no" question. That way, I could nod or shake my head without having to speak. Something I sincerely appreciated since my throat felt like it was on fire.

As I had nodded, she smiled. "Bōnūs, Bōnūs. Now, I'm going to run some tests on you, okay? I need to make sure you are healing properly."

I nodded, and she spent the next two hours testing me. The tests didn't hurt, but they sure were weird. I've forgotten everything that happened at that time due to the drugs I was on, but I do remember her taking a blood sample.

After it was over, my eyelids were heavy. I yawned and blinked.

She straightened from her crouched position and said, "There, now. All done. You rest, and I'll see you tomorrow. Nŏctūs Bōnūs, Alaĕna!" She walked out of the room.

The lights turned off, and I conked out.

CHAPTER 6

Life of Songs

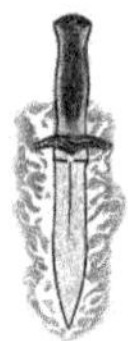

While I was asleep, I had another dream where I was walking on a dark forest path with a man and a boy. The man had long, black hair and a full beard, while the boy had light brown, shoulder-length hair and a clean-shaven chin.

As the man was teary-eyed and red from crying, I questioned him, "Why are you sad, father?"

"Oh, my sweet girl, I'm sad because our people are doomed." He sniffled, the moonlight reflecting off his numerous tears. Soon, his sniffles were joined by those of the boy who seemed to be around my age.

Confused, I asked, "What are our people doomed to, and what has doomed us?"

Wiping his eyes with the back of his hand, the man, who I somehow remembered was named Glenrick, explained, "My dear girl, we are doomed to a slow death by those who hunt us.

We can no longer make weapons or even hold them. We are defenseless, save turning our enemies into animals.

"We're doomed to this because of our own foolish mistakes. Because our people, save you, Quintus, and I, have betrayed our Protectors by murdering the Old One and Īncĕndīūm Fĕrŏx."

I gasped, covering my mouth with my hand. "Why would anyone do that?"

"I don't know, Alaĕna. But I did try to stop them, but they would not listen. Now, I grieve at the loss of the friendship of the wisest beings in all of the Earth, the Ūnīcornĕs Vōlătīcĕs, who are our protectors and our strengths. We also grieve over the loss of a great friend." He shook his head and sighed.

"At least you tried," I said as reassuringly as possible.

At that moment, a bright white light appeared before us. It said in a voice as firm as thunder yet as soft as the rustling of leaves, "Glenrick Bombyx, Quintus Cōr, and Alaĕna Bombyx." The being was female, that much I could tell by the voice.

Glenrick and Quintus kneeled before the magnificent creature, and I did the same.

"Yes, Ălă Lūnă, Moon Wing," Glenrick responded.

"Yes, shining one," Quintus answered.

"Yes, merciful one," I replied.

"Your people have betrayed us." Her echoing voice was harsh and filled with grief and anger. "They have killed both my Pătĕr and my Cŏnīūnx. You know your people will suffer my wrath and the wrath of my kind." The magnificent being's voice softened. "Yet you still try to set things right. Why?" She seemed honestly curious.

"Because our kinds have been together for the longest of times, and I don't want us to separate. We need each other, though we both might not like to admit it. Măgī Latīnī and Ūnīcornĕs Vōlătīcĕs are meant to be together," Quintus explained. "And because we felt that we needed to avenge our fallen friend."

"The boy is right," Glenrick stated. "Our kinds need each other. Your kin need a gentle hand while ours needs strength and protection."

The light grew brighter as Glenrick finished.

"I am delighted with your answers, Glenrick Bombyx and Quintus Cōr, but my kind will not be delighted with what I am about to propose to you; for my kind can and will hold grudges for the longest of times.

"The proposal is a pact. My Lĭbĕrī, Născī Flămmărūm, and Vīta Lyrārum, will be the first of my kind to bond with a human and those humans will be one of your descendants, Alaĕna Bombyx and Quintus Cōr. In exchange, none but that one descendant will be able to use Magic or become a Latin Magician. When that human appears, he or she will have the full use of the power of the Măgī Latīnī and more. Will you agree to my terms and give up your ability to use Magic?"

"I agree to your terms, for they are most fair and serve as a hope for our kinds," Glenrick said.

"I agree, as well, most fair and beautiful one," Quintus understood.

"I agree, noble one, your terms are most just," I promised.

She nickered. "Good." I heard the flap of wings and another, light blue light landed next to her which was singing a beautiful song.

I could not understand what it was saying, but it was exquisite, and I assumed the being was Vīta Lyrārum. "Sălvĕ, Alaĕna, Chosen One," she said. Her voice sounded like a flute, a violin, and a harp combined to become greater than even the loveliest of symphonies performed by the most famous of the professional orchestras. It was nigh to impossible to describe because of its interchanging notes which were constantly overlapping each other in a difficult yet harmonious rhythm.

Then another larger, reddish light landed next to her. My heart flipped in its presence. I could feel its gaze upon me. Its voice was deep, warm, and comforting. "Show them."

I gasped because it was the voice I had heard the day I received my name and it was the voice I had heard at least four nights before. From the tone, I could tell the being was male.

His light dimmed slightly, allowing me to see his outline. He was completely red, and he looked like he was made of flames. He possessed glorious wings that could put even the largest and most handsome bird to shame. His mane and tail looked like flames of the deepest shade of red. Upon his forehead lay a one-foot-long ivory horn that seemed to glow in a blue tint. He looked a bit like a Phoenix, that legendary firebird that rises out of ashes.

"Show them, dear one. Show them who you are. Show them the woman you are destined to become." He stepped forward and nuzzled me in my heart. "Be strong, dear one, and show them your true self." The trio of Magical beings partially reared and flew off into the night in a dazzling dance of colorful lights.

I woke with a start and groaned as pains enveloped me. Because of the dream, the questions, and the pain, I wasn't able to fall asleep but, after half an hour of lying on the hard bed with my eyes forcibly shut, I heard a song. Its tune reminded me of a flame, flickering from low to high. The lyrics, no, verses, were in Latin, the best and most beautiful Latin I had ever heard. *Sleep, my little one, for the sun utters farewell. Yes, sleep, my dear one, for the moon calls you to dream. Sleep, my small one, for the day when dreams are forbidden draws nigh. So, sleep, my love, for the time of imagination will soon disappear. Sleep, my Light, and dream with no fear. Sleep, my child, for my heart is with you forever more. Sleep, now, sleep for the moon calls to you. Sleep, now, sleep for the day is done, and night has begun. Now, sleep, my dear, dream while you can in a painless slumber.*

As the song faded, I quietly drifted off into a deep, painless sleep filled with wondrous dreams. Although, before I fell into that deep, peaceful sleep, a thought occurred to me. *Quintus Cōr, Dīcărĕ Cōr. Dīcărĕ's a descendant of Quintus Cōr, and he's a Latin Magician. He must be one of the Chosen Ones! Wait, wouldn't that make me the other?* A cool sensation rushed through me, and I felt… free. *Well, that's not helpful.*

No more realistic dreams happened for the next day or week—I hadn't the slightest clue since time is irrelevant when one is heavily drugged. I learned that very quickly during my stay at that accursed hospital. Dumb drugs.

"Sălvĕ, Isabella," I greeted my nurse as she walked into the room for what must have been the hundredth time.

"Sălvĕ, Alaĕna." She trotted toward me and sat down on the cold metal chair that rested next to my bed. "How are you today?"

"Better. How long has it been since I first arrived here—in the hospital, that is?" I intuitively queried.

She made a face, pulled out her smartphone, checked it, and then said, "About a week."

I nodded. "When do you think I can get out of here?"

She looked at her clipboard, which she always had with her, and said, "In four to five days, depending on how fast you recover. You've already recovered remarkably fast. Your injuries were as follows: a two-inch-wide, two-by-one-half-inch deep hole in your left arm; a fractured collarbone; a dislocated shoulder; and, to top it off, second-degree burns that covered your entire body! I was amazed that you made it through the day."

"A blessing of healing," I muttered.

"What?" she asked.

My big fat mouth and those dumb drugs do not mix! I scolded myself. "Oh, nothing, just the ramblings of the mentally delusional caused by a stream of morphine."

She was about to say something when out of the room came…

"Incoming!" A few screams and "watch-outs" came from outside. Then, through the bleached door, came a bandaged boy in a wheelchair being pushed by a beaming Jacob.

Isabella sighed and rolled her eyes. "Pūĕrī."

I blinked and saw that Bartholomew was the one in the wheelchair. I smiled and raised my hand in greeting, wincing with the movement, "Sălvĕtĕ, Bartholomew Ĕt Jacob." Turning my full attention to my brother, I asked, "How are you, Bartholomew?"

He shrugged and winced. "I've had better days." He looked at my shoulder and then at my arm. "And you?"

"Me? I've had better days." I smirked and let out a sighing, pain-inducing laugh.

His eyes lit up as he said, "I learned from Jacob that about all of the Măgī Latīnī are calling you 'The Bane of the Sĕpīa Vōlătīcă'." He grinned, and Jacob nodded.

"And that's not anything to be taken lightly, either," Jacob assured. "The VS are a tragedy to MLs. They've been plaguing us since the Īmmanīs Lacĕrta disappeared. I'm guessing that the Īmmanīs Lacĕrta hunted the VS and, when they were killed by the knights, the VS went crazy and started to take over the world." I raised an eyebrow in disbelief, and Jacob sighed. "*Okay,* so they didn't take over the world, but they did decide to make MLs their favorite prey since we are defenseless against them. The Damsels knew this. So, they've been breeding them in secret. At least, that's a theory."

I smiled sadly. "That's a conspiracy theory to remember."

"You really do like conspiracy theories, don't you?" Jacob asked.

Nodding, I replied, "Yeah, I do. They're so interesting, and there's no end to what they might contain. There's this huge conspiracy about the mayor of Wetly, Colorado, which is my hometown. Well, this is what it is: you see, we all believe— strike that, *know*—that the mayor used a fake passport to fly in from Saudi Arabia. He's a terrorist. Everyone in Wetly knows it. Though Bart there can't seem to get it right." Bartholomew turned red. He hated it whenever I called him that. "He *always* says that he used a fake name."

Bartholomew made an unintelligible sound like her-humph and crossed his arms over his heavily bandaged chest.

Jacob and Isabella laughed.

"Touchy, touchy, Bartholomew," I chuckled. *I wonder if they know anything about the Ūnīcornĕs Vōlătīcĕs,* I thought, and then looked at Isabella and Jacob seriously. "What do you know of the Ūnīcornĕs Vōlătīcĕs?"

Isabella and Jacob looked at each other, and, with a dark, enigmatic look on her face, Isabella asked, "How do you know of the Flying Unicorns?"

"I heard a tale of one once," I replied calmly.

She eyed me suspiciously. "Uh-huh, well, I do know that according to a legend the Măgī Latīnī relied upon them for strength and protection. We need their strength because, well, in your studies later on, you'll see. It's rather depressing. We need their protection because we can't defend ourselves from a lot of creatures. Then, for some reason, they killed the Grudge's

'Old One', and the Mǎgī Latīnī were cursed."

I put up a finger and asked, "What about Īncĕndīūm Fĕrŏx?"

She was speechless and began to look around nervously. "Alaĕna, don't speak of him here. We're not allowed to."

I tilted my head in confusion. "What do you mean I can't speak of Wild Conflagration? Why?"

Isabella sighed and replied, "Because *they* will kill us if we speak of him."

"Who are the 'they'?" I asked.

Jacob shook his head, his eyes wide with fear. "The Grudges."

"Why do you call them that?" I inquired.

Jacob pursed his lips and explained, "The ancient MLs murdered the Old One, and the Grudges placed a curse upon the MLs. Now we cannot make weapons or harm our enemies, creature or human. That is the reason why we are defenseless against the VS and the Damsels. Oh, and turning Damsels and other humans into animals doesn't count as harming them. Don't know why though. One would think that it would, but it works out well for us. I suppose that it was their idea of mercy. Though, there is another legend, just gossip really, that a man who I can't remember the name of…"

Isabella cut in, listing, "I'm pretty sure his name was Genrick Bones, or, no, Jrenick Bombis; no, that's not it. Wait, Glenrick Bombyx! That's it! That is definitely his name."

Jacob nodded in approval. "Yeah, that sounds right. Anyways, he stood up against his people and tried to stop them. It's said that Glenrick Bombyx made a pact with an Ūnīcornīs Vōlătīcīs which said that one of his descendants would be fully bonded with an Ūnīcornīs Vōlătīcīs. This has never happened in the history of MLs or Grudges. No one knows what will happen." He gloomily looked away. "But that's just an old tale."

"Hey, Alaĕna, your last name is Bombyx. What if you're one of his descendants? Wait, that would also make me one of his descendants, but I'm not a Măgūs Lătīnūs, so I suppose that counts me out. Bummer." Bartholomew wilted.

Isabella rolled her eyes. "If she were one of his descendants, then she would have to be the one bonded to the Ūnīcornīs Vōlătīcīs."

Jacob grinned. "I learned this a few weeks ago from one of my friends in the Anthropology department: the thing is that Glenrick Bombyx had a daughter whose name was Alaĕna, and, apparently, she was a lot like you. Only, she loved her father more than anything."

Bartholomew laughed. "Same or different or somewhere in between. I guess your name isn't as original as you thought. Jacob, do you know if it has a meaning? Alaĕna says that her name doesn't have a meaning. I personally think that it means something really embarrassing."

"It means 'Came from Wings'," I mumbled.

"What?" He tilted his head and cupped a hand around his ear.

"I said my name means, 'Came from Wings'," I repeated a bit louder. "My full name is Alaĕna Ĕx Bombyx, which means 'Came from Wings of Silk' or 'Came from Wings out of Silk'."

Isabella seemed to recognize something when I said my name but didn't say anything.

"Uh," Bartholomew said, "you said your name didn't have a meaning."

"Well, I also told you I gave myself my name, didn't I?" I snapped. His mouth dropped open, and I shook my head. *Oops! Drugs… big mouth… ugh!*

"Alaĕna…" Bartholomew looked shocked and angry. "You

said for all of your life that you named yourself! But if you didn't, then who did?"

I turned red. "Well… I can't tell you. Not now, maybe not ever."

Bartholomew fumed. "What do you mean not now? Why can't you tell me now?"

"If I told you now, I would die!" I yelled back at him. "You know what happens if I get too close to that truth. Remember when I collapsed?"

"Well, I don't want you to die. I just want answers!" He glared at me.

"Bartholomew James Healdton, stop complaining! I saved your life." I scowled.

"I know you did! Would I be here listening to you not giving me answers if you didn't?" he said matter-of-factly.

"That's my point. And, if I told you anything about Frŏns and Pătĕr and…" I gasped because I should have been writhing with pain by now. *Why… oh, duh, I found out that Dīcărĕ was the one bonded to the Flying Unicorn, or possibly me, or both. Grr!*

"What?" Bartholomew asked, looking concerned.

"Oh my, I can talk again. I can tell you what happened," I exclaimed, looking extraordinarily surprised.

"What do you mean? I thought you would die?"

"No, I found the thing that would allow me to tell you. Oh, Dīcărĕ, I can save you now!" I said daringly and was pleasantly surprised when I didn't even flinch.

Isabella and Jacob jumped in recognition, and Isabella asked, incredulously, "Dīcărĕ? How on earth would you know Dīcărĕ?"

I looked at her questioningly. "You know him?"

Isabella nodded. "That's what I'm asking: you know Dīcărĕ, too?"

"Oi, this is confusing." I groaned, putting my hand on my forehead.

Puzzled, Bartholomew asked, "Who's Dīcărĕ? I am so confused. Your life puzzles me. First, you can't tell me what happened because you would die, and then you can tell me what happened. Then you start talking about this Dīcărĕ guy! Was he the one that you hung out with all the time, the one at the Age of Old: Metallurgy Shop?"

"Bartholomew, were you following me around?" I questioned suspiciously.

"I am not a stalker, if that's what you're thinking. And who's this Dīcărĕ guy and why couldn't you tell me earlier?" he nearly demanded.

I huffed and waved him off with a flick of my hand. "In good time, Bartholomew, but now, I would like to know why you were following me around."

He frowned. "I went off-topic. Let's get back to the other one."

"Bartholomew James Healdton, how dare you follow me around!" I glowered at him.

My brother shook his head. "You walked off in a weird direction after school, and I wondered where you were going and wanted to make sure you were okay and no weird thing was going on with you. Can we please go now?" he whispered to Jacob.

"That's no excuse for stalking me!" I glared at him.

He quickly countered, "Oh, I was not stalking you."

"You were following me around without my knowledge of you doing so," I insisted.

"That's still not stalking. I was just making sure you were okay," my brother said, trying to make it sound sweet.

However, I asked, "Why would you care?"

His voice turned stern. "Because I care, all right! I was worried about you. My mom wasn't the one who was sincerely worried about you. I was." He glanced at me funny, then looked away. "I felt—and still feel—responsible for you. I feel like I have to take care of you since no one was there to. That's why I followed you. And that *boy* worried me. I didn't know what you were doing or getting into." He looked sincere, then shocked. "It is Dĭcărĕ. Dĭcărĕ is that boy."

I stared blankly at him. "So, you're just figuring that out?"

"Humph, what relation do you have to him?" he asked apprehensively.

"How 'bout I tell you later when I can think straight? I'm rather tired, and this is the most talking I have done in a long time. So, why don't you get back to recovering, and I'll explain when I get back to my room?"

"All right…" He seemed disappointed then, motioning to the door, announced, "Well, wheel me away, Jacob!"

Jacob shook his head, like shaking off a fog, and rolled my brother out the door.

I leaned back into my raised bed. *Well, at least I now know what he meant earlier and can finally tell them, though this does seem a bit too easy, hmm. Why didn't Vīta Lyrārūm and Născī Flămmărūm show me this before?* I thought.

Isabella leaned forward. "I know it's not really my place, but… how did you know Dĭcărĕ and do you know what happened to him?"

"First," I said, "can you explain how you knew him?"

She sighed and nodded. "He came here when he was very, very young. It was after his mother died. He became one of us, and we loved him like a sibling."

"So, what did you mean when you asked me if I knew what happened to him?" I inquired.

She looked down and said, "Jacob explained to me that after a fight with Mr. Cĕtĕră, he stormed off. He said something about trusting him. I never saw him again."

"When was this?"

She thought for a moment then replied, "About two years ago."

My face turned ashen.

"What's wrong?"

"I'll tell you with the others."

She sighed. "All right, I'll wait. We were friends, Dīcără and I, but Jacob was his best friend. They were always together."

I nodded sadly. "I'm not surprised. Jacob reminds me of him."

It might have been the way I said it or just a wild guess, but Isabella asked, "Did you love him?"

I almost fell off the bed when she asked that. "Of course not! He was just a friend, besides I'm way too young for that! I'm barely more than thirteen."

She smirked then said sarcastically, "Sure. One thing I need to know is if the boy at the Metallurgy shop was really Dīcără."

I looked away. I knew even a blind person could see the pain on my face. "Yes. He lived there with his brother, Frŏns, and his father, who we all knew as Pătĕr. Dīcără helped me out, and so did his brother. The incident prevented me from telling anyone their names, plus, they didn't want me telling anyone their names, anyway. They are the ones who…" I stopped.

She leaned forward and urged me to continue by asking, "…who what?"

I was hesitant and didn't know what to say, so I asked that voice what I should do. Warmth rushed through me and I knew exactly what to say. "…made my knife."

"Oh." She looked surprised. "So, you made your knife."

"Well, sort of, I guess, suppose, kind of…" I said.

"Oh?" She looked at me suspiciously. "But still, I wonder how you were able to battle and kill the VS. I mean, it goes against the curse."

I shrugged. "Maybe they are lightening up the punishment. It has been almost forever since they first put the curse in place."

She nodded thoughtfully. "Maybe, but they hate giving up grudges, thus their nickname."

"Maybe one of them thought of the man, boy, and girl that tried to save their leader, and, since I share the last name with the man and Bartholomew is my brother, they took pity on him and decided to let me save him," I said, trying to think of a good reason.

"I suppose, but it wouldn't be like them to do it and, wait… a boy? I never heard of a boy in the legend." She looked a bit surprised.

"Quintus Cōr was his name," I replied.

"Quintus Cōr?" She pondered for a moment and then inquired, "Just curious, what was the surname, or last name, of Dīcărĕ? He never told anyone what it was."

"Cōr, Dīcărĕ Cōr," I answered.

"Okay, you seem to be in the heat of things. Are you saying that… hmm… that's odd. Alaĕna Bombyx and Dīcărĕ Cōr, Dīcărĕ Cōr and Alaĕna Bombyx…" She was lost in a train of thought.

I smashed that train by saying, "Would you mind if I slept some?"

She shook her head and said, "Yes, you need to rest. My curiosity sometimes gets the better of me." She walked over to the door. "Now, get some sleep." She turned off the lights and walked out of the room.

The next three days were uneventful and rather boring, so I was glad to be out of the hospital and into my room.

When I entered the space once again, I found my knife on my nightstand. I picked it up and felt its comforting weight. It was all I had left of him. It was my past, my present, and my future all in one leather scabbard. "I will keep my Promise, because when I make a Promise, I keep it, even if it means my life." I took the knife, slid it into my belt, put on some normal clothes, and sat on my bed.

I was so tired. I hadn't slept well the past three nights and, so, fell asleep very quickly, even though I didn't mean, or want, to sleep in my clothes.

CHAPTER 7

Truth Be Told

The next morning, I woke up to a pair of eyes attentively staring at me. "Oi-ya-whoa!" I yelped and then thought, irritably, *How are you people getting in here? Go ahead. Don't worry, just barge in. Who cares? My box had more privacy than this place.*

"Sorry, Alaëna, ma'am, but I was just wondering what you looked like. Everyone says you are hideously scarred with burns and cuts. Some say that, with your beauty, you charmed the Sēpīa Vōlătīcă into a sleep-like trance, causing his supply of Magic to end, therefore making him fall, which made him die from a lack of oxygen. You're pretty, but not that pretty."

I looked at the person with a rather young voice, and she seemed to be about seven or eight years old.

"My big brother Jacob says that you just beat it with your extreme talent and your awesome knife. What does it look like? I've never seen one because Măgī Latīnī can't make weapons.

At least, that's what my sister told me anyway. By the way, I'm Kīanna, but my brother calls me Garpix, which he got from Gărrūlītăs Pīxīs which means Chatter Box, basically. I don't know what he's talking about. I don't talk that much, do I? Well, if I do, sorry. I can't help it. My dad told me I was like spaghetti and whatever solid conversations I had were meatballs." She sighed. "I miss him."

I blankly stared at her, trying to process all that she had said, and then, when I had processed her one-sided conversation, put a hand on her shoulder, "Kīanna, what a pretty name."

She beamed like she had just been given a pony with all expenses paid. "Well, at least you think so. My brother doesn't. He thinks that I'm a pain in the rear end and that I need to talk less. I heard that you have a brother. His name is Bartholomew, right?" she continued before I could respond. "I think he's really cute and super brave for taking on that VS. Without him taking it on in the first place, who knows what might have happened?" Before I could roll my eyes and make a smart quip, she babbled on, "Well, I'm hungry, are you? Of course, you are. Who wouldn't be after what you've been through with taking on the VS and arguing with your brother about some puzzling thing? A kid heard shouting in there. What happened? Oops!" She clamped a hand over her mouth. "I'm not supposed to ask that. Oops, I'm not supposed to tell you that either. Oh well, so are you hungry? I make a mean Pop-Tart, especially when my brother acts as the toaster." She hopped off the bed and skipped to my fridge.

I groaned with exhaustion and stretched. Having slept in my clothes, I could feel the nice red indents on my side from my belt and scabbard. I took a deep breath and swung my feet off the bed. "So, you're Jacob's sister?"

She looked over at me and frowned. "Unfortunately. He

picks on me all the time, though I get him back by tackling him into the ground," she preened.

I got up, staggered over to her, and asked, "So, you're making Pop-Tarts?"

"Yep." She scrunched her nose in thought. "Though I can only get them out of the packages. Jacob has to cook them. So, I need you to cook them with Magic."

I was surprised by the statement. "Don't the Măgī Latīnī use their abilities more… cautiously?"

"I dunno. I'm not one. I just live here. I might be a Măgūs Lătīnūs, but I don't think so. Usually, only one family member becomes one. Goober is an anonamaty, anonalty, animaly…"

"Anomaly," I corrected.

"Yes, that, thank you. Well, I think you'll be fine." She smiled broadly.

I sighed. "All right, where are the Pop-Tarts?"

"Right here." She held out a plate of four Pop-Tarts.

I closed my eyes and focused, pursing my lips with concentration. After a moment, I commanded, "Cŏxī Hīc Cībĕ Ăd Pĕrfĕctīo!" The Pop-Tarts began glowing with a bright white light and turned golden brown. Before I touched one, I asked, "Are there peanuts in this?" She shook her head no, and I picked one up and bit into it. It was delicious, especially since it was the first one I had ever eaten.

"Oh, Pūĕr, these are *so* good, even better than my brother's. And that's saying a lot!" she mumbled through her mouth full of gooey, warm, jelly, flaky, crunchy goodness. I am sorry for those of you who are completely starving by the continuous reading of my book. I know with that description, you might want to eat the page… okay, you wouldn't, but you get the point.

Now, anyone watching me would have laughed their head off if they had seen me then with jelly sticking to my face and the crust sticking to the jelly. I looked like a baby eating a strawberry pie.

The door creaked open, and Jacob called, "Garpix! Garpix! Where are you? Are you bothering Alaĕna?"

"Come in if you don't mind getting sticky," I said with a tongue that stuck to the roof of my mouth.

He walked in and covered his mouth with his hand in an attempt to stifle a laugh. It ended up coming out as a loud snort. "What did my sister do to you?"

Kīanna giggled as she hid behind me, trying to avoid her brother's gaze.

Smirking with amusement, I said, "She introduced me to all of the stuff covering my face. One would think that this Pop-Tart thing wouldn't get all over you but no."

He laughed. "Oh, Garpix, what am I going to do with you?" Then to me, on a serious note, he asked, "Mind if I talk to you… privately?"

I looked discerningly at him, trying to figure out what he was thinking. "Sure, but why don't Kīanna and I wash up first?"

He nodded, and I walked over to my bathroom to wash my face. Using a soft towel, I cleaned Kīanna's sticky, gooey face which was extremely hard since she squirmed the entire time. Once finished, I hurried her out of the room with a "thanks for teaching me how to eat Pop-Tarts,', which made her giggle. I shut the door and wiped the few remaining water droplets off of my face. "So, what did you want to talk about *privately*?" I walked over to him, put my right hand on the right side of my hip, and put my weight on my right leg.

He appeared a bit nervous but had the courage to ask, "What was up with you and Bartholomew the other day?"

"Oh, that. We usually do that. We have what we call the-saurus matches whenever one of us says a word that could be improved. Like when he said 'radical' when we first arrived here, I started spouting off synonyms for it. We do keep score on who thinks of the most."

He shook his head. "That's not what I was talking about, but that does explain something." Chuckling, he added, "Though it does remind me of when my dad and I used to play this game. It was silly, but fun. We would lie on our backs in the grass in our backyard and, since we lived near the air base, we always had aircraft going over us. Anyways, we would see a flying speck and try to figure out the type, model, and year of the object. My dad always won that game. Always." He looked lost in memories.

I smiled sadly. "I wish I would've had a real father like that. I did have one that was like a father to me. He was Dīcărĕ's father. He was great."

Finally, Jacob asked, "What happened to him?"

"Don't want to spoil the fun come the time when I tell you the tale of Dīcărĕ and Alaĕna. Er, Dīcărĕ slash Alaĕna. Er, never mind. Anywho, I will say that Dīcărĕ found me and gave me a home. I couldn't stay there, for reasons that are, uh, hard and rather embarrassing to explain. But they were my family, the kind of family that would give their lives to save mine."

He grinned. "That's a good family. Although, sometimes I would like to lock my sisters in our house and throw away the key. I love them and would give anything to save them if they were in trouble. Just don't tell them I said that."

I smiled and let out a small laugh.

"You know, you have a pretty smile," he said.

I looked at him threateningly and declared, "If that's an attempt at a flirt…"

He looked startled and stuttered, "Oh no! I was just trying to be nice."

I sighed. "Yep, you definitely are like Dīcărĕ. So, that's all you wanted to know?" He hesitated, so I continued, "So, Kīanna is your sister, and you have another?"

Jacob seemed to be a bit relieved. "Yes, Garpix. And, guessing by the way that you two looked, she was teaching you how to eat a Pop-Tart. Did she make you cook them?" I nodded, and he continued, "Yeah, even if you have a toaster, she loves Magically cooked Pop-Tarts. They seem the same to me, but, oh well."

I shrugged. "They seemed tasty enough. By the way, what's your other sister's name?"

"Her name is Wilanira," Jacob replied. "I call her Wily. So, what's up with the thing on your belt?" He pointed to my knife.

"Ah, Căpĕrĕ Flămmaĕ, To Contain the Flames. She's all I have left of him."

"Him who?" he asked.

I scowled. "Oh, stop trying to spoil the story that I'm going to tell you later!"

He sighed. "Is there anything you can tell me?"

I thought about it for a moment as I leaned against the wall next to me. "Well, I can tell you that the pigeons in Wetly are the most idiotic creature in all the world since they dare each other to get hit by cars and if someone calls anyone a Wetly Pigeon, then that would be calling him or her the most idiotic creature in the world. I once turned Peter Pan into a Wetly Pigeon." He was looking a bit confused, so I explained, "Peter Piper Pan was his name. Nowadays, we call him Pigeon Peter. It wasn't my greatest accomplishment."

He snorted.

After an awkward silence, I told him that he needed to go get the rest of our party.

Jacob complied and walked out the door.

I sighed and thought to myself, *What will they think after I tell them the story? Should I tell them about that man or what should I do?* I sat down on the floor and shook my head. The familiar warmth flooded through me. "Show them."

I waited for three hours. During that time, I took a nap; ate a chocolate bar, which was really good; and just sat around. It was about noon when I heard a knock on my door.

"Alaěna, it's the 'party'!" Jacob announced.

"What 'party'?" I heard a boy's voice, presumably Bartholomew's, ask.

"Come in," I said, sitting down on a chair next to my table. They entered, and I announced, "Welcome to the Log Cabin of Luxury!" I spread my arms out and then set them on the wooden table.

Isabella walked in and said, "Okay, Alaěna, I think we've waited long enough."

Jacob and Bartholomew nodded in agreement.

I smiled. "All right, you might want to sit down for this. Feel free to sit on the bed or the chair."

In response, Jacob sat on the chair while Bartholomew and Isabella sat down on the bed.

Incidentally, Bartholomew blushed when he accidentally bumped into her when they sat down. "Sorry," he stuttered and sat at the opposite end.

I rolled my eyes, and Jacob smirked.

"Okay, Michelangelo," I said, teasingly, as Bartholomew looked down with red cheeks. Closing my eyes as I remembered the scenes, I began, "Let's start at the sad beginning which Bartholomew partially knows:

"My birthday had been only yesterday, and my dad had promised me a big surprise the next day. So, I was really excited. Only a couple minutes before, my father had told me that we were going somewhere, and he was now pushing me into the car, saying, 'Let's go, sweetheart.' He lifted me into my car seat and clicked the seatbelt in place. I asked him where we were going, but he didn't answer. Instead, he hopped into the front seat and backed out of the driveway.

"We drove to a part of the city I had never been before. It was terrifying. There were men with tattoos on their arms and guns in their hands, men like Banana Bear, Cheeky Monkey, Breaker, and Apple Arm. I asked my dad where we were, but he didn't answer.

"As he had stopped near a macabre building with a lot of graffiti, I repeated my question.

"He sighed and said, 'Sweetheart, you'll be staying here for a while. I will return for you… soon.' He got out, walked around the car, opened my door, unbuckled me, and picked me up. He held me close and promised he would come back for me before setting me down on the ground next to the road.

"I was so confused. Between sobs, I asked my father what he was doing.

"He ignored me, jogged over to the driver's side of the car, and drove off.

"I tried to follow him, but he was going too fast. I sat down on the side of the road and cried. I waited there for two hours, but he didn't come back. I watched the sun begin to set, which caused the shadows to grow larger. The noises were terrifying. At times, I heard gunshots and screams. Eventually, it overwhelmed me, and I curled up in a little ball and bawled.

"At around midnight, two boys, one was seven and the other was ten, walked up to me.

"The older boy asked, 'What's wrong?'

"'My daddy left me here. He said that he'd come back for me but he hasn't,' I replied. I looked so pitiful with my little pink pigtails; my high, girlie voice; and my polka-dot dress.

"They looked sad, and the younger boy inquired, 'What's your name?'

"'I don't have a name, just a last name: Bombyx,' I replied.

"Their eyes widened, and they shared a look. The older boy put a hand on my shoulder and said, 'Why don't we give you one then? But first, I would like to say that my name is Frŏns and that this is my little brother Dīcărĕ.'

"The younger boy waved shyly before looking up. It seemed as though something was talking to him, but I brushed the thought off as he said, 'What about Alaĕna Ĕx Bombyx? It means 'Came from Wings of Silk'. It is a very beautiful name. It speaks of the Ūnīcornĕs Vōlătīcĕs, Flying Unicorns.'

"I nodded. 'I like that name. It's pretty.'

"'Yup, just like you,' Dīcărĕ said.

"I giggled—yes, Bart, I giggled. Now, shut up.

"Frŏns rolled his eyes and shook his head.

"After the rather embarrassing moment, Dīcărĕ offered me his hand and helped me up. They took me to their Metallurgy shop. It was large, with an immense chimney at the far end of it. As we entered, the smell of burning hickory and pine filled my nose, making me sneeze.

"By what I learned was a forge, a large man looked straight at me with his large, brown eyes. He had a warm smile, like the coals of a fire which, with no doubts, I can say Dīcărĕ inherited. The man had broad shoulders and very muscular arms from forging metal for years upon years. He wore a thick apron over a leather-like long-sleeve shirt and a pair of worn jeans. 'What have we here?' he said. 'A little girl in pigtails? A sweet girl like this shouldn't be wandering around all by herself, especially around this place.' He knelt at my level.

"I hate to admit it, but I hid behind Dīcărĕ. He was tall, I was small, and the man was new and scary.

"Dīcărĕ took my hand and told me that the man was his father and that he was a kind and generous man who had a heart of gold.

"Frŏns explained what happened, and the man looked sad. He reached out to me and said, 'It's all right. I'm not going to hurt you, Alaĕna.' I slowly walked forward into his arms, and he gently picked me up. 'I'm going to take care of you now. However, you will have to do two things for me: first, you'll never go out after dark, because it's too dangerous for a little girl like you out in the big, wide world. Second, I would love if you would sing for me every once in and while. Why, my wife had the most beautiful voice the world had ever heard.'

"I found out later that she had died from an unknown cause. It was a cause that I never got Dīcărĕ or his brother to answer.

"I told the strange man that I was sorry about his wife and that I would do as he asked.

"The man smiled and said, 'Please, call me Pătĕr.'

"I smiled. He was my adopted father. I miss him." After a moment of silence, I grinned, "Now, the next day is when I met Bartholomew."

"Oh, please, don't bring that up!" Bartholomew begged. "It's so humiliating."

"Another reason to tell it," I said, rubbing my hands together, and Bartholomew flopped backward onto the bed, covering his face.

Jacob snorted, and Isabella leaned over my brother, concerned.

Clearing my throat, I resumed my story, "Dīcărĕ and Frŏns had dropped me off at old Wetly Kindergarten through High School for Needy Children. Apparently, my dad had already made plans for me to go there but had to get rid of me early. I was six-and-a-half when I first went to school. Spending time with the Cōr's helped me mature a bit. So, instead of wearing a dress and pigtails, I was wearing the normal Wetlian attire that you saw me in when I first arrived, minus the sword, knife, and squealing Damsel-rat. So, I was walking down the hallway, though it was more a really fast walk, close to a run really, since I was close to missing class when WHACK, WHAM, BANG, CRASH!" I clapped my hands together for dramatic effect and continued, "I groaned as I realized that someone had run full force into me and was now on top of me. As his face was close to mine, I demanded, 'Get off me!'

"The person on top of me shook his head. 'Oh, you should watch where you're going.' He groaned and rolled off me.

"'Me?' I asked incredulously. 'Try you! Now I'm going to be late for my first class ever because of a stupid, idiotic, puerile boy!'

"'Wow, you don't need to recite the whole thesauris, the-sorus, thesaurus—yeah, that's right—to describe yourself,' the boy said.

"'Humph, you sure don't make very good first impressions, jerk.' I crossed my arms and looked away.

"'Well, neither do you, brat,' he grumbled as he got up and, though he didn't seem to like me, he offered me a hand up. I took it, and he lifted me.

"'Thanks, what's your name?' I asked.

"'It's Bartholomew James Healdton,' he responded and inquired, 'and you?'

"'Mine's Alaĕna Ĕx Bombyx.'

"'Huh,' he grumbled, 'your name's a lot more original than mine. I'll have to tell my mom that.'

"I chuckled. 'And say she has no imagination?'

"'Well… no… erg! Let's get to class,' he said with a sigh and tried to lead me to the classroom, but I fell when I put my weight on my right leg.

"'Oh, great! I think my ankle's sprained!' I exclaimed.

"Bartholomew sighed and asked, 'Want me to carry you to the classroom? The teacher can help you.'

"I thought about it for a moment and reluctantly agreed. He picked me up and carried me to the classroom like a knight-in-shining armor carrying away his damsel-in-distress." I couldn't help but chuckle at my simile. Holding back even more laughs, I continued, "We arrived at the classroom, and a man, presumably our teacher, looked rather startled. He asked what happened.

"'Well, the incompetent boy here ran full force into me and sprained my ankle,' I said.

"'You ran into me!' Bartholomew argued.

"'I was walking, speed walking, possibly, but not running,' I corrected.

"The man took me from Bartholomew's arms and said, 'Either way, she has a sprained ankle that needs to be tended to.' He walked over to a desk, set me on it, grabbed a bandage from his desk, and wrapped it around my ankle so that it couldn't move.

"'What's your name?' the man asked.

"'My name's Alaěna Bombyx. You are?'

"He seemed to recognize the name and replied, 'Cětěră, Măgīstěr Ět Cětěră. You may call me Mr. Cětěră.'

"I nodded. 'Mr. Cětěră.' And that is how I met Bartholomew… and Mr. Cětěră." I concluded.

"Why was that humiliating to you, Bartholomew?" Jacob asked.

Sitting up and sighing with relief, Bartholomew shook his

head. "You don't want to know."

I nodded in agreement. "To continue the story, I'll skip to when we, as in Dīcărĕ and me, were ten and nine years old, respectively. That is when something happened; something I have never described to anyone. Not Bartholomew. Not to Mr. Cĕtĕră. Not anyone. An attempted murder is what happened, and I was part of it." I winced in the memory, which was still fresh. "You see, I was walking home, well, that is, if you can call a cardboard box a home. I didn't stay with them for, uh, complicated reasons. Anyways, on the way, I saw a couple of men corner a boy, who was about ten years old. I didn't get a good look at him at first.

"They shoved him against the wall under gunpoint. One of them said, 'Ye 'ave violated our laws.'

"'What did I do? I've obeyed the laws for my whole life!' the boy pled as he looked around for any route of escape.

"'Oh, you poor rat. You've disobeyed the laws by being born.' The man sneered.

"I knew I had to do something. So, I knocked over a metal trashcan and hid in a nearby dumpster.

"The boy ran when they came to see what happened, and the man who had squished the boy against the wall yelled, 'You get back here, rat! You hear me?!'

"I smirked and, after a bit of looking around in the dumpster trash, noticed a metal pipe. With pipe in hand, I jumped out and cried, 'Hey, idiots! Over here!'

"The boy looked at me, and I recognized his eyes. It was Dīcărĕ! I mouthed Run! and he hesitated but ran behind a building.

"'Wait, I know you,' the man stated, squinting his beady eyes in recognition. 'You're one of them... one of those mutations, vermin that infect us. And you're a powerful one, too. The

D-A-M-L will be most pleased if we bring you in.' He smiled an evil, gruesome smile.

"I stood my ground and commanded, 'Stay where you are!'

"However, they came closer. Their eyes narrowed, and they charged, letting out a ferocious battle cry.

"Hastily, I swung the pipe with all my might and heard the sickly crunch of a humorous breaking.

"The evil man's scream rang through the still air.

"Quickly, I dropped the pipe. Its sharp ring joined the shriek in a sickly duet. Sprinting at full speed down an alleyway, I unknowingly entered a dead end. As I looked about for a way out, I noticed that there was a metal ladder that led up to the rooftops at the end of it, but it was ten feet off of the ground. Before I could turn around and bolt out, the other unharmed man ran after me, gun in hand. The loud bang of a gun being fired echoed through the narrow alleyway, and a bullet whizzed by my head as I ducked to avoid the deadly metal pellet. Directly above me lay the ladder, and I wished with all my might it would slide down, but nothing happened.

"The man stepped closer, drawing his sword.

"I was trapped.

"'Your head is worth more than I could make in a lifetime,' declared the man. 'Time to give it up, girl.'

"I shook with fear but I stood straight and put a foot forward. 'I am not afraid of you murderers!' He laughed and pointed his gun at my head and was about to pull the trigger when I heard the sliding metal ladder coming down at me.

"'Heads up, arms up!' Dīcărĕ had released the ladder while he was standing on it, and the crazy kid was going down fast. After the ladder reached its limit, he grabbed both my arms, pulled me up onto the ladder, and helped me climb up. As soon as we reached the top, we quickly pulled the ladder up and ran up the stairs and onto the rooftops.

"The man swore and cursed with frustration like there was no tomorrow .

"I thanked Dīcărĕ, and he rested on his knees, panting. 'No problem,' he said.

"I said, 'Well, Dīcărĕ, now I owe you twice.'

"He shook his head and replied, 'Nope, only once since you saved me from those Damsels.'

"We laughed a nervous laugh.

"'You know, that was really brave… for a girl,' Dīcărĕ teased with a toying smirk stamped on his face.

"I elbowed him in the side. 'That was pretty brave of you to pull me up… for a boy.'

"Once again, we laughed.

"Dīcărĕ erected himself and said that we needed to make something to help defend myself and that his dad would be able to help. So, I followed him to his shop.

"His father said to us after both of us told him what happened, 'You were brave saving him, for that I am grateful. That ML bounty hunter and D-A-M-L Agent would have blown a hole in his head if it weren't for you.'

"I shook my head. 'Same would have happened to me if it weren't for him.'

"He nodded and put an arm around his son. 'Yes, that's my boy, brave and daring! But I agree. You need something to defend yourself with. However, you also need to know how to defend yourself.' He stroked his black beard and said, 'Here, why don't we do this: I'll teach you some of my works, and maybe you can actually sing a song, which you have yet to do.' I looked sort of guilty. 'I haven't heard a song sung since…' His shoulders sagged.

"I pointed out how he had yet to tell me Dīcărĕ's mother's

name, and Frŏns, who had just come in the door, said, 'It was Elenor.'"

I thought Bartholomew was going to explode. "Eleanor, that's my mom's name! Er… our mom's name." He jumped off the bed.

I looked up thoughtfully. "I guess it is, but I never thought about it 'til now."

"Why on earth didn't you tell me?" he demanded. "I could have long lost brothers. Wait… that would mean my mom had a *really* busy social life."

I grimaced, stuck out my tongue with disgust, and said, "Well, her name was spelled E-l-e-n-o-r."

"Oh, no, my mom's name is spelled with an 'a' in it. So, sorry to insult your already almost non-existent honor, mom! Go ahead, continue my one and only sibling, I hope." He waved me on and sat back on the bed.

I sighed and continued, "All right, well, I agreed and sang a song for him. If you're wondering about the song, I kinda blocked out the memory, so I don't remember what I sang." I shuddered. "Anyways, in exchange, he taught me his trade and Frŏns and Dīcărĕ taught me how to sword fight.

"After a visit from a couple more bounty hunters and Damsels, the time added up to two years ago when Pătĕr said to me while getting ready to forge a knife made with the best steel he had ever worked with, 'I need you to do something for me, say a few words while I make this knife, all right?' I nodded, and he began to forge it by first melting the metal, cooling it a bit, then softening the metal, folding it, softening it, folding it over and over until he took me and said, 'Speak to it, let the words pour out. Make it what you want it to be.'

"Dīcărĕ was there watching very attentively.

"I took a deep breath, stood over it, and then sang an

enchantment in Latin. I have no idea where it came from. It just flowed out like a gentle stream. And when I had finished reciting, the metal became like a crystal, and it seemed as though flames were trapped inside of it. But that's only when it's on, when it's off it looks like…" I unsheathed my knife and showed it to them. "This. So, I didn't make it. I just improved it a bit."

Isabella and Jacob had wide eyes and dropped jaws.

"Well, now that the prologue is over, time for the climax. The epic battle of good and evil, when Mr. Ratty first appeared. I remember it like it was yesterday: every detail, from the cool breeze to the color of the bricks to the whispered words that floated around in the air. Every single one." After a moment to allow myself a bit of time to prepare to share the story, I slowly began, "As I walked down the dirty backstreets of Wetly, Colorado, I pressed my school books tightly against my chest. I stumbled on a stray beer bottle on the road. 'Can't you people throw it next to a building, at least?' I grumbled, kicking the bottle into the side of a moldy, brick building which shattered it into millions of tiny pieces that sparkled like jewels in the late-afternoon sunlight.

"I made sure to avoid Breaker's place since he was a bit, um, sensitive because his business had just arrived, and he usually takes on this mode in which he will kill anyone who gets near him. Also, I made sure to stay clear of Cheeky Monkey, a malicious man who uses his well-trained monkey Cheeky to murder VIPs at zoos and the like, and Banana Bear, who is actually a nice guy but was just at the wrong place at the wrong time. Anywho, it was just another day in Wetly," I said sarcastically.

Bartholomew snorted with amusement.

Smirking, I continued, "The police were too scared to come down that way, but it was the only way to the Age of Old: Metallurgy Shop.

"When I arrived at the old brick building, I called, 'Dīcărĕ, I'm ready for my lessons.' He didn't respond, and I called once again. 'Dīcărĕ, are you there?' I stepped into the dark doorway. The door was softly swinging in the wind, foretelling another Wetly thunderstorm.

"'Alaĕna run!' Dīcărĕ yelled from inside.

"I stepped back. He knew I could handle myself, and if he said run, it had to be bad. I tried to turn and bolt, but an arm wrapped around my stomach and yanked me back, slamming me into the wall.

"I gasped for breath as the man squeezed my neck, saying, 'Where're ya goin', girlie? Tink ye can get away?' The man said, drawing close so that his face was just three inches away from mine. His breath stank like cigarette smoke.

"I almost threw up.

"'I know wat ya are. Yer one o' 'ose rats 'at infest te world. An' rats don't deserve te run away, 'ey deserve te be exterminated.'

"I could see Dīcărĕ struggling to get free.

"Frŏns and his father were nowhere to be seen.

"'We've already got yer father an' yer brothers. Now, we were just waitin' fer ya te come walkin' inte our trap.'

"'They're not my blood family.' I responded, struggling to slip from his grip.

"'Ah, so yer all alone. Ain't ya, girlie?' He laughed. 'Looks like no one will miss ya wen yer dead.'

"'Leave her be!' Dīcărĕ demanded, driving his elbow into his captor's stomach.

"The man groaned and crumpled to the floor.

"He grabbed the sword the man was carrying." I paused for a moment and inquired, "Why do they carry swords?"

Shrugging, Isabella plainly responded, "Because guns don't

work so well on us and swords do."

"And why?" I asked, motioning for her to explain more.

"Whenever someone fires a gun at a Măgūs Lătīnūs, the ML has the instinct to move out of the way of the bullet. It comes in handy," she explained.

I shrugged and continued, "As I was saying: and he raced over to me.

"The man holding me unsheathed his knife and held it at my throat. It cut my skin, and hot, sticky liquid ran down my chest.

"'One step closer, lad, an' she'll be visitin' yer mother.'

"Dīcărĕ stopped and looked at me. The look of helplessness in his eyes was something that I had never seen before.

"'Ya 'ear me loud an' clear, lad: ya drop yer sword an' come quietly an' I'll let te girlie go!' The strategy was so predictable, but what I did wasn't.

"I kicked the man in his private parts and rammed into him, knocking him onto the floor.

"The man cringed, but immediately got up and drew his sword fast enough to block the downward cut from Dīcărĕ.

"I ran as fast as I could to the workshop and grabbed the knife that we had made: Căpĕrĕ Flămmaĕ. I dashed from the room and came in to see the full-out swordfight between the man and Dīcărĕ.

"The movements and grace were hypnotizing.

"'Hey, you big, ugly, chunk of rotten rat meat, over here!' I yelled, and he immediately turned his attention to me, letting Dīcărĕ place a shallow cut on his left thigh.

"The man screamed in pain and weakly blocked the next onslaught of cuts, slices, and stabs.

"'Căpĕrĕ Flămmaĕ, Ăccĕndī!' I hissed, and the knife burned almost as hot as the sun. I tried to help out as much as

I could, but his defenses were impenetrable, so I just distracted him so Dīcărĕ could injure him further. Thankfully, he was getting weak fast.

"We were on the brink of winning when… Dīcărĕ yelled something, but I didn't hear anything. The sharp tip of a knife blade entered my stomach, and then it quickly disappeared with the sharp sound of steel sliding out of my back. I couldn't scream or move. A moment passed before I collapsed.

"As I lay on the floor, Dīcărĕ cut the sword arm of his attacker and raced over to me.

"I was shaking. The world was blurry with pain. I saw a sword at the neck of Dīcărĕ.

"His voice cracked with emotion as he said, 'Let me save her, please, and I'll go with you without any more trouble.'

"The men agreed but made Dīcărĕ swear an oath in Latin first.

"I couldn't hear what the oath was, but, when he finished, Dīcărĕ whispered to me, 'Grab my hand and don't let go of it, because if you do, I'll know you're dead.'

"I nodded and weakly held onto it.

"He then began to chant sentences upon sentences of healing in Latin. It worked, and the pain began to subside so that it was enough for me to speak.

"Before Dīcărĕ could finish, the wounded man said, 'The girlie will 'ave te swear te never 'ell yer name, yer father's name, ner yer brother's name te anyone. An' she'll never speak o' 'at 'appened 'ere te anyone. Only then, will we let ya save 'er.'

"He looked at me and said, 'It's the only way you can live.'

"I nodded and repeated this in Latin, 'I promise that I will not speak the name 'Dīcărĕ', the name 'Frŏns', or the name 'Pătĕr'. I will not speak of what happened here to anyone.' And I said in a quieter tone which only Dīcărĕ and I could hear,

'Until I discover who the Ūnīcornīs Vōlāticīs is bonded with.'

"'All right, she did it,' Dīcărĕ declared once I had finished.

"The men nodded for him to continue, and he did.

"He was about a sentence away from finishing when the non-wounded man started to pull him away and said, 'That's enough, scum, she'll be fine. Let's go.'

"Dīcărĕ looked confused. 'I thought you were taking her with us?'

"The non-wounded man shook his head. 'No, she'll be more useful to us here. You will tell us just what we want when we have her as… motivation. Many crooks here will accept the smallest amount of pay to get his hands on her, maybe even none at all.' He grinned an evil, rather gruesome grin that made my skin crawl, and a fearful lump form in my throat.

"Dīcărĕ hung his head, and they pulled him up, but before they could, I pulled him by his hand, pulled his ear close to my lips, and said in Latin, 'I promise I will rescue you. I promise on my life, for it is yours since you saved it.'

"He looked like he was about to say something, but they pulled him away and walked to the door.

"'Wait,' I held up a hand and asked, 'who are you?'

"The wounded man smiled, 'We're the D-A-M-L, the Defense-*Against*-Măgī-Latīnī. Just remember te name o' our group, girlie, so it'll haunt ya in yer nightmares.' And with a spine-chilling cackle, they briskly walked out the door and into the darkened street.

"I curled up into a ball and put my head on my knees. I whispered to myself, 'I promise, Dīcărĕ. I promise I'll find you and rescue you from those D-A-M-L agents, and they will pay dearly.'

"For three minutes, I stayed in that position until I began to wonder what happened to Frŏns and Pătĕr. So, I wandered about until my pondering came to an end when I noticed a bloody hand poking from behind a door. I gulped to attempt to calm my churning stomach as I reluctantly opened the door. The sight was almost too much for me to bear. Frŏns and Pătĕr were dead by beheading." I shook my head and pursed my lips. "I carried…" I could barely finish the sentence at the thought of the scene. Eventually, I was able to compose myself enough to finish the sentence. "I carried them out and buried them beside Elenor."

After a moment of silence to remember the dead, I clapped my hands, causing everyone to jump. Isabella even yelped with fright. "And that is the story you have been waiting to hear. So, now may I go to the Magology Center?"

Isabella said, her voice close to a squeak, "Yes." Clearing her throat, she continued in her normal voice, "Yes, I think that would be a great idea."

Jacob and Bartholomew were still registering everything I had said, although my brother looked a bit queasy.

I got up, trotted over to the fridge, and grabbed an apple. "Any of you guys want something to eat?"

"No, I think your words were filling enough," Jacob replied, and Bartholomew nodded in agreement. His face was turning a bit green, most likely at the thought of two beheaded bodies.

"So," I began, "I hope this explains me to a certain degree."

Isabella seemed to recognize something. "Wait, since you can speak their names and tell that tale, then you must have found the one whom the Ūnīcornīs Vōlătīcīs has bonded with!"

Jacob snapped to attention while Bartholomew looked confused and a bit intrigued.

I wonder… One who is bonded to Dīcărĕ, can you hear me? I waited a moment.

Yes. A musical voice responded. It was Vīta Lyrārum.

After taking a moment to recover from the fact that my dream wasn't a dream, that I had actually seen three Ūnīcornĕs Vōlătīcĕs, and that I was talking to something telepathically like in some sort of Sci-Fi show, I said, *I have an idea as to how we can save Dīcărĕ.*

I felt a feeling of fascination and intrigue.

Go on, Alaĕna. I am listening, she insisted.

CHAPTER 8

Promise Keeper

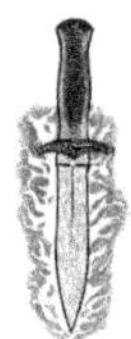

After a few seconds of explaining my plan, the Ūnīcornīs Vōlătīcīs mare replied, *I agree. You are a most interesting filly, Alaëna, and I am glad that Dīcărĕ chose you. Let us hope that this scheme of yours works!*

I was puzzled by her comment but shook it off. The Majestic being remained present as I told the party of three, "Yes, I found him. I'm surprised you haven't figured it out yet. Dīcărĕ was a Măgūs Lătīnūs like us, and yet he fought with a sword and actually made them. 'How?' you may ask. The answer is quite simple. What do you think, Vīta Lyrārūm?"

"Who's…?" Bartholomew started, but Life of Songs interrupted him telepathically.

Sălvĕ, Bartholomew, Frăter of Alaëna, Filīūs of Bombyx and Healdton. Sălvĕ, Isabella, Filīa of Walsh and Taylor. Sălvĕ, Jacob, Filīūs of the Courageous Tĕrră who has earned the respect of both my Frāter and me. I am Vīta Lyrārum, Life of Songs, Filīa of Ălă Lūnă, Moon Wing, and Īncĕndīum Fĕrŏx, Wild Conflagration, also the Germăna of Născī Flămmărum, To Be Born of Flames, and Catēnă of Dīcărĕ Cŏr, she grandly introduced. *I have come to you to ask your help. As you heard, Dīcărĕ, your friend and kin, was taken by what you call Damsels. The man Alaĕna turned into a rat and brought here has the answers you need to be able to find Dīcărĕ. I will help as much as I can but am afraid my people will kill both Dīcărĕ and me as soon as they find out that I have bonded with a Măgūs Lătīnūs. Please, rescue him, for the Heart must live so that the Light may fulfill the Prophecy and the Promise. I bless that you will find my Catēnūs and rescue him from the clutches of evil. Vălĕrĕ Īubĕrĕ.* And Vīta Lyrārum departed.

"What was that?" Bartholomew asked, still a bit shaky.

"That, my dear Bartholomew, was an Ūnīcornīs Vōlătīcīs mare. She glows like a blue moon and sings more beautifully than any songbird," I said.

"You sound like you've seen her." He smiled, seemingly joking.

"I have," I stated, ignoring his sarcasm. "Except, not in person, but in a dream. She was beautiful."

Isabella immediately jumped up and ran over to me. "Alaĕna, you must come with me immediately, to the Magology Center. Though my people are experts, they might accidentally blow the Damsel-rat up. It's happened before." She shivered in the memory. "So, we better hurry. Come on! If Dīcărĕ really is bonded with this Vīta Lyrārum, then we must go and interrogate that man. Jacob, Bartholomew, speak of this to no one."

"Yes, ma'am!" Jacob said enthusiastically.

"Yes, ma'am," Bartholomew said, with less enthusiasm.

Isabella nodded and motioned for me to follow her out the door.

I did as Isabella requested and said to the mare, *I don't*

believe it worked, Vīta Lyrārum! You were great! Though, I'm not sure where the Heart and the Light thing came from.

Do you not know the Prophecy? she asked. A hint of incredulity was in the melodies which made up her voice.

No, should I? I waited for a reply but none came.

We ran to the door, but, before we exited, I looked back at Bartholomew and waved. "Vălĕrĕ Īubĕrĕ, Frăter!"

He held up his hand, seeming sincerely confused as he flopped down backward onto my bed, which bounced him up and down with his weight.

Too much to process, I figured. Continuing our journey to the Magology Center, we sprinted to the elevator, pressed the '-1' button, and went down. *Huh, I thought there were only positive elevator numbers.* Then the elevator music kicked on, and I plugged my ears. It was some pop music band that I'd heard a boom box playing a few years back.

There was an audible *ding*, and the door opened, revealing a long hallway. At the end was an old, beat-up, termite-infested, rotten, and rusted door. "The Magology Center door," I whispered to myself. "Guess that lady didn't get to fixing it." *It's the door from my dream!* I thought excitedly.

Isabella walked to the door and whispered a password in Latin. "Tĕrră Sīlvărum Ĕt Flūvīŏrūm Dīvīsī Īn Bōnūm Ĕt Mălūm." The door opened, and I heard animal sounds. There were trumpets, squeals, neighs, the clip-clops of hooves, barks, yowls, and squeaks coming from inside the center.

That's odd, the password is different. Why would it be different? I pondered.

"Isabella, what brings you here today?" A girl who seemed to be sixteen years of age appeared from behind the door.

"It's imperative that I speak to Dūx and Iūīlīa. The matter is urgent," Isabella answered.

I looked behind the door with wonder and couldn't help but finger the hilt of my knife. Who knew what weird creatures lay beyond the door?

"I'm sorry, ma'am, but I'll have to know the name, age, and purpose of your counterpart. Extra security measures have been taken since Mr. Walsh has yet to return from his trip." She moved so that her body was blocking the doorway.

A bit of worry showed on Isabella's face, but she shook it off and said, "And it's great that you have taken these measures. This is Alaĕna Ĕx Bombyx, she's thirteen, and she has some questions she would like to ask the Damsel."

The girl looked at me suspiciously but allowed us to pass. She quickly shut the door and sat down on a chair to the left of the door.

"Come, Alaĕna, this way." Isabella grabbed my arm and pulled me on toward the hallway to the left.

There were seven hallways connected to the original chamber, which I had first come into. The one we traveled into led to the prison. "This is where we will interrogate the Damsel-turned-rat," she explained. "Once you turn him back into a man, that is, since no one has been able to do so. It's very strange. Luckily, we have not blown him up… yet. But, come, we'll leave those questions for later."

We traveled through hallways left and right, straight and diagonal, north and south, east and west, until we finally reached it.

I heard the voices of several people coming from the dark cell to my left, which was lit by only a light bulb hanging from the ceiling. It smelled like the nest of a rat.

"Rĕdĕ Īn Vīrūm!" a girl-sounding voice commanded, and I heard groaning.

"No, Iūīlīa, try this: Rĕdĕ Vīrĕ!" a boy-sounding voice corrected. Nothing happened, and the girlish voice—apparently named Iūīlīa—laughed.

"Wasn't that impressive?"

Isabella entered first, and I followed.

"Isabella Walsh-Medici, it's been a while since we've seen you in this dark hole!" The boy chuckled. He was wearing a red T-shirt and black pants while the girl Iūīlīa was wearing a light green T-shirt and dark green pants. They were both sitting on the floor next to a rat that was imprisoned in a tall, electrified fence.

"Hello, Dūx, how's it going with him?" Isabella asked, walking toward them and then kneeling next to the fence.

Dūx sighed. "Oh, it's going…"

"…Terribly!" Iūīlīa finished. She groaned. "It's like trying to squish an army ant with your boot. Well, except for you, Alaĕna, probably."

I nodded, confirming her statement.

"So, why are you here?" Dūx interrogated.

"Alaĕna needs to ask the rat some questions," she replied.

The two wanna-be rat-to-man turners snickered in amusement. "Ha. Well, she'll need to speak rat if she wants to ask any questions and, in turn, get answers."

I huffed. "Amateurs." I walked over to the fence, pulled out my knife, sliced the fence in two, reached inside, and grabbed the rat, which was squealing its little head off. Taking a deep breath, I focused and commanded, "Mūs Mălūs Cūm Ŏcūlī Rūbĕrī Mūtă Īn Vīr Impurī Fūīstī, Sĕd, Dīcăs Mē Rēspŏnsă Ăd Hŏc Īntĕrrōgătă: Ūbī Dīcărĕ Ĕst?!" Subsequently, I set him on the ground and backed away.

He slowly grew larger and into a man. The details are kind of gross, so I'll leave those out. Basically, he turned back into a man who was standing up, holding his sword at the ready. The other Măgī Latīnī jumped up and took four large steps back. The man looked at me and immediately swung his sword.

I jumped back. "Stop! You are surrounded by Măgī Latīnī! Do you want to be turned into something worse than a rat, Mr. Ratty?"

"Why, it's ye, girlie. Where am I?" He lowered his sword and sheathed it.

"That doesn't matter," I retorted. "I need you to answer a few questions for me, quickly and efficiently. The tides have turned, and the time has come for you to tell me where he is."

"Ya tink I would tell ya where de lad is? Naw, I don't tink I will. Ye can turn me inte anythin' ye want te an' I'll never tell ya." He grinned as he stood tall and defiant.

I grabbed him by the scruff of his shirt and held my knife to his throat. "How 'bout I cut you with this?"

Mr. Ratty looked dispassionately at the blade. "Yes, it was ye."

My eyes narrowed.

"Ye…" he began, but I cut him off by pushing the blade harder against his bristly skin.

"You know what happens when I cut someone right here. You remember, don't you?"

He stared into my cold, dark eyes and shivered.

"Listen to me," I hissed near his face, "you better tell me where Dīcărě is or you'll be dead before you can say no."

The man squared his jaw and clenched his fists, preparing for death.

"Tell me, rat. I command you to tell me!" I demanded, pressing my knife against his throat. A bead of blood slowly fell from his neck across my blade, plunged, and landed with a quiet 'pong' as it hit the hard, cold concrete floor.

His eyes glazed over, and he cried out, "No, no!" Ignoring

me, he put his hands on his head, fell to the floor, and screamed, "In Saudi Arabia, 131 miles west of Layla, 145 miles southeast of Afif!" He began to glow then *poof*! He was gone. I looked around for him and all that was left was a small, red bead on the floor.

I apologize, Alaěna. That was my own doing. I felt Dīcărě in pain. I couldn't wait for him to respond, so I took matters into my own hands. We need to hurry before it is too late, Vīta Lyrārūm explained.

It's okay. You just ended up puzzling a couple of kids and a technical adult, I answered.

Bōnūs. She didn't say anything more following that.

"That was the most interesting thing I have seen in my life," Dūx announced as he sat down on the floor.

"Saudi Arabia, huh," I said as I wiped my knife on my pant leg and slid it into its sheath.

Iūīlīa shook her head with amazement and declared, "Wow, you're a puzzle."

"Yep. Now, I'm even more of a puzzle. I'm going to Saudi Arabia, 131 miles west of Layla, and 145 miles southeast of Afif. Wherever that is. No time to explain, only time to pack and to tell Bartholomew." I started to jog off, but Isabella caught me by the arm.

"Oh no, you don't. I'm coming with you. And, I'm assuming Jacob is as well. He is a pilot and engineer which would come in handy over there. And I'm a linguist, which means I can speak Arabic along with many other languages. I am also trained as a nurse, which would also come in handy."

I looked at her and groaned. "Fine, you can come. Probably need a technical adult anyways, but, if we do rescue Dīcărě, you will take Dīcărě as far away as possible and leave me in Saudi Arabia."

She frowned and asked, "Why?"

I glowered at her, and she turned away.

"Iūīlīa, Dūx, don't tell anyone what happened. Okay?" the woman instructed.

They nodded. "Yes, ma'am."

Dūx whispered to his counterpart, "Besides, no one would believe us either."

The girl snorted. "No kidding."

Consequently, Isabella and I sprinted off into the deep, dark depths of the M-L-P-A Home Base.

It took about thirteen minutes, but we arrived back at my room. Jacob and Bartholomew were still there talking, which they abruptly stopped doing once we entered the room.

"What happened?" Bartholomew asked, and I explained everything.

"Saudi Arabia? Damsels? Danger? I'm in!" Jacob avowed.

"Well, don't forget me! I must be good for something," Bartholomew said as he stood up.

I thought about it for a moment and said, "Well, I'm pretty sure you can move around quietly, since you could follow me without me knowing about it, thus stalking me."

He glared at me. "I was not stalking you. That would mean I would either want to harm you or I would…" We shivered at the thought.

"Well, looks like we have our crew: Jacob Tĕrră, the Pilot and Engineer; Isabella Walsh, the Linguist and Doctor; Bartholomew Healdton, the Stalker." Bart glared at me, but I ignored him and placed a hand on my chest. "And me, Alaĕna Bombyx, the Protector and much-needed Backbone. Now, all we need is a name for our party," I said.

Jacob frowned but soon smiled his huge, white grin. "How about 'Servărĕ'? It means 'To Keep a Promise' or 'Promise Keeper'. What do you think?"

We all nodded.

I smiled at the thought. *How fitting: Servărĕ, Promise Keeper.*

CHAPTER 9

I Hate Airplanes

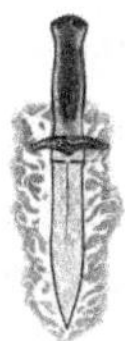

I rested my forehead against the cold window of the airplane. By that time, I had learned that I had a knack for developing brain-splitting—I don't think that's a used comparison, but that's how it felt—headaches when on an airplane. And, to make matters worse, I had a terrible peanut allergy which is a real quandary when everyone else was munching and crunching the ghastly things on that accursed aircraft.

After the whole fiasco with Mr. Ratty, our party of four ended up having to sneak out in the middle of the night because Mr. Cětěrǎ wouldn't have let us leave the M-L-P-A Home Base. Following our most likely illegal act, we waited for *five hours* for the plane to get ready. We just sat there twiddling our thumbs, which I suppose was a good thing since it meant that they hadn't noticed the rather massive knife underneath my jacket and the sword in my suitcase. Why they didn't find them is because I had placed a spell on the sword which would prevent both X-rays and metal detectors from picking up on the blade. However, since the knife was already enchanted, it was invisible to metal detectors.

Security on planes these days is horrible. A drug dealer could have had ten pounds of cocaine hidden in his hat, figuratively speaking of course, and no one would notice! It's just plain sad.

Anywho, at that stage of the journey, we had hit fourteen hours of airtime and eight hours of getting-ready-for-airtime time. Four of those airtime hours were spent on the first plane from Mulpa, which resides in a lesser-known Washington mountain, to the beaches of the tip of Florida—Miami, to be exact.

After that, we waited for three hours—much better than the first time—and then we were in the tenth hour of the flight with no land to be seen. *Oh, how Bartholomew can like this kind of stuff and how Jacob can make this his lifetime passion befuddles me,* I groaned.

Soon after that thought, I realized I was suffering from an extreme case of boredom, and what didn't help was the fact that everyone, save me, was happily asleep, including Isabella, who was sitting next to me. Unfortunately, my headache and throbbing ears prevented me from sleeping… period. So, I began to recount everything that I had in my luggage. *All right, I have several pairs of pants, shirts, and other stuff; a traditional Saudi Arabian girl's clothes for any undercover work; my leather armor; my sword; my knife; and my jacket. Okay, looks like I'm good. What do you think, Vīta? Think I forgot anything?* I mentally asked.

Her voice echoed in my mind. *I would not know since I do not know what you had with you before you left.*

I thought about it for a moment and declared, *I think I forgot to bring a chocolate bar. Bummer. I'm guessing they won't have any over there.* I frowned. *Do you really think we'll be able to rescue Dĭcărĕ? I've missed him over the past years… in the way that a friend would miss a friend, of course.*

Oddly, I could parse some of her emotions through our connection. *Amusement?* I thought.

I am sure you do, Alaëna, she said, *for I miss him as well. I will meet you soon. You know where to go.*

Yes, I remember.

Good. Now get some rest.

I can't. I have an awful headache.

Then why do I not sing you a lullaby my Măter once sung to me when I was but a suckling? My Frăter eventually learned to sing it, but to me, he sounded more like a dying ember than an orchestra. The mare laughed.

That's weird, I muttered. *I heard a voice like that when I was in the hospital. It sang like what you described. I would like to hear the lullaby and see if it was the same one.*

Hmm… interesting, Vīta hummed. *Nevertheless, I will sing.*

Thanks.

A moment of quiet passed before she began humming a tune that first went low, then medium, then low, then high, then medium, then very high, then high, then very high, then high, then medium, then low. It repeated a few more times before it formed into gentle, harmonious words which immediately lulled me and rocked my weary mind to and fro as a calming, spring breeze does the branch of a dogwood. *Sleep, my little one, for the sun utters farewell. Yes, sleep, my dear one, for the moon calls you to dream. Sleep, my small one, for the day when dreams are forbidden draws nigh. So, sleep, my love, for the time of imagination will soon disappear. Sleep, my Light, and dream with no fear. Sleep, my child, for my heart is with you forevermore. Sleep, now, sleep for the moon calls to you. Sleep, now, sleep for the day is done and night has begun.*

Now, sleep, my dear, dream while you can.

I yawned. *That was close, but the ending was…* I fell asleep before I could finish.

When I awoke three hours later, there was land on the horizon. "Isabella, look!" I excitedly whispered as I nudged her.

She woke up with a start. "What?" the woman grumbled in her Italian accent as she rubbed her eyes.

"Look, land!" I grinned. "Finally, we're close to being done with flying."

My hopes were dashed when she said, "No, we still have a long way to go. This is only the coast of the Western Sahara. Right there in front of us is the city of Dakla. We'll land there and grab another flight to Ain Salah, Algeria, and then we'll be off to Benghazi, Libya. Lastly, we'll travel to the airport near Dawadmi, Saudi Arabia."

I sighed, slouched in my seat, and crossed my arms over my chest. "Oh Pūĕr, how wonderful: flying in airplanes! What a novel idea it was to think of airplanes!" I declared acerbically.

"Alaĕna, it would take a lot longer to go across the country by vehicle, then across the ocean on a boat, then back on a vehicle or even possibly a camel to cross the continent of Africa, then on another boat to cross the Red Sea, and then getting on another vehicle or camel to cross the desert and into the heart of Saudi Arabia. That would take months, maybe even a year! We don't have that kind of time according to our source," she argued, and I put my hands up in resignation.

"All right, but, wait, did you say, 'Benghazi, Libya'? Isn't that…"

"Yep, it's the place where all of *that* happened. Excuse me, I need to use the restroom." Isabella slipped out of her seat and walked down the hallway to the tiny bathroom.

I shook my head. *She's trying to give me something to think about during the flight. It's working, but I'm still bored.* I leaned my head against the headrest.

Suddenly, I thought of something as I looked at Bartholomew, who was snoozing in the seat in front of me. I smirked at the Machiavellian plan I had concocted for him. Slowly, I stood up and leaned over his seat.

Jacob, who was sitting next to my brother, saw what I was doing and tried not to laugh.

I got right next to my ear and said, "Hullo, Mr. Snooze!"

He jumped and bumped his head on the baggage cubby above his head.

I fell back into my seat, laughing, and Jacob was bent over his seat holding in a loud laugh, which ended up being his famous and brilliant white smile.

Over the few days, I had begun to figure him out some in that he had a good sense of humor he disliked most of the airplane snacks, and his snore sounded like the rumble of an angry elephant.

"Alaëna! Oh, come on! Seriously? I couldn't take a single nap without you scaring me out of my wits?" Bartholomew scowled, causing me to laugh even harder.

Some of the other passengers were staring, but I didn't care.

"Cowboy Up! We're going to land soon, in Dakla, Western Sahara to be precise," I said, slapping him on the back.

He stroked his chin. "Hmm…" He grinned then grabbed me with his arm and gave me a noogie.

"Bart!" I chortled as he let me go. "Bartholomew James Healdton, what has gotten into you?"

"I'm treating you like family. That means I can do stuff like that." He smirked. "You can kiss me, so I can give you a noogie. Girls give hugs and boys give noogies. That's how it goes."

Jacob shook his head. "Actually, Wilanira punches me all the time, and she kicks me, too, but then Kīanna tackles me. For some reason, all of my younger siblings like to beat me up. Thank goodness, I don't have more sisters."

"Oh, really? I guess I've been acting like your sister all along, Bart," I teased.

"Please, stop calling me that," he pled.

"Bart, Bart, Bart, Bart, Bart. There, I called you Bart eight times."

"Uh, that was five," he corrected.

I frowned. "No, eight. I counted the last ones."

He stuck out his tongue and crossed his eyes.

I messed up his hair.

Waving his hands around, he declared, "Hey, don't mess with the hair! If you can't help but hurt the rest of me, just leave the hair alone. You can mess with Jacob's hair."

Jacob looked puzzled, and I chuckled. "He doesn't *have* hair to mess around with, Bartholomew."

Jacob scowled. "I have hair, just not Barbie doll hair like Bartholomew." The boy grinned as he gently patted Bartholomew's close-to-shoulder-length, dark brown hair.

"Barbie doll hair, eh?" Bartholomew rolled up his sleeves. "Oh, you're going to pay for that one!" He looked like he was going to tackle him onto the aisle, but Isabella came rushing into the scene.

"Bartholomew! What are you doing? This is not a wrestling mat in a school gym! This is an airplane!" She glowered at him.

"Uh, I wasn't *going* to tackle him," he opposed. "I was just going to make him think I was."

She stared at him in disbelief.

"Okay, I was going to tackle him. On an airplane or on the ground, it doesn't matter to me. I was born to fly!"

I hung my head in shame. *That was one of the cheesiest statements I've ever heard from you, brother.*

"Jacob, when are we going to land?" Isabella questioned, exasperated by my brother's antics.

Jacob climbed over Bartholomew and looked out the small, square-ish window. "We look to be about fifty-five miles out, so about half-of-an-hour at this speed, which is extremely slow. Oh, how I miss my baby." He sighed.

"Yep, at least I was able to bring my baby." I patted my knife, which was sheathed and hidden underneath my jacket. A faint smile crossed my lips when I touched the warm pommel. It reminded me of Pătĕr, Frŏns, and Dīcărĕ.

"Yeah, and I'm still wondering how it got past the… Ouch!" Bartholomew exclaimed when Jacob stomped on Bartholomew's foot.

Isabella gave him a stern look.

"Sorry?" Bartholomew shrugged.

I rolled my eyes and tried to get comfortable in my seat. A minute passed, then two, three, four, five, six, et cetera. No, not Mr. Cĕtĕră, et cetera, as in, etc.… that kind of thing. It gets confusing when you have a teacher named that, which I highly doubt you would.

When fifteen minutes had passed, the electronic voice of the pilot boomed through the plane in two languages. The first was English, and the second, I believe, was Arabic. I hadn't heard Arabic before, so I wouldn't know. No offense to Arabic speakers, but it sounded like someone was hacking up a hairball in some of the words. However, that was just my perspective since I was able to speak only English and Latin.

"Attention passengers, this is your pilot speaking. Our previous destination of Dakla has been changed. So, please make yourself comfortable." I looked at Jacob with a confused look, and a "light bulb" moment hit us at the same time.

Immediately, we jumped up and ran over to the cockpit.

As I caught up to him when he had entered the room, I heard a deep, familiar-sounding voice ask, "What are you doing in here, boy?!"

"What are you doing in here?" Jacob countered.

I was hanging by the door, listening, when it hit me. I jumped into the room and saw him. Astonished, I asked, "Banana Bear?"

A large, gruff-looking man turned around and instantly recognized me. "Sharp Hand?" he examined.

Nodding, I responded, "Fancy meeting you here on a plane. Long way from Wetly, eh?"

Jacob looked from me to the gruff man and then back to me, trying to make the connection.

Banana Bear nodded and said, while pointing his pistol at the pilot, "Yes, it is. What are you doing here?"

I shrugged. "Business. You?"

He shrugged. "Business."

I nodded. "My business is in Dakla. So, you'll have to drop the gun, sit yourself back down in your seat, and let the pilot and copilot do their job. All right? Don't want to end up like Apple Arm, now, do we?"

Banana Bear laughed. "Well, I guess that I don't have much of a choice then. Either I go to Dakla and get arrested or I go to my previous destination and get rich, but then end up like old AA. So, I think there's *one* option since the first involves police officers, which would be messy, and the second involves you. Sorry, Sharp Hand, looks like neither of us is going to our destination."

As I saw that he was aiming at and preparing to fire a bullet into the control panel, I immediately drew my knife and tried to prevent him from completing his task, but I was too late.

Sparks flew everywhere, and I heard people start screaming behind me. Before he could fire again, I tackled him to the ground and put my knife to his throat. I'm feeling a serious sense of Déjà vu, here!

I leaned down and whispered in his ear, "This is a chance for you to get a new start. Serve your time and start a new life. I suggest you take it." He tried to throw me off, but before he could, I hit him in the temple with the pommel of my knife, knocking him unconscious. Once I had wiped the blood off of the pommel, I sheathed my knife and stood.

Jacob's jaw was dropped, as were the pilot and copilot's.

I tried to snap them out of their shock as the plane began to go haywire and plummet down to the sea. As a last resort, I cried, "Jacob, do your job!"

Jacob shook his head, shaking himself, and declared, "Listen to me. We've lost control and will go down if you don't let me take control. I'm a professional."

The pilot shook his head, also shaking himself out of his trance-like state, and waved off the gathering smoke. "Listen…" cough "…boy, even if you are, it's too late for this piece of junk. I told them before we left that we needed a gun in here, but no! They refused. Isn't that right, Jimmy?"

"Yep, absolutely!" Jimmy responded and coughed. "And if we're not careful, this thing might…"

"Blow up. Yes, I can tell by the smoke. It's not that hard to fix if you know what you're doing," Jacob finished, rather cockily at that.

"Look, kid, if you can do something, then go ahead and do it. We're going down anyways," the pilot insisted, which I'm sure was sarcastic.

"All right, then. Get up from your seat and let me teach

you how to fly an airplane!" Jacob grabbed the man by his arm, pulled him up, and then plopped down in the seat. He started to push buttons, flip switches, and also speak some Latin to fix some internal damage, which, I'm sure, puzzled the pilot and copilot. I'm assuming they thought the words were curses. The big dumb-dumbs.

"Is there any way that I can help?" I asked.

Jacob nodded. "Get Bartholomew 'cause I need him in the copilot's seat."

I nodded and dashed off to get Bartholomew.

"What's wrong? What was that noise?!" Isabella asked.

Instead of answering, I grabbed Bartholomew and yanked him off his seat and down the hallway to the, uh, room thingy.

"What is it?" he asked with a worried expression on his face.

"Banana Bear, gun, dumb pilot and copilot, and that sort of thing," I said, even though both the 'dumb' people were right next to me.

Nodding, Bartholomew followed me back to the room.

As we scrambled up the aisle, I explained, "Jacob needs you as copilot, though we should be able to land before we blow up."

"Blow up?!" he cried as he abruptly stopped in his tracks.

"Yes, I've faced worse things in Wetly. Now, come on!" I pulled him into the cockpit.

Jacob nodded to Bartholomew and motioned him into the empty seat, which Jimmy had been nice enough to vacate.

Hastily, Bartholomew sat down and also started pushing buttons and flipping switches, but did not speak Latin.

While they were doing their duty in ensuring that we didn't crash into the ocean, I did my duty of making sure that Banana Bear didn't wake up by occasionally thwacking him with the metal butt of my knife. Thankfully, I only had to do it twice since, within two minutes, there was no smoke, and we were flying smoothly.

"There you go, fixed and smooth," Jacob declared as he put the plane into autopilot and stepped out of the chair.

"Smooth as cream," Bartholomew confirmed as he erected himself and stood beside Jacob.

The pilot and copilot were in utter disbelief.

"Parker, I have never seen anything like that," said the blank-expression Jimmy.

Parker—a.k.a. Pilot Guy—nodded in agreement.

"Well, you're welcome." Jacob did a slight bow and walked out of the room.

Bartholomew did the same.

Laughing at the priceless expressions on the men's poor faces, I followed my counterparts to their seats.

As I sat down, Isabella gave me an enigmatic look, and I explained what happened. The woman smiled and put a hand on both of the boys' shoulders. "Those are my boys. Mr. Cĕtĕră would be proud."

Bartholomew blushed, and Jacob said, "It was nothing, just the basics."

Isabella nodded, and the flight went on.

———◆———

"I wanted to thank you again for saving the lives of our passengers. They would have surely died if you hadn't stepped in, taken down that man, and fixed the plane!" a medium-height man thanked us for the millionth time.

We had landed safely at the airport, and Jimmy and Parker had told the owner of the aerodrome what had happened. The man had a long, black beard; an odd hat that wrapped around his head similar to what girls do when they dry their hair; a white-and-blue-striped robe, which looked like a dress; and sandals. His skin was bronzed due to the blazing sun, and he had deep-brown eyes that spoke of troubled times.

"Please, sir, it was nothing but simple mistakes that could easily be fixed if you had the right training," Jacob insisted.

Jimmy shook his head. "No, there was something else. You were speaking Latin as you fixed it. No amount of button-pressing and switch-flipping could fix that bullet hole. You're one of those Latin Magicians!"

"Me?" Jacob feigned shock.

Parker nodded. "Yes, I agree. I heard you mumbling Latin. You must be one of those rats!"

"Rats! Măgī Latīnī are not rats! It is those D-A-M-L agents that are rats!" I yelled. *Me and my big fat mouth,* I scolded myself.

"So, you are one of them!" Jimmy assumed.

I sneered. "So, what if I am, buster? What will you do about it? Jacob, Bartholomew, and I saved your ungrateful lives, and you accuse us of being Măgī Latīnī negatively; the kind of way that the Măgī Latīnī have been murdered by. What great hospitality this city has!"

The man in the robe glared at Jimmy and Parker. "She is right. We do have great hospitality here, even if they are Măgī Latīnī. Which are they? We will not turn you in to the authorities if you are, of course." He looked very proud and dignified with these words. I had heard that in some countries, good hospitality was part of their culture.

Isabella spoke at last in her Italian accent, which was particularly strong that day. "I am Walsh. I would like to admit that I am a Măgūs Lătīnūs, along with my traveling companions Jacob Tĕrră and Alaĕna Bombyx. We come in peace and do not want to harm you or your people," she slowly said that part to make a point to me. "That is why Jacob, Bartholomew, and Alaĕna saved the plane. We are not terrorists, but quite the opposite. Jacob invented the un-failable engine."

Jacob beamed with pride as a confirmation.

The man offered a slight bow, saying, "I am very impressed. I am hoping that you will be most comfortable in my own house for a meal or even a night, if you will accept. My wife loves to cook for guests. She was raised in England. A most interesting accent she has, almost as beautiful as yours, Ms. Walsh."

I tried not to laugh.

He was either trying to flatter her or just being courteous. Either way, it seemed to have had a positive effect on Isabella.

"My son, Kharim, is a very bright student and would love to meet you and ask questions about America and Italy."

"Thank you, sir. Your wife and son sound very nice. Begging your pardon, what is your name?" she asked, smiling.

"Oh, goodness, I forgot to introduce myself," the man gasped. "I am Abu Kharim."

Isabella nodded slowly.

Ka-ka-ka-ugh! Pŭĕr, I'll never be able to pronounce that right! I declared to myself.

"Now, come, I will get your luggage and bring you to my home. But first, I will call my wife and inform her of our arrival. She gets extremely angry with me when I bring in guests without telling her. I suppose it is because she is British. If not that, then I do not know."

Jacob nodded. "Yeah, my mom gets mad all the time when I invite friends over without telling her. My mom… it's been a year since I've seen her." He sighed.

Abu Kharim frowned but didn't ask anything. Instead, the man led us over to the inside of the actual airport.

Since everything was tan, I couldn't tell the building from the sand. This was the case with almost all the other buildings in Dakla. Once we were inside, I discovered the temperature was a few degrees cooler, which amazingly made it feel like I was walking into a refrigerator. After my eyes adjusted to the indoor lighting, I saw that the building was not that large, with it being about a hundred feet wide and two hundred feet long.

We retrieved our luggage and exited to the parking lot. It looked kind of like an oval or a rectangle with rounded edges. It was prettier than the flat-out straight parking lots we had in the US, or the ones which I was used to.

He took us to his SUV, loaded our stuff in, and even opened the car door for me! Nice guy. I just hoped that he wasn't one of those nice-to-you-then-kill-you people. He drove out of the parking lot and down the short road, took a left, and drove on for about four minutes.

I studied his car as he drove: it was white, lots of white, with wood paneling on the doors and dashboard. *I hate white,* I groaned. *Of course, Vīta, no offense to your beautiful Māter.* I expected her to respond, but she didn't. *I hope she's all right.* I had a very concerned look on my face, and Bartholomew noticed.

"What's wrong?" he queried.

"It's nothing, just some thoughts," I responded. He didn't say anything else, but I knew that he didn't believe me and that he would know that I probably wanted to tell him later when there weren't so many people around. So, I continued to think about the reasons Vīta wasn't responding, pondering every option, until she finally answered.

With a rather weary tone, she said, *I am sorry if I made you worry. I have been having family trouble. My Frāter left one week ago without telling me. I am afraid that either he has been kidnapped or has finally been killed for agreeing to bond with a human. This has never happened before, never. I am worried about him.*

I was relieved to hear from her, but I was also concerned

about her Frăter. *Maybe he heard something Mr. Ratty said and went to look for Dīcărĕ. He is a Bonded One, after all, and I'm sure he wants Dīcărĕ to suffer as much as we do.*

You do not understand. My Frăter was forbidden to enter your world. The rest of my kin and I may go freely, but my Frăter did something awful: he spoke to a Măgūs Lătīnūs before he was bonded. Even my Măter would have been shocked.

What's the difference? I inquired.

You could not understand. Our politics and rules are very different from yours. After a long pause, she quickly said, *I must go, hastily, before they discover our plans. Vălĕrĕ Īūbĕrĕ, Lūx Aĕtĕrnă.* The light blue, glowing mare spoke no more.

I internally groaned. *Great, yet another nickname!*

As the vehicle stopped, Abu Kharim stepped outside and opened the doors for us. After our luggage was collected from the back, he escorted us to the front door. The man entered and motioned for us to follow.

Stepping indoors, I gawked at the magnificence of the sight.

It was a huge room with two stairways. One was near the left wall, one was near the right wall, and they both curved upward. Marble, brick, and beautiful crown molding lined the archways and ceilings.

White, why is it always white? I asked myself. *Oh well, at least he's not trying to kill me, hopefully.*

"Welcome to my home! This is my wife, Susan," Abu Kharim said as a very pretty, middle-aged woman strode over to his side.

She was dressed in a long brown skirt and blouse. She had a black garment wrapped around her head that covered all of her face and hair except for her hazel eyes, which glittered with pride when her husband described her education and upbringing in England. After some more introductions, she motioned for us to follow her as she floated to the steps and began to ascend with her long, coffee-brown skirt billowing back with the motion.

We lifted our bags and suitcases and trekked up the stairs, which seemed more like a journey to the moon than to the second floor. Once we had reached the top, I was panting a bit and felt like flopping down on the steps, but I had a reputation to uphold. I couldn't do stuff like that! So, I Cowgirled up and followed Susan.

The others were panting and sitting down, but quickly stood and pursued the two non-panting people.

She motioned to the girls with her right hand and said, "This is your room." She gestured with her left hand to the door on the left side of the hall and said for the boys to go into the room on the left. "The bathroom is at the end of the hall. Let me know if you need anything." She curtsied and left.

I looked the opposite way of Bartholomew, scooted next to him, and then punched him in the arm.

"Ouch!" he exclaimed. "What was that for?"

"Nothing," I responded, and he glared at me with a vengeance. Laughing silently to myself, I marched over to the girls' room and entered.

Shaking her head, Isabella sighed and followed.

The room was about two times the size of my room at Mulpa and had an infinite amount of white. "White, white, white, why is everything white? I'm going to go insane soon because of this blankness!" I exclaimed, flopping on my bed with white sheets and white pillows. Vīvūm, even the headboard and footboard were white! "I mean I can deal with black, purple, even pink! But not white."

Isabella looked quizzical as she asked, "Why do you hate white so much?"

I sighed. "Because it reminds me too much of when I almost…" I put my hand over my stomach, which still held the scar of when a Damsel stabbed me in the back with a long knife.

"Oh… that. What was it like? I don't mean to be insensitive or anything like that, but I am curious," Isabella said.

I sighed, closed my eyes, and focused. "Dark… then light. Flashing colors and sounds. I was thirsty… then I felt nothing and then something. Finally, I saw white, pure white, with no black, gray, or any other colors. That is until I saw this being. It was large and glowed a white that made its surroundings look black. Its eyes burned right through me. Then I snapped out of the trance and saw Dīcărĕ. That's why I hate white." I spat the word 'white' like it was a curse.

"I'm sorry that I brought it up. I know that must have been hard for you. That being, do you remember anything else?"

I shook my head, "No, noth… wait. I remember. He said this to me: 'Fear not, Lūx Aĕtĕrnă, for your time has not come.' Once, when I was alone, Vīta called me that. What is Lūx Aĕtĕrnă? I wonder if…" I stopped as my mind trailed off into a world of thoughts.

Isabella snapped her fingers, and I jumped. "Well, while I try to figure out what on earth Lūx Aĕtĕrnă is, let's change the topic to something that's been bugging me: was Dīcărĕ really your…"

"No!" *Well, that wasn't suspicious at all. I am so bad at this.* "Of course not. I was way too young for that. We were only eleven and twelve years old. I mean, I was *eleven years old*, much too young."

Isabella smirked. "All right."

I glared at her. "Not like that. Oh, phooey this is frustrating." She started laughing, and I turned red. "Just don't forget that I still have Căpĕrĕ Flămmaĕ, okay?"

She stopped her merry giggling and glowered at me. "Stop threatening people with that, okay?"

"Why? Why should I stop? It's the only way no one will harm me. Do you know how dangerous it is to be a thirteen-year-old girl in this world? Very dangerous. Now plug in the fact that a good many men want my hide, and there you go! A paradise for me to become rat-soup." I flopped down backward onto my bed.

"Oh, stop being such a drama queen," she said sarcastically.

"I am not a drama queen. If you want a drama queen, talk to Bart."

She sighed and began to check her suitcase.

Nothing else was said between us as we checked and re-checked our luggage over and over again. Nothing was missing, nothing, but something felt wrong, and it was all going well until I heard Bartholomew scream. *Oh no. Not again!* I ran outside to see what was wrong. Bartholomew was face-to-face with the largest beast on four legs I had ever seen.

CHAPTER 10

I Almost Die, Again

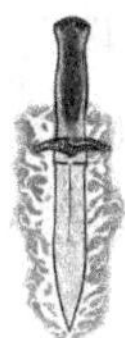

I was laughing so hard I thought that I was going to either cry or pass out. "Oh, Bartholomew, what a cute friend you've found!" I laughed. "Oh, what a hoot this is!"

Bartholomew glared at me. "Alaĕna, this is not funny!" He tried to say more, but the four-by-ten-inch tongue interrupted him with a slobbery kiss. My brother was sitting on the ground next to the largest dog I had ever seen: a Great Dane, to be precise.

"Of course, it's funny! You're being licked by the largest tongue in the world!" I burst into another laughing fit. "And here I thought you had been attacked by another Sĕpīa Vōlătīcă."

Jacob and Isabella had come out right after me and were cracking up. Isabella had more control over her laughing fit than Jacob and I did.

"Oh, go ahead and laugh! See how you like being covered

in drool and spit." He grunted and flailed his hands about. "Get off, dog! Go away, shoo!"

The dog whimpered, gave him one final lick, and trotted over to me.

I knelt down, and she sniffed me with her huge, wet, black nose. She was white with large, black spots. Her eyes were the most beautiful shade of light blue.

"Gracie!" A young man about eighteen or nineteen years old ran up the stairs to the Great Dane and grabbed her collar. "I'm sorry. I'm surprised my father didn't warn you about her. She's large and can be a bit scary at times, but she's just a big softy!" He scratched her head, and Gracie happily yipped. The man was wearing black pants, a white shirt, and a black tie as if he had just come from a cubical or something. With black hair, a lighter skin tone, and a black-and-white outfit, he looked a lot like Gracie. "I'm Kharim, by the way. Pleased to meet you!"

I stuck out my hand for me to shake and, instead of shaking it, he kissed it like the gentlemen of old. I was very surprised by the gesture and probably looked astonished. I quickly shook my head. "Now, why didn't you do this when we first met, Bartholomew?" I asked jokingly.

"I was too busy carrying you to do *that*," he said, looking pretty red. "Now, here's my hand for you to *shake*. I am Bartholomew, age thirteen, and brother to Alaĕna, who you are still holding onto." He glared at him, and Kharim released my hand and took his.

"I'm sorry if I have offended you in any way. Is it not normal in your country to do that? I did research and thought that this is how you greeted," he explained.

I shook my head. "No, not these days. Well, not to the extent of my knowledge, anyway. We shake hands when we meet a person."

He nodded.

Thank goodness, he didn't research French greetings, ugh! I thought.

He turned his attention to Jacob, who was closer than Isabella, and asked, "You are?"

They shook hands, and Jacob replied, "Jacob Tĕrră, pilot and engineer. That pretty gal over there is Isabella. She's a linguist *and* a nurse." He pointed with his thumb at Isabella.

Isabella put out her hand and said in a strong Italian accent, "Sălvĕ, as Jacob said: I am Isabella, a nurse and linguist. I am pleased to meet you."

This time he took the girl's hand and shook it.

"Nice to see you learned your lesson. Do anything like that to Alaĕna and she might slug you… or punch you if you don't know what a slug is in that context. She is well known for doing that."

Bartholomew nodded.

The man seemed puzzled by me.

"Yes, I am puzzling." I grinned. "The more you know me, the more I puzzle you because I am a conspiracy."

"Isn't that the truth?" Bartholomew shook his head.

Kharim blinked with confusion, then kneeled next to the Great Dane. "As you probably heard, this is Gracie. She is a Great Dane, a very large one at that, and eats about a bag of dog food each day." She wagged her tail and barked. "She also has a very loud bark." He scratched her side, and she licked him. "Dinner is ready, and we prepared an English dinner that my mother experienced in her days in England. We hope that it is close to your American food."

Jacob looked like he was going to burst out laughing but was able to keep his mouth shut.

It would be very, very rude if we refused anything they

gave us, or so Isabella explained. So, I just hoped that nothing they gave us had peanuts in it. To Alaëna who was slain by a peanut-butter cookie. Now, that's the stuff of legends.

With one last pat, Kharim left Gracie and escorted us down the left staircase then behind it. Through a white hallway, we came to the dining room. The kitchen was to the right of it and was behind a wall with expensive-looking art hung on it.

A large oak table lay before us, with a total of six chairs placed at each end and two on each side. Six places were set with white napkins folded in triangles. Beside the napkin was a large plate, which was underneath a medium plate that was underneath a smaller plate, which was underneath a teacup. To the right of the set of plates were a variety of forks: a long fork, a short fork, and a middle fork. Next were spoons, which came in all shapes and sizes. Then, you had a rather pathetic-looking knife which looked similar to what the embryo of my knife would look like. Everything was on top of a white placemat trimmed with cream-colored flowery lace.

In the middle of the table was a vase of red roses, orange petunias, white daisies, pink tulips, purple snapdragons, and a single sunflower in the middle. It smelled like a day during spring in a wildflower field. The smell reminded me of the night when the blue moon was out and these glowing flowers popped out of the snow on the Wetly mountainside, creating a look that only the glittering heavens above could compare to. That happened the night that Pătĕr and Frŏns died. It was like someone was trying to comfort me, but that was illogical and improbable.

As we approached the table, Isabella whispered to me, "These people must hold a more modernized Muslim belief system. Normally, the women do not eat with the men."

I was confused but didn't ask for more.

Abu Kharim sat at the far end of the table, Kharim sat

on the left side of him, and Susan sat across from her husband. Bartholomew was next to Kharim and Jacob was next to Bartholomew. I sat down next to Susan's chair, and Isabella sat next to me.

"All right, now, it is time to eat!" Abu Kharim exclaimed.

Susan stood, strode into the kitchen, and brought in a teakettle that was steaming hot.

I hadn't a clue what to do since I had no manners, no training, nothing.

Isabella, undoubtedly, saw my confusion, so she said to Abu Kharim, "Please, excuse Alaĕna if she has no manners. She was, um, abandoned at the young age of six by her father and grew up in the dark alleyways of Welty, Colorado."

Abu Kharim seemed shocked. "Why would he abandon her? She seems nice."

Bartholomew almost laughed out loud. "Wait until you get to know her!"

I glared at him.

"What do you mean by that?" Abu Kharim asked.

"Don't you two start," Isabella warned menacingly.

I nodded reluctantly, and so did Bartholomew. So, we quietly continued our dinner. First was a cup of tea and then a salad dish, which was followed by a soup dish. Next, a couple of sandwiches, which were complemented by some cookies that were finally supplemented with a shot of mint tea. Afterward, we thanked them for the meal and went upstairs.

As I lay down in my bed to take a nap, Isabella went with the boys and talked with them for a while about something that I didn't care about.

A while later, I awoke to see Gracie attentively eyeing me with her large, inquisitive eyes. Smiling, I scratched her behind her ears and sat up. "What time is it?" I whispered. Hearing Isabella's quiet breathing in the bed next to me, I assumed she was asleep. It was dark, and I had slept into the depths of the night. I wasn't tired, so I knew I wouldn't be able to sleep. Therefore, I decided to wander around a bit and stretch out my legs.

While being as silent as possible, I crept out of bed and began to tiptoe out the door, but, for some reason, I grabbed my sword from my suitcase and sheathed it in my belt. I had this feeling which made me uneasy.

I always trusted that feeling.

I continued out the door with Gracie happily trotting behind me. Luckily, her nails were trimmed so they didn't make any noise on the marble floors. After I had made my way down the hallway and the stairs, I stopped and looked at the door. Hearing scuffling and a few whispers outside the door, I drew my sword as a precaution.

The door jiggled and unlocked.

Hastily, I ran over to the space behind the door and hid.

Gracie followed close beside me.

They opened the door, and I moved with it. It was dark, but I could see their faces. It was Parker and Jimmy! They had swords at their left sides and a long knife—or a hunting knife in Jimmy's case—on their right. Also, small handguns were in their hands.

Damsels! I mentally exclaimed.

Parker quietly shut the door and started toward the stairs with Jimmy.

Stealthily, I snuck behind the men and put the point of my sword at Parker's neck. "What do you think you're doing?" I asked rather loudly.

Jimmy dropped his gun and drew his sword. "Rat, what

are you doing up so late?"

I smirked. "What are you doing here? Now, before we continue this conversation, I will say that this sword is one of your own, Damsel, and it's sharp. Do you really think I care about one of you Damsels? You already know what I did to that man, so I would recommend sheathing your sword and getting out of here as fast as you possibly can." I pressed the sword harder against the pilot's neck.

He gulped down his growing fear.

Jimmy's eyes widened with recognition.

"I could also turn you into an animal, maybe a cat for Gracie to play with?" I smirked as Gracie growled and barked, creeping closer to the copilot. She barked once, twice, thrice. I heard Abu Kharim running through the halls. "Last chance."

"We have orders, and I intend to follow them!" He swung his sword, and I blocked.

The cling of metal hitting metal rang through the room and echoed through the house.

In an instant, Bartholomew, Isabella, and Jacob were on the balcony, watching the fight.

Parker quickly began shooting at them, and they dropped to the ground to avoid the deadly bullets. They couldn't do a thing, and I was too busy to do anything about Parker's shooting gallery.

Jimmy sliced vertically.

I blocked and that time with that fight took the offensive. Adrenaline pumped through my veins as I thrust at his stomach, and he barely brushed it off, although the sound of ripping fabric echoed in my ears.

He sliced at me from the left.

I blocked and countered with a torrent of cuts, slices, and thrusts that made him fall backward. My blade was pressed against his throat the moment his sword hit the ground with a sharp clang. It had only been thirty-five seconds, but it felt like a lifetime. I was breathing slowly and calmly as I firmly commanded, "Drop your weapon or your counterpart feels my blade."

Jimmy looked at Parker with pitiful, pleading eyes, and the man complied and dropped his gun.

Slowly, I lifted my sword.

Jimmy scrambled up, and the two wannabe assassins, who seriously needed lessons from Breaker, ran out the door.

Abu Kharim was standing in the hallway with a rifle. "What happened?" he demanded.

I twirled my sword in my hand and said casually, "Oh, your pilot and copilot were trying to kill us."

Abu Kharim looked surprised, and Bartholomew said in a shaky voice, "See what I mean about getting to know her!"

I glared at my brother. "For the second time, you have done this. I have saved your life, and you thank me with criticism. Typical," I said as I sheathed my sword. As I walked to the door to close it, a knife flew through the air toward me, and before I could move, it hit me. I was knocked to the ground. I couldn't even scream.

Take two on extreme pain!

Gracie was immediately at my side, licking me.

I groaned, "Oh, not again." A small cry left my lips as I tried to sit up, causing an unbearable pain from the motion to consume me.

"Alaĕna!" Bartholomew yelled as he sprinted down the stairs to get to me.

As fast as he humanly could, Abu Kharim raced to the door, slammed it shut, and bolted it.

Bartholomew looked at the damage. He was trembling badly as he kneeled next to me. "Germăna Mĕa, Nĕ Dĕrĕlīnqŭăs Mē. Qŭaĕsō Sōrōr Nŏn Mōrī, Sīs!" I thought he was going to cry.

"Don't worry, Bart. It's only a scratch. I'll recover in no time." I weakly smiled as Isabella rushed to my side. I shook from the blood loss. Shock set in. Glancing over, I noticed that the knife was to the left of my head. I blinked once. It was going dark, then a bit light.

Alaĕna! I heard Vīta yell in my head. *Alaĕna what happened? Nevermind, let me see.* To my surprise, I felt a being in my head, presumably Vīta, searching my memories for what happened. *Oh, Alaĕna, why do you do this to yourself? I… I cannot do anything! If I was there, I could. However, not even I can perform a healing spell that will work telepathically. Oh, Alaĕna, I am so sorry!*

It's okay, maybe now I will… I didn't have the strength to continue.

After a minute, a song, like a flickering flame, echoed through my mind. *O Ūnă Vulnerătă, Ămō Tĕ. Ūnă Vulnerătă, Vīvă Ĕt Spīră! Aŭdī Ăd Vōcĕm Mĕăm! Aŭdī Ăd Cŏncōrdīăm Mĕăm! Aŭdī Ĕt Sănă! Aŭdī Ăd Cărmĕn Mĕūm! Aŭdī, Ūnă Vulnerătă, Ŏb Ămō Tĕ, Lūcĕm! Live and breathe as I do, dear one.*

The wound began to heal at an alarming rate.

My brain cleared, and I asked, *Vīta?*

Her musical voice filled my ears. *Oh, Alaĕna! You are alive! How…*

I thought you had figured it out.

No, I did not. What happened?

I explained everything.

Interesting, she muttered. She did not speak after that.

After a moment, I opened my eyes and waited for the world to come back into focus. As soon as I could count the ceiling tiles, I jerked up, readying myself for a fight, just in case the men had come back while I was dying.

The rapid movement made everyone around me jump with fright.

"Alaĕna, you're alive!" Bartholomew exclaimed with joy and disbelief.

"Yeah, I'm alive, and now I remember the song Dīcărĕ sang to me that day."

"It must be a very powerful song because you were dead for sure. The knife had pierced your heart!" Isabella cried out, tears in her eyes.

"Yeah, so stop gawking! Now, I owe him two favors and need to settle those debts. Come on, no need to stick around here since we're only putting our host in even more danger. You think that they're going to disappear?" I tried to get up, but I noticed something. I still had the knife in my shoulder. So, I took it out, it was as clean as a whistle. I smirked. "Another souvenir for my collection." I tried to stand up but, in the process, almost fell over. Although, I recovered my balance in time so that I didn't fall backward onto the red-stained floor.

Bartholomew offered me some support.

Soon, Isabella also helped me.

Jacob, who had been talking with Abu Kharim, was still standing next to the man in shock.

"How many weapons do you have now?" asked my brother.

I thought about it for a moment. "Three. Here, Bart, you can have this one." I handed him the knife. It was a nice hunting knife with a serrated edge on the top and a regular edge on the bottom.

Bartholomew gulped as he took it. "Sharp, very sharp."

"I know that. I felt how sharp it was," I replied coldly. Bartholomew looked as if he felt quite badly about his statement, so I reassured him, "It's okay, Bart. I'll be fine. I told you

I would be fine, and I am, right?"

He nodded solemnly.

"I can't believe you're alive!" Jacob cried as he rushed over to me. He had just come out of his shock and was back in the real world.

I rolled my eyes and waved it off. "Yeah, yeah, I keep getting that. It's really annoying."

The young man rolled his eyes but didn't say any more.

Abu Kharim was sitting on the bottom step of the right staircase with his head in his hands.

This whole thing had only taken two minutes and Kharim had just arrived at the scene. "What in the world happened?!" he exclaimed, looking at his father and then at me.

"Oh, look, he said something American!" I pointed out.

My supporters shook their heads.

Isabella was the one to explain everything that happened.

"Wow, so that's what it's like to be a Latin Magician." Kharim's eyes were wide. "Anything else that's bad about being a Latin Magician?"

Isabella nodded and said, "Yes. We have anger management issues. We have those Damsels constantly hunting us. Plus, we have only forty years to live."

Bartholomew and I jumped. "What?" I continued solo for the rest of the sentence. "What do you mean I have 'only forty years to live'? Nobody ever told me that!"

"You weren't told?"

"No, I spent most of my time in the hospital. What a depressing thought for someone who almost died for the seventh time in their life! Oh, why does this always happen to me?" I plopped back down on the ground and sighed with contempt.

Bartholomew nodded unsympathetically. "Yeah, this stuff always does seem to happen to you."

"Thanks, Bart," I said sarcastically. "Well, at least I now know why we need their strength."

"Yes, that's why, and it stinks." Jacob sighed.

Confused, Kharim asked, "Who or what is '*they*' in '*their*'?"

Isabella frowned. "That is information that should not be made known unto the public, or that's classified."

He sighed.

"Well, no use staying in this Popsicle Stand. Let's get out of here. I've had enough of these pilots and copilots who want to be banes of Latin Magicians. I'm sorry about any damage to your house, Abu Kharim, but we should go now to offer you some protection from the maniacs who want us dead. Dĭē Bōnă, Abu Kharim, Kharim." I stood, nodded to them, and ran up the stairs. *I don't care if I have to walk to Saudi Arabia because I am not getting on another plane!* I declared to myself.

CHAPTER 11

Abandoned

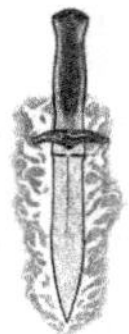

On my face was a scowl only Cruella De Vil could match as I walked into the plane. Somehow, they had convinced me that I should go on the plane, that not all pilots and copilots were similar to the ones we had encountered previously, and that it would be too slow to journey on land… *Oh, who cares how long it takes? I would've walked to Saudi Arabia if it meant not going on another accursed plane.* I glared at Isabella, the main instigator of my intricately planned demise. *Oh, Vīta, how can you stand to fly?* I thought.

I cannot stand it. I welcome it, love it, and enjoy it, she corrected. I huffed. *Smart Alec.*

She whinnied, amusement coming through our connection.

Once we were seated, a fancy assistant lady with bright red lipstick, dark brown hair, unnaturally white teeth, a large smile, and a skirt that was too short and too tight for her walked in and said, "Please remain seated as we take off and, please, turn off all cellular devices." Her voice was one of those annoying ones that made me want to knock her pretty little lights out, but that was just my mood.

The lady, with no sense of modesty, disappeared into the back, and the plane began to move forward. Then her voice was on the speakers, "Seat belts, everyone!" Oh boy, that voice was torture, but Bartholomew seemed to be fine with it. That time, he was sitting next to me, and Isabella was sitting in the row in front of us next to an old, bald, fat guy with a Hawaiian, button-up T-shirt that said *Call Me.*

The man had just conked out when his head fell over onto her shoulder.

Isabella turned to me and mouthed, '*Help me!*'

I shook my head and put up my hands.

She scowled, snapped her head back into her forward-facing position, and pushed the man over so that he was leaning on the window instead.

Jacob had better luck since he was sitting in the row to the left of us next to a fourteen-year-old girl who was wearing a long, flowing blue skirt and blouse. He was trying not to pay attention to the fact that she kept on glancing at him.

I rolled my eyes and shook my head.

Bartholomew was trying not to laugh when Jacob blushed because the girl had fluttered her eyelashes at him.

"I think that I'm going to be sick!" I whispered to Bartholomew before covering my mouth with my hand.

He snorted. "Oh, so you don't like that kind of stuff?"

"No, it's so… *gross.*" I shivered.

He smirked. "So, that means you never…"

I cut him off. "Don't finish that sentence, no, never! *Never,* and I'm not lying."

He rolled his eyes.

"What?" I tilted my head.

He sighed. "Nothing, Alaĕna, nothing. You've just acted very suspicious ever since you first mentioned that Dīcărĕ guy."

"Suspicious? How and in what way?"

"Well, whenever you mention him you either get touchy or distant, sometimes trailing off. It reminded me of your dad when he was speaking of mom and how he trailed off when he spoke of her."

I shook my head. "Bartholomew, he was a friend, like a brother to me."

"Does that mean you treated him like you treat me?" He seemed curious. "What would you do if we did rescue him? What will we all do? What did he mean to you?"

I sighed. "I didn't treat him like I treat you. I was more… distant. And if we rescued him, I don't know what I'd do. I might help him recover. Introduce him to you. It won't be like one of those cheesy love stories where I go running into his open arms, so gross, and so unsanitary. And the latter… he was a good friend, family… one way or another." I turned my head to the window and said no more.

Bartholomew was the only one who knew what I meant by that, and he consequently put a hand on my shoulder. "Alaĕna, don't worry. We'll find him. Do you think you can describe him?"

I turned back to him and nodded. "He was my height the last time I saw him and had short, light brown hair. His sense of humor matched mine, which you have no idea how hard that is to find. His eyes were blue, not baby blue or sky blue, but sapphire blue like yours are emerald green. He's the only one left alive to ever hear me sing. He used to beg me when we were younger. He said it was like hearing his mother's voice again. Of course, I only sang *real* songs to him, not to anyone else, for reasons that I can't really explain.

"I remember him sitting by the fire of the forge, flames flickering. He was always smiling a smile that even Jacob couldn't compare to. He loved to make old and broken things into new and beautiful things. Like me," I said and faintly smiled at the memory.

"You know, Alaĕna, you're truly smiling," Bartholomew said.

I shrugged, and my smile disappeared. "I suppose I was."

"I have to admit that I've never seen you actually smile. Did he make you smile like that?"

A moment passed before I said anything else. "Well, my time of remembrance is done for the day," I abruptly stated as I snapped out of my dream-like state. "All those warm and fuzzy feelings will have to wait for the next flight, all right? I will tell you more if you'd like, but not right now."

He nodded, staring forward and slightly down.

Just as I had leaned my head against the headrest, the voice of the attendant rang through the air once more, but I barely noticed, for memories were flashing through my head.

One of the memories was when I made my first snowman without my father, and Dīcărĕ had accidentally melted it when he got too close to it with a hot hammer. He then fixed it and made it a hat out of scrap metal. Another memory was the time when he started to teach me how to swordfight, along with Frŏns, of course. I could never match him. Then, the thought occurred to me, *He could have easily won that duel the day that he was taken and escaped. But he didn't. Instead, he stopped and saved me, and that song that he sang to me. What was going through his head?*

To my surprise, Vīta replied in a sympathetic voice, *I know. But it is up to you to decide.*

I felt angry at first. *Well, that thought also went through my head, but it's illogical.*

Indeed. After a pause, she inquired, *Have you thought about the meaning of his name?*

His name? No. Why?

I think it might have some clues into his thought process that day. Think about it. She left me to think it over.

Oh, how I didn't want to become a soap opera, ugh. I hate those. That is why I was in complete and utter denial.

Even so, I took her advice and thought about it. *His name… Dīcărĕ. Maybe his full name. Pūĕr, I haven't thought of that one in a while. Let's see… Dīcărĕ Ădservō Cōr. 'Di' he got from Dīlūcĕsĕrĕ which means 'Grow Light'. 'Cărĕ' he got directly from Cărĕ which means 'At Great Cost' or 'Sacrifice'. 'Ădservō' is a direct word that means 'Save Life Of '. And 'Cōr' is a direct word which can mean 'Heart' or 'Soul' or 'Person' or… 'Sweetheart'. Sweetheart… Dīlūcĕsĕrĕ Cărĕ Ădservō Cōr, 'To Grow Light at Great Sacrifice and To Save the Life of the Sweetheart'. Me. I guess that is living up to your name's sake. But 'Grow Light at Great Sacrifice', what does that mean? Another mystery for another day, he used to say. Oh great, now I'm a poet.*

Dīlūcĕsĕrĕ Cărĕ Ădservō Cōr. So much was said in such a little name. I don't know where he got his nickname. He was just called Dīcărĕ, much easier than saying his full name I suppose, like me, as my name is Vĕnī Ă Ălaĕ Ĕx Bombyx. It means 'Came from Wings of Silk' or 'Came from Wings out of Silk'. Alaĕna is actually a nickname. Squishing some of the words together to make a first name happens a lot if you have complicated and long names. I know that Vĕnī as a first name sounds weird which is the reason why I have Alaĕna as a name.

"Bartholomew?" I asked.

He turned his head. "Yeah?"

"You know, my full name sounds funny. Want to hear it?" I

asked and, when he nodded in reply, continued, "Věnī Ă Ălae̯ Ĕx Bombyx. That's what it is if you put it all together in the right order."

He looked surprised. "Really? Your first name is Věnī?"

"I know, but 'Alae̯na' is really my nickname, like how 'Dīcăre̯' is Dīcăre̯'s nickname. It works when you have long names. You're lucky because your name is just Bartholomew James Healdton, much easier to say."

"Well, then, I guess that's why you say it all the time." He smirked.

Shaking my head, I said, "No, just because the occasion occurs often."

He rolled his eyes and inquired, "So, what's his full name?"

"That is for a later…" The look he gave me was enough to tell me that he wasn't in the mood for anything of the sort. "Fine. Dīlūcĕsĕre̯ Căre̯ Ădservō Cōr. That's his name. Unfortunately, he's lived up to part of it."

"Oh, that." He looked down. "I just hope that he's all you've explained him to be since we're risking our necks to save his. Particularly you, Alae̯na, since you seem to attract danger and evil to you."

"Tell me about it." I sighed, and, to Bartholomew's surprise, rested my head on his shoulder. "I'm glad you're my brother. I couldn't stand it if it were anyone else."

Sighing, he rested his head against mine. "Me, too, Alae̯na. Me, too."

Quite quickly, I was able to fall asleep.

Thankfully, I was asleep the entire flight to Ain Salah, Algeria. Another thing to be thankful for was that the stay there was brief, about four hours, and only in the airport. This meant no evil pilot-assassins but less time on solid ground. We took off from the airport around eight o'clock US mountain time—I say that because that's the time I'm used to.

As I rested my head on the headrest again, *I thought to myself, Another flight… another very long flight.*

Bartholomew tried to cheer me up by asking me questions about my times with Dīcărĕ. It was nice recalling the days that I had with him, also a bit weird. But the only true escape I had from that dreadful place was sleep, and sleep I did.

------ ◆ ------

"Seat belts, everyone!" the flight attendant exclaimed again as the flight to Benghazi ended.

I jumped at the sound of her voice and glared at her and her getup. It annoyed me to the point that I wanted to lock her up in that room of hers that she kept on walking out of. *Humph.* In the last day and a half, I had talked to Vīta quite a lot. Apparently, we had many things in common, like the fact that we both had annoying brothers whom we deny loving to anyone but ourselves.

When we landed and had retrieved our luggage, we walked down a very dark hallway, and, suddenly, the lights started flickering as a loud *BOOM* came from outside.

Hastily, I rushed down the hallway and to the door that led outside. It was a minefield out there! "What's going on?" I yelled over the noise.

"I don't know!" Isabella cried in reply.

As I heard people screaming and yelling in Arabic, I saw her rearing and screaming with such ferocity that only I could not cower before her. She was Vīta Lyrārūm. Even in the daylight, a faint glow emanated from her light blue hide. Her ivory horn was of the deepest blue, and her eyes were as bright as the North Star.

She seemed to be battling against something, but I couldn't see and thus began walking forward.

Bartholomew caught my arm and frantically asked, "Are you crazy? You can't go out there!"

I shook him off, dropped my luggage, and ran out. I still had my knife, if necessary. As I trotted along, I saw that the beast she was battling was not a single creature but a pack of predators which I did not expect to see. "Manībī Ŭngūībī…" I whispered.

They were roughly three feet tall, with pebbly, leathery hides. They had long, middle claws on their feet. The rest of the claws were long and sharp, but not as thick as the middle one. They had long arms that could grasp prey and a petite head with long, sharp teeth protruding behind thick, lizard-like lips. Long tails and muscled bodies completed these terrifying predators.

Vīta was scratched and bleeding all over. Her nostrils were flared, and the whites of her eyes were showing. White lather covered her withers and neck, and bubbling froth covered her mouth, dripping to the ground like wet snow.

There were two Manībī Ŭngūībī, well, twelve if you count the dead ones that had been trampled by the sharp hooves of the Ūnīcornīs Vōlătīcīs, had been bitten by sharp teeth, or gored by a long, ivory horn. And, to add to the madness, people were throwing grenades at Vīta and the Manībī Ŭngūībī to try and destroy the threats to public safety.

I ran over to the middle of the battle, put my hands up, and yelled, "Stop, Sīstă!"

The Manībī Ŭngūībī eyed me with lime-green eyes that contained only narrow slits for pupils and stopped.

The men throwing bombs stopped and started commanding me to get out of the way.

Vīta trembled with fury, but it subsided, and she said in

her musical voice, *Sălvĕ, Alaĕna, you've changed since the last time we met.*

I was curious about the meaning of her comment, but the hungry Manībī Ŭngūībī on my left overruled any thoughts I might've had. "Vīta, get out of here as fast as you can. You are wounded and weak. I'll take care of the rest. Did you succeed?"

She nickered a yes.

"Good, you know where to meet me."

She reared, screaming a final, shrill war cry, and took off toward the sea.

I drew my knife out of my pocket and commanded, "Căpĕrĕ Flămmaĕ, Ăccĕndī!" It flickered with light as the flame warmed the blade. "Game on," I said as I motioned for the Manībī Ŭngūībī to come and get me.

They happily obliged my simple command. Running at me from front and back, they attacked. One jumped at my back, and I stabbed it in its middle with my knife. The creature screamed with pain as it began to disintegrate at the stab spot. Soon, it was gone completely.

The other one was more cautious and bought its time by getting close and then backing off. Its eyes glared at me with a mix of hatred, desperation, and fear. Finally, it made its move and jumped, letting out a shriek that would mean either victory or defeat.

With lightning-like speed, I caught it, held it in front of me, and whispered a command to it in Latin, "You must listen and obey me! I am letting you live so that you may know that humans and Latin Magicians can be merciful. Listen and obey, for I now name you Mănūs Ăcĕr, Sharp Hand, after me. Bear it well and go freely, but be ready to come to my or my brother's aid when either of us summons you for you owe me your life, and, one day, you'll need to repay it. Now go!" I released him, and he, looking positively baffled, ran off into the vast desert to my right.

I walked back over to the others and saw their extremely puzzled looks.

"What was that?" Bartholomew asked, plopping down on the ground and causing a dust cloud to fly about him.

"Oh, nothing. Just a few Manībī Ŭngūībī and… oh!" I held my knife up and commanded, "Căpĕrĕ Flămmaĕ, Exstīngūī!" The knife went cold, and I sheathed it in my belt. "Well, those Manībī Ŭngūībī won't be bothering anybody else now. I thought they were extinct, though. Oh well. One owes me his life now, just to let you know. Although, I don't think anyone would guess that Vīta would be there in mortal combat with the beasts." I put my hand on my hip and put my weight on one leg. "Well, now you know what happened. Now, I'm going to find her and figure out what she knows about Dīcărĕ."

Isabella stepped forward. "What about our flight? It's in only thirty minutes!"

I smirked. "Well, for you, it is. I'm not going on any other planes."

"That was your plan all along, wasn't it?" Jacob frowned.

"Things changed, Jacob, and so do people. I'm not going on another plane, might as well swim than fly on a plane!"

His eyes widened momentarily, but his features relaxed, and he picked up his bags. "Let's go then. I'm not leaving your side until we get back home."

"I don't have a home, Jacob. Bartholomew knows that. As soon as we get 'home', I'm leaving!"

"But why?"

"I have my own agenda, and it doesn't include staying in the uppermost tip of Washington," I said. *The time is now, and I must leave them to meet Vīta.* I thought to myself.

"What agenda?" Isabella pressed.

I shook my head and stepped back. "Looks like we're going to have to part sooner than planned."

"What do you mean?"

"You really think I would take you into the hands of the Damsels when you can't even lift a butter knife? No! I would never endanger you like that. So, this is where we part. Vălĕtĕ, Servărĕ." I picked up my bags and bolted off toward the sea. In the smoke, I had to dodge both people and dead Manībī Ŭngūībī to keep from falling flat on my face.

Over the anxious cries of terror and shock, I heard Bartholomew calling me. "Wait! What are you doing, Alaĕna!"

I didn't even turn back to look at him. It was too dangerous for them to continue. When I first contacted Vīta, we immediately started working on a plan to rescue Dīcărĕ. I needed Isabella and Jacob to get this far. However, with Bartholomew, I had no choice on the matter.

Vīta had extracted even more information from the ratman after he had disappeared. I had no clue what happened to him afterward and assumed it was something that was not very pretty.

During the week or so on the road, Vīta had taught me how to hide my thoughts from her kind, since she had heard something that unnerved her. Unfortunately, the mare never told me what it was.

As I turned a corner around a building, I grinned because everything was falling into place, and all that I needed to do was get to Vīta. However, Bartholomew was running full speed after me, along with Isabella and Jacob.

Ignoring them, I kept running onward, into dark alleyways that lay between the sand-colored buildings, and over asphalt roads and dirt roads.

Tirelessly, they followed me.

Stopping next to an abandoned warehouse to catch my breath, I put down my luggage, unzipped the large suitcase, and took out the leather armor. Piece by piece, I put it on and, when I was finished, placed my belt over it. During the flights, when everyone was asleep, I had made a sheath for my sword.

I took a deep breath. Now was the time for my disguise. I dressed myself in the black outfit that Islamic girls wear. It was instantly scorching hot inside the dress and robe, but that was how no one would be able to recognize me.

I squished all the food and water I had packed into my smaller bag, which I had stored in my suitcase into a satchel that I swung over my shoulder.

Alaĕna, are you ready? I am circling above you. I heard Vīta Lyrārūm say.

Yes, I am. I've said my goodbyes, I replied. She dove at high speed and landed gracefully next to me.

Sălvĕ, Alaĕna, how are you doing? Vīta inquired.

A bit sad, excited, and nervous all at once.

Do not worry, Alaĕna, you will be fine.

After a brief moment, I asked, *May I, Vīta Lyrārūm, have the honor of being the first to ride you?*

She whinnied and tossed her long, wavy, feathery mane. *Of course, you may, Amīca Catēnī.*

I slowly walked up to her faintly glowing body. I reached to her neck and stroked it. Her skin twitched as we touched, and I felt my heart lift. I was finally able to get a perfect picture of her. There was a bluish tint to her short, soft fur. She had feathers around her fetlocks; her mane and tail were soft blue feathers that were about a foot-and-a-half long; her horn was of the darkest blue, like the midnight sky; and her wings were made of silken feathers. It reminded me of what my name spoke of.

Still puzzled at why my name spoke of such a thing, I cocked my head and inquired, *Why would my name have anything to do with your kind, Vīta?*

I am not positive in this, but I believe it is because you are… Vīta was interrupted by a noise behind us. She pricked her ears and studied the shape forming in the dust cloud.

Bartholomew's frantic and desperate yell echoed clearly, "Alaĕna, don't go!" My brother was right behind me.

I turned my head and locked gazes with his watery eyes. "I have to go, Frăter, because it's either life or death for *us*. Dīcărĕ is a Bonded One and my family, and I *must* save him because if I fail, *we* will die. Only Vīta and I can do it. Farewell. We may never meet again."

In denial, he shook his head. "No, I have to go with you. *We are family*, and I won't allow you to go alone. Come on, you have just one more flight to go. Please?"

I nodded. "Yes, I do."

He shook his head. "No."

"Vălĕ, Frăter Mĕūs, Nōs Cŏnvĕnīrĕm Rĕrsūs, Ūtinăm, Sĕd Prōmīttō Rĕddĕrĕ Ăd Tĕ, Ūtinăm Pŏssūm." I mounted the mare, positioning myself so that I was lying flat on her back with my hands grasping her mane and my legs squeezing her back and flanks.

He ran the remaining distance to me, and Vīta Lyrārūm galloped away. Her wings slowly disappeared, and she looked like a normal horse; she had even changed colors into a white Arabian mare with a black muzzle and socks.

Hastily, I changed my position so that I was sitting on her as I would a regular horse.

Riding such a gallant creature was an exhilarating experience, and a grin snuck upon my lips. However, I looked back at Bartholomew, who was kneeling in the dust with his hands clenched, and the feeling disappeared. Something about him was different than it was a few minutes before, though I wasn't sure what could've changed.

CHAPTER 12

The Prophecy

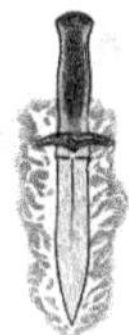

We ran for days until we came to the coast of the Red Sea to rest for the night. It was mostly me who needed rest. I was hungry and tired and didn't feel safe precariously perched upon her back while she was speeding like a freight train with hooves. Plus, I was dying in that disguise!

I hunkered down on a dune about a hundred yards from the shore. The waves were gently lapping against the shore, glittering in the light blue moonlight. "Vīta, does your Māter look like the moon?" I asked as Vīta lay upon the soft, tan sand.

Yes. She was brilliantly white with a gray muzzle and fetlocks. Her mane and tail were speckled with white and light gray hair. She was beautiful. Her eyes dimmed for a minute as she finished.

"You speak in past tense?" I noted as I stroked her neck and grabbed an apple out of my bag.

She sighed. *Yes, she was killed two years ago.*

I looked down. "I'm sorry. I suppose you lost two loved ones that year."

She blinked, and her light blue forelock fell over her star-like eyes. *And you lost three.*

I violently shook my head. "Oh, no, just two. Well, not *just* two, but, well, I… he was just a friend."

You may say so, but he thought differently. Why do you think he gave himself up for you? Vīta hinted.

"Because he was my friend. Bartholomew would do the same," I stated, still in complete and utter denial.

Alaëna, he was your friend but he loved you more than a friend would, the mare pressed.

"Oh no, I'm not a girlie girl. I won't go into that. I'll wait until I'm older to deal with that. I'm still a young kid, really young. Can't I wait until I'm at least fifteen?" I pled.

You cannot do a thing about it, Alaëna. It chooses you.

"Well, I don't want to be chosen! Don't you even wonder why I don't want that? I don't want to be loved like that. As a brother-sister thing, I'm fine. But *that*? No! I'm no girlie girl that's going to have to…" I curled up in a ball and bit my apple.

Alaëna, what is it? Vīta Lyrārūm nuzzled my ear and pushed me a bit.

I sighed. *I don't want to end up like my mom, and not the insane bit; I can handle that.*

She closed her eyes and touched her horn to my heart. *Alaëna, do not worry about this tonight. Trust your bosom and trust your heart. You will know what to do when the time is right.* She pushed my bangs aside with her muzzle and tickled me with her soft whiskers.

I tried not to laugh. "One thing I do know is that you're the only one who seems to care about my troubles. No one cared about my troubles until you came around. No one was ever there for me in the way I needed them to be. People always thought I was this *tough* girl who had no problems on the inside at all. But… I have so many I can't keep track of them all."

She nickered sympathetically. *Well, I do not care what those hooligans think. I think you are a misunderstood and troubled girl who needs a Pătĕr and a Mătĕr to take care of her and comfort her. Unfortunately, you have neither because of the accursed politics you were caught in the middle of.*

I leaned against her side. "Thanks," I said in a tone that was between sarcastic and an actual thank you. After a second, I inquired, "Want the rest of the apple?" It was a half-eaten Red Delicious apple.

Ĭtă, Tū Grătĕs. She ate the apple whole and, seeming quite pleased, shook her mane, ruffling her wings which had reappeared along with all her unnatural features in our solitude.

"Ĕs Grătūs, Vīta Lyrārūm," I replied as I wiped my hand on my black garments.

Taking a deep breath of the cold, salty air, I closed my eyes and soaked the sounds of the ocean water soothingly lapping against the sand, the breathing of Vīta Lyrārūm, and the cry of a lonely seagull. They put me in a trance-like state and, to my own surprise, I quietly began to croon Vīta's lullaby. "Sleep, my little one, for the sun utters farewell. Yes, sleep, my dear one, for the Moon calls you to dream. Sleep, my small one, for the day when dreams are forbidden draws nigh. So, sleep, my love, for the time of imagination will soon disappear. Sleep, my Light, and dream with no fear. Sleep, my child, for my heart is with you forever more. Sleep, now, sleep for the Moon calls to you. Sleep, now, sleep for the day is done and night has begun. Now, sleep, my dear, dream while you can." That was the first time I had sung since the time of Dīcărĕ and me.

Vīta stirred and looked at me drowsily.

"I am sorry if I disturbed your peace," I said.

She snorted. *No, I thought for certain I would fall asleep to that old lullaby. My Fräter loves singing it, though he will never sound as good as I do, or you do, for that matter.*

I was a bit embarrassed. "Vīta, the only time I ever sung was around Dīcărĕ. And Dīcărĕ, well, he always knew how to flatter me. He would kiss my hand and bow slightly whenever we met. He would always open doors for me and pull back chairs for me to sit in then push them back in. Never once did he make me uncomfortable. He was—oh, how can I say it—handsome on the outside but, on the inside, was he even more so. He was kind and had a loving heart, but, to tell you the truth, I'm worried that if I get him back, he'll be different." I had never told anyone that, not even myself.

I was hoping that Dīcărĕ was all right wherever he was in the Deserts of Saudi Arabia. Just thinking about Dīcărĕ reminded me of home and of my old life, the one where I could breathe without worrying. Sure, in Wetly, there were gangsters and murderers. That's just something you have to deal with. Unfortunately, the Damsels thrive there like infectious vermin, teaching the already illegal people there to be evil. The city was sick, and I knew that anyone could tell that, but I wanted to fix it. That was just one of the many thoughts that went through my head. I never slept well at night since it took me forever to get my over-active imagination to settle down.

To help, I focused on the beating of Vīta's heart and the sound of the surf hitting the turf. It aided my struggle some, but I never did get to sleep that night. Instead, it was Vīta who slept soundly. I didn't want to disturb her in any way, so I slowly and quietly stood up and walked down the shore. Taking in the smell of the sea, I breathed deeply and exhaled slowly. I looked out into the water. The moon was reflecting off of the dark-black abyss and back onto my face.

I looked back to Vīta and thought, *Tomorrow, we will enter Saudi Arabia. Then, the day after, we will hopefully find the Damsel base. Who knows how long it'll take to rescue Dīcărĕ. I wonder if he'll even recognize…* I turned my attention to the blackness that surrounded the ocean. Something was watching me. Something that was ancient. Something that was… hungry.

Two white, glowing eyes stared at me from about fifteen feet up above the surface of the water. The silvery orbs were about three feet apart and approximately the size of honeydews.

Grasping the hilt of my sword with my right hand, I readied for the fight of my life.

The creature growled, and the splashing seawater not two feet from my boots grew larger and larger until they were full, seven-foot-tall whitecaps. Eventually, a breaker splashed over my feet, thoroughly soaking them.

My heart pounded with fear as the eyes came closer to the shore.

Its body was hidden from sight until the moon peeked out from behind its cloudy blanket.

The sight I beheld was awe-inspiring: the head was like a crocodile, except it was three-and-a-half feet wide at the eyes and eleven inches wide at the nostrils, which were blowing out pitch black smoke. It was seven feet from its scaly shoulders to the tip of its prickly nose. A great fin stretched from in between the nostrils to its broad, muscular withers. Being well-rooted and serrated, the teeth were built for catching and tearing through prey. Its neck was like the trunk of a hundred-year-old tree, five feet in diameter and close to twenty feet in height, since its entire neck was now exposed from its watery home. The body was about sixty feet long from the tip of the nose to the tip of its tail, and its color matched that of the sea which surrounded it.

The thing that stood out was its scales, which reminded me of thousands of shields melted together to make an impassable barrier that not even air could get through, but that was on the back. On the underbelly were millions of sharp, pointy scales which faced outwards.

Vīta! I called out with my mind.

She snapped to attention and whinnied. *What is wrong Alaĕna?* I showed her the creature, and she replied, *This creature has another name, but my kind knows it by the name of Īnsŏmnīum Mărīs, Nightmare of the Sea, a being of the time of the ancients. This one is named Cīnnabar, Dragon's Blood. He was known to eat dragons in days of old and, now he is desperate for nourishment and will eat anything that dares to cross into his territory. Did you touch the water?*

No, I hesitated but then corrected myself, *Well, yes. It got closer, and a wave splashed over my shoes.*

Stay where you are. I will come to you. Vīta commanded.

Yes, ma'am, I replied then privately thought, *I just hope that I'll be able to live that long.*

As I finished my thought, the Īnsŏmnīūm Mărīs reached the shoreline.

Throwing my head back, I managed to gaze up at the giant head looking down upon me. His blood-stained teeth glimmered in the moonlight. Drops of seawater rained down on my face, and I drew my sword.

Cīnnabar's stomach began to convulse, and he opened his jaws and let loose a stream of fire.

I tried to jump into the water to escape the flames, but its five-foot-high tail blocked my path. "*Vīta!*" I screamed, and the creature whipped its enormous head down to my level.

Spit dripped from in between its sharp fangs, splashing onto the sand, creating craters the size of my hand in the wet sediment.

I tried to stab it in defense, but he snapped his tail around the blade, wrenched it out of my grip, and threw it into the ocean. I tried to run, but he grabbed me by the stomach with his tail and yanked me into the sea. Before I was pulled underwater, I cried out one last time, "Save Dīcărĕ!", and we plunged into the icy cold depths.

It was dark, with no light whatsoever. I could feel the pressure of the water crushing me as Cīnnabar jumped from the shore and dove into the depths of the Red Sea.

I tried to reach my knife, but the tail was too thick to be able to reach across, and the grip was too tight to be able to slip my arm under the trunk of the appendage. The beast let loose a jet of fire, lighting the water for a moment and warming our frigid surroundings. Below us, on the sea floor, I saw chariots and what looked like bits of bones, human and horse to the looks of it, which were being circled by a couple of sixgill sharks that scattered into the darkness, trying to escape the bright light and giant sea monster. *What are those chariots and skeletons doing at the bottom of the sea?* I wondered, but the thought was too tiring. In the end, I focused on the more important matter of slowing my heart rate to preserve the precious oxygen.

Finally, after about two minutes, a light appeared above us. My lungs felt funny, my head started spinning, and, as the light got closer, I blacked out.

———◆———

When I woke up, the first thing I saw was a decaying person next to me. I yelped and tried to jump up and away from the grotesque thing, but a thick braid of seaweed pulled me back and on top of the deceased human. It would take months after that day to stop having nightmares about it, so I won't describe the thing in detail to you.

I leaped backward, trying to get off of it but was once more pulled back by the elastic-like seaweed ropes that were bound to my wrists; although, that time I was able to aim myself next to the person instead of on top of it. I shivered and suddenly thought, *My knife! Oh wait, it's not there. What a surprise. How on earth could a sea creature do these things? I suppose since it's a Magical being, it can do things like this. Why did I have to get kidnapped by one of the few Magical beings in this world? Why not a regular creature, one that can't take away your knife? Ugh!* I slouched against the cold rock wall.

Looking around, I saw that the gravelly ceiling was covered with stalactites and the smooth floor with stalagmites. At the far end of the chamber was a deep pool that lit the room in an eerie blue glow. *I wonder where I am.*

You are in my home, a deep voice rumbled in my mind. It reminded me of…

Cinnabar, I spat. *So, you can speak. Why have you taken me here? What good am I to you since you don't eat your captives?*

He chuckled then added, *The reason why I took you here is so that you might help me and so that I, in turn, may help you.*

How could I help you and vice versa? And even if I could and you could, I don't have time! I have to meet up with Vīta, and we have to get to Saudi Arabia to complete our mission before it's too late.

He chortled. *To complete your mission would bring great misfortune upon you and your kin.*

I was confused. *How would you know? You don't even know what my mission is! Wait, do you?*

Once more, he laughed. *Your mission is to rescue Dīcărĕ, is it not?*

How would you know?

For I know what has passed, what is, and what will be. I am the one who foretold the Prophecy which tells who you are and, more importantly, what Dīcărĕ will do.

I looked around for him and commanded, *Show yourself!*

The surface of the water began to bubble and foam, and out from the surface came his enormous head then his body followed. In his jaws was a fish about as large as I was.

Gently, he laid the great fish on the ground and said, *This is a coelacanth, one of my favorite meals. I had to travel all night to get it since it is now mostly found in South America. Here, I will explain everything as you eat.* His stomach convulsed, and his mouth lit up as a stream of yellow fire engulfed the fish. Within the second, Cīnnabar closed his throat, stopping the stream cold. Heavy black smoke came from his nostrils and jaws.

Looking at the fish, I saw that the scales had formed a shell that could be peeled back all at once and that the meat was cooked gently.

Thanks, I guess. Will it kill me like that guy? I pointed with my thumb to the deceased person next to me.

No, Cīnnabar replied, *That was a man who had tried to steal my children who still lay within their shells. His story is not important to you.*

I shrugged. *Okay… Where's my knife and sword? And can you get this seaweed off of me?*

He waddled up to me and snapped the ropes in half, releasing me from the wall. *There, I know you are going to ask why I tied you to the wall. I did so for your protection. My mate is very protective of our children, and if you were able to go free, then she would have killed you on sight. Your sword and knife are hidden away for now.*

I sighed and cautiously walked toward the fish. Though he had told me to eat, I still felt a bit uneasy about eating it since it was too close to fish tacos, which I will never eat again after tasting those rotten ones. So gross! But, because it would be rude not to, I took a bite. I almost threw up trying to get that little sucker down, but I was eventually able to. As I tried to take another bite, Cīnnabar began to speak, er, telepathically, of course.

To begin, I must tell you the entire Prophecy:
'By sad countenance do I plea,
'In my home forlorn in the sea,
'A bitter offering to those,
'Whose minds the future only knows.
'For one abandoned by her blood,
'A promise made in crimson mud,
'A Heart in rhythm shall divine,
'A way to keep the Light aligned.
'The Light shall promise to keep and break,
'Lives shall she spare, lives shall she take.
'Protect and save shall the Heart act,
'All through the war shall their pact enact.
'From death's hold, the Light will redeem.
'Sword aglow, the Moon's Rock shall gleam.
'And death shall be her fated friend,
'Following her through to each end.
'The Heart a path will he then find.
'An acute cry, last of her kind.
'Great evil will conquer in war,
'And Bŏmbyx's will be no more.
'Only then will she find reason,
'As Queen of Magic and its seasons,
'The Master of Magic's creatures,
'For 'ternity and forever.'
And that is the Prophecy that I foretold nigh to four thousand years ago. Many thought I was a crazy fool, but I know what I saw. He saw my ashen face and asked, What is wrong?

That's what Dīcărĕ knew that would change everything: he knew the entire Prophecy, he knew who that girl was… Finally I managed to spill the beans to the confused creature. *Tell me who the girl is!*

Cīnnabar paused, thought for a moment, and then said, *You will find out soon enough.*

I rolled my eyes and groaned but then said, *Here, you can have the rest.* Standing up, I stepped back from the fish.

He stretched his neck, grabbed the coelacanth, and commanded, *Follow me so that we may go to the location where you shall aid my mate and me.* The being waddle-walked into a large tunnel that lay behind a huge wall that was partially covered by long, sharp pillars of rock. Since he was out of the water, I noticed that his legs were long, wide flippers used for steering and extra speed.

Why on earth didn't I see that huge hole in the wall before? I asked myself. *Oh well.* Then, to Cīnnabar, I inquired, *I was wondering, how am I able to help you?*

I want you to make my children hatch. If they stay in their eggs any longer, they will die, the Īnsŏmnīum Mărīs replied.

But how can I make them hatch?

He looked at me and explained, *You will feel what is right when the time comes. For now, I will tell you the tale of the last Vătĕs Fūtūrōrūm, Seer of the Future. It is a sad tale, but one that must be told to understand that Prophecy:*

Once there was a time, very long ago, when all was perfect. During this time, two adult Īnsŏmnīum Mărīs were created by our Creator. Ironic it is that the first Vătĕs Fūtūrōrūm was the first of its kind and will be the last of its kind if you do not succeed. No, I am getting ahead of myself.

Some time passed, and then the world fell into chaos and evil. Our Creator became angry and sent catastrophes to kill the unfavored. The Vătĕs Fūtūrōrūm was one of the few sea creatures that survived the catastrophe, but during the calamity, he saw his kin die. Every day was a struggle. The *Vătĕs Fūtūrōrum* wished that he had died that first day, but something in him told him to keep going, even if he would be the last of his kind. Fortunately, three of his kin survived, which were his truest friend, *Fŭrōr* meaning Rage, the *Vătĕs Fūtūrōrum*'s mate *Stlăttărīa* meaning Sea-Borne, and the *Vătĕs Fūtūrōrum* himself.

It took years upon years for them to recover their home, but eventually they were able to live in peace when the *Cūstōs Fătī*, Guardian of Fate, finally agreed to transport us to our homeland. After many wars, there came a time of peace. This was the time of the reign of the Old One when the *Ūnĭcornĕs Vōlătĭcĕs* made their peace treaty with the *Măgī Latīnī*. This was also the time when *Vīta Lyrārum* was born, as well as her *Frăter, Născī Flămmărum*.

During this time of prosperity, the *Vătĕs Fūtūrōrum* had a vision of the time to come and he called upon his kin to stop what was to come. But alas, they did not succeed, and chaos reigned once more, and they were all banished by the rulers of old from that land of beauty and peace. Families were separated. Friends were torn away from friends. The *Vătĕs Fūtūrōrum* lost *Fŭrōr* that day but, luckily, he was able to keep his mate.

But the same day he entered the new ocean that would be his home for the next three-thousand years, he told the *Măgī Latīnī* and the *Ūnĭcornĕs Vōlătĭcĕs* that same Prophecy; although, only part of it, for he did not want to cause the destruction of the girl. He told the trusted leaders of both kinds the entirety of the Prophecy, he would regret it all of his life.

He waited for years with his mate, and eventually she laid a clutch of eggs, which brought joy into his life. But they never hatched, for it had been a part of the peace treaty between the *Ūnĭcornĕs Vōlătĭcĕs* and the *Īnsŏmnīum Mărīs* that a clutch of eggs would hatch only if an *Ūnĭcornīs Vōlătĭcīs* touched them with his or her horn. Unfortunately, they were born down here in this cave, and the *Ūnĭcornĕs Vōlătĭcĕs cannot swim in water, for they will drown. That is why I called you here.*

I thought about all he had said and replied, *But what do I have to do with anything since I'm obviously not an Ūnīcornīs Vōlātīcīs?*

He laughed. *Yes, indeed, you are not. But I shall tell you this: you are more than you appear.*

I tilted my head. *What's that supposed to mean?*

He just chuckled and waddled faster.

I sighed and followed.

Within five minutes, we reached a large chamber with a ceiling fifty feet high.

I felt a fresh breeze and knew there must be some sort of ventilation shaft. It was too dark to see until that very same shaft was uncovered. I was glad for the light until I saw what had been covering it. It was the giant head of Stlăttărīa, Cīnnabar's mate. *Ugh, one of the many creatures that wants to kill me,* I thought to myself. Turning to the giant sea creature next to me, I said to him, *Please, make sure your mate doesn't eat me for lunch.*

He chortled and tossed the fish to his mate.

She sniffed it hesitantly at it and, after looking to her mate for reassurance, bit off half of it. The being swallowed and finally tossed the other half to Cīnnabar, who caught it in midair with his behemoth jaws and slid it down his enormous gullet.

Who is she? Stlăttărīa asked sharply, and Cīnnabar explained who I was and what I was doing there.

When he had finished, she sighed. *You may try, but if you harm them in any way...*

I cut her off. *Then you'll harm me in every way. I know the deal. Where are they?*

She glared at me as she motioned toward a small alcove at the far end of the room.

I trotted over to the eggs. There were two of them, about

two feet tall and three feet wide at the broadest; both were lying on a bed of dry seaweed and other aquatic plants. As I kneeled down next to them, I thought for a moment. *Okay, now what do I do? Hmm, first let's find out whether or not they're still alive.* Quickly, I commanded, "Lūx, Splĕndĕ Īn Ŏvă!"

A light appeared and allowed me to see into the eggs.

They weren't moving, so I gave them a jumpstart. "Lībĕrī Cīnnabarī, Spīră!" They kicked a flipper, but that was all I got. The embryos had outgrown their shells and had run out of air, but, still, they wouldn't hatch.

"That's it, little guys. It's time for you to come out!" I focused really hard on the task at hand, laid a hand on each of them, and commanded, "Ēvēnī Ŏvă Tūă, Lībĕrī Cīnnabarī, Ēvēnī Ĕt Vīdĕ Lūcăm! Ēvēnī Ŏvă Tūă, Lībĕrī Cīnnabarī, Ĕt Cŏntīnŏ Pătūm Tūūm Ĕt Mătūm Tūūm! Ēvēnī Ĕt Cŏntīnŏ Tĕrrăm!"

Cracks appeared in the deep blue shells, and, slowly, miniature Īnsŏmnīă Mărīūm made their way out and into the world.

They plopped down onto their leafy bed.

I picked one up and stroked it. Pleased with my fondling, it cooed softly. I put the Chow-Chow-sized infant back into the nest and looked upon his parents. "I made them hatch. Now, tell me who the girl is!"

Cīnnabar gave me a smug look—if that is at all possible—and replied, *Is it not obvious? If not, then I think I will wait a bit more before I tell you.*

I was fuming. *I don't believe this. I made his dumb eggs hatch, and he pulled this trick on me. Humph, never trust a sea serpent, which should have been a given.* Glaring at Cīnnabar, I demanded, *Get me out of here, since you have no further use of me.*

He nodded. *As you wish, Lūx Aĕtĕrnă. One day, we will meet again; that I am sure of. Now, close your eyes and you'll be back on the beach. Vălĕrĕ Īūbĕrĕ, Alaĕna, Pro Īăm.* And just as I closed my eyes, he said, *Be warned, never trust...* His voice disappeared, and I blacked out.

CHAPTER 13

Deserted in the Desert

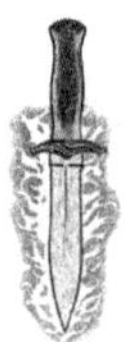

When I opened my eyes, I realized that I was sitting in knee-deep seawater. In a knee-jerk reaction, I sprinted out of the water, only to find myself feeling cold, sticky, and itchy from the salt in the seawater. *Never trust whom…* I then called out, *Vīta!*

She quickly came to me and asked what had happened to me. I then explained all that had occurred. The mare snorted and shook her feathery mane. *It is good to see you once more. I was very worried about you. I looked all night and beyond for a way to follow you. But alas, the only way into the caves is through the water. My kind cannot swim. It is an unfortunate disadvantage when at war with sea serpents.*

Yes, that would be a disadvantage. For now, we have to leave. We've already lost precious time, and we can't afford to lose any more, so let's get a move on. I mounted her, and we flew across the Red Sea.

During the flight, Vīta seemed tense. Lather was forming

around her withers and neck; foam dripped from the corners of her mouth; her ears flattened against the back of her skull; and her lips pulled back, revealing gleaming white teeth.

I attempted to communicate with her but with no success.

Once over, she landed softly on the sandy ground.

I dismounted and asked, "What's wrong?"

She grabbed the bags I had placed on her withers and dropped them on the ground. Vīta shook her mane and stepped away. *I am truly sorry, she said, but we must part ways now. I will only be a hindrance to you for the rest of your journey.* It seemed to me that she was acting as a robot would with someone pushing buttons on a fancy remote control. She grimaced in pain and then galloped off, flapping her great, glowing wings until she was soaring back across the sea.

That was sudden and weird, I thought. *Looks like I'm walking the rest of the way. I sure hope that nothing… nope, I'm not going to say it because if I say it, something will go wrong. Oh, Pūěr, this is bad. I'm talking to myself, having an argument with myself about talking to myself. Ugh.* I sighed, picked up my bags, and walked.

It was early morning, and the sun was barely above the horizon. Beautiful arrays of colors ranging from deep reds to blackish blues and purples to vibrant pinks and oranges painted the sky in a picture that even a million-dollar painting painted by the best artist in the world couldn't compare to. Unfortunately, this also meant that it was getting hot—quickly! One of the annoying things about the desert is its extreme temperatures, with it being beyond freezing in the night and exceeding sweltering in the day.

Luckily, for me, it was in the in-between phase of things, which meant that it was a good temperature for walking across the desert. Well, if there is a good temperature for walking across the desert.

Anywho, I stuck close to the ocean so that I could walk in the water to cool my already over-heating body and, although there was a road about four miles due east of my location, I never traveled toward it because the blacktop was extremely hot. Hot enough to cook an egg! Trust me when I say that it's not an exaggeration.

By noon, I had walked close to ten miles, which is pretty good, I would say, for traveling on foot. Regrettably, I was forced to stop then because it was too hot. I ended up drinking the last of my water and eating the last of my food since I had only planned on it taking a little over a day to travel from the beach to our destination and therefore packed that much. But *no*, Vīta had to fly off and leave me stranded there in one of the hottest places in the world. *Maybe I should've stayed with Servărĕ*, I thought, but I quickly shook my head. *No, I did it to protect them. I can't let them get hurt. I can defend myself, and they can't.*

After the short break, I kept on walking until I hit the city of Almuwaylih or Almowailih—the English spellings for Arabic names can differ since the Arabic writing looks nothing like English writing unless it's cursive because then there's a tiny bit of similarity, but that's it. I stopped right before the city, made sure my disguise was secure and looked realistic, and finally decided that I really should've robbed a bank or something 'cause I was flat-out broke. *Well, I look like a poor girl. Maybe somebody will take pity on me and give me enough money to buy some food and water,* I thought to myself.

As I stepped onto the dirt road, a couple of people in black garments stared at me from inside their houses. I fingered the hilt of my sword, ready to pull it out at a moment's notice. I saw a couple of boys about my age throwing rocks in the street.

As soon as they saw me, they whispered something to each other in Arabic and, when I walked by, they stood, then walked over to me.

I stopped and turned around, saying quietly in as much as an Arabic accent as I could muster, "Look, I don't want any trouble. I'm just passing through."

They were startled by my English and glanced at each other and then at me. Once more, they whispered to each other.

Slowly, I backed off and walked away.

The boys seemed a bit angry as they raced back to their house.

I looked back and saw them standing in front of a large man, who was wearing traditional Muslim garb, pointing at me. I quickened my pace into a run, since I didn't know what exactly they were going to do. Who knows whether they would offer me a place to stay for the night or do something else like chop my head off? I never found out. However, I did learn that they were not angered by my English but by my speaking. Apparently, according to strict Muslim law, women are not allowed to walk by themselves or speak to men unless under certain circumstances.

At about five in the afternoon, I reached the city limits and kept on walking. This time, I walked on the side of the road, and every time a vehicle passed by I gave a thumbs up. Thankfully, by the fiftieth vehicle, there was a tourist who understood what I meant and parked next to me on the side of the road.

"What are you, a little American girl, doin' here?" She was about twenty years old and was wearing a pink tank top, khaki shorts, and white tennis shoes. She also had a Coloradan accent.

"Uh, my story's my own. But I would like a ride. I've been walking all day without more than two sips of water and an apple. My ride abandoned me about thirteen miles up the coast," I explained.

She hesitantly nodded, and I jumped in the vehicle, taking off my headdress. The woman frowned. "Huh. That stinks.

Where're you headed?"

"Well, it's a bit specific, 131 miles west of Layla, and 145 miles southeast of Afif," I replied, clicking my seatbelt into place.

"That is specific. Why are you heading there?" she asked, driving back onto the highway.

As I looked around, it occurred to me that there were a bunch of Arabic-to-English and English-to-Arabic translation books in the back of her Silverado. I couldn't imagine how expensive it would be to rent that particular vehicle. Shrugging, I uttered, "Well, um, I would recommend not getting involved with my business. It can get messy."

Her eyes widened. "Oh. What can a girl like you get into?"

I smirked. "Oh, you'd be surprised. Besides, I'm from Wetly."

She nodded. "Ah, Wetly, Colorado, the crime capital of the US. I thought all the kids there were psychopaths. No offense to you, of course," the woman quickly added.

I chuckled. "Yes, all except two are: me and another kid there. He's not half bad once you get used to him."

"I know that this might be pushing it too far by asking this question to a girl who I don't even know the name of, but I was wondering… Did you run away?" She looked at me inquisitively.

I shook my head. "No. My parents abandoned me. Enough about me. I want to know who you are, with your permission of course."

The girl's eyes had softened, and she shrugged. "Eh, not much to tell. I have good parents and background. My boyfriend is studying to become a, what was it again… oh yes! He is studying to become a, I think this is how you pronounce it: 'Mag-olo-jist'. I think he's insane for believing in Magic, but I love him. I'm actually driving to meet him in Yanbu."

Grinning, I said, "A Magologist: one who studies Magic

and its beings. Beings such as the Sĕpīa Vōlătīcă, Ūnīcornĕs Vōlătīcĕs, Īnsŏmnīă Mărīum, even the Măgī Latīnī."

She looked me over suspiciously. "How do you know so much?"

"Damsels... er... D-A-M-L agents are everywhere in Wetly. We actually had an ML until they captured him and beheaded his family. I knew that kid. He was nice, and so was his family." I shook my head at the memory. "Well, I suppose I should finally introduce myself. My name is Alaĕna. For security reasons, I won't give out my last name since, uh, I'm still not too sure what my last name is; whether or not to use my father's surname or my mother's. Oh well. So, whom, if I may ask, is my chauffeur?"

She rolled her eyes. "Well, Alaĕna, my name is Alyssa, though most call me Aly."

I nodded, and, as I turned my head to the window, the thought struck me that I hadn't been in a vehicle since Mr. Cĕtĕră. I smirked as I thought of the semi going off of the cliff, and the look of horror, then relief on my and Bartholomew's faces when we saw that the driver had jumped out in time to escape the soon-to-be bomb. It seemed so long ago, although I knew it had only been a few weeks.

I sighed quietly and thought, *I'm sorry that I couldn't let you come with me, Bart. The reason I left you behind was to keep you safe and sound. However, I do really miss you. Maybe, I'll get to see you again one day, just maybe, when all of this craziness ends, when my Promise is fulfilled, or when I finally rescue Dīcărĕ from the D-A-M-L Home Base. Just maybe, Bartholomew, I'll be reunited with you.* I then rested my head on the headrest to try and get some rest. After about an hour of driving, I reluctantly fell asleep from the pure exhaustion of the day's hike.

———◆———

When I woke up, I noticed that we had stopped at a small building. It was on the outskirts of a large city which, I assumed, was Yanbu. I looked outside and saw that the sun was just beginning to peek out above the sandy horizon.

"Rise and shine, sleeping beauty," said a voice that sounded familiar, but I couldn't quite put my finger on it.

Oh right, I almost forgot that I'm in, what's-her-face… oh yes! Alyssa's *truck.* I rubbed my eyes and stepped outside. *At least the door wasn't stuck,* I thought to myself. Once outside, I noticed that a guy in dark blue jeans and a white T-shirt was looking very weirdly at me. "What?" I asked.

"Why are you wearing *that* if you're American from Wetly?" he asked, pointing to my getup. "I mean, I know there're American Muslims, but it's Wetly."

"It's my disguise as I run from the government that wants to kill me," I stated.

"Ooookay… Hey, Aly! Where'd you pick up this odd piece of personality?"

While shaking her head, Aly trotted over to us.

I observed that she had changed into brown slacks and a tan T-shirt.

With a hint of sarcasm, the woman said, "On the side of the road where I picked you up."

"Ha ha, very funny. So, what're you doing way out here?" the man asked me.

I frowned. "I'm running away from the government that wants to kill me."

He sighed and shook his head. "I'm Leo, Aly's boyfriend, and you are?"

"Alaĕna is the name, and pain is my game." I offered out my hand, and he hesitantly shook it. "No offense, but do you have anything to eat? Or drink? I haven't had anything since yesterday morning."

He nodded and led me into his sandy home.

To the back of the house was a small kitchen with a refrigerator, a microwave, a stove, and a sink; to the far right was a couch and small TV; to the far left was a desk with a Sony laptop with a tablet next to it; to my immediate right was a small cot; and to my immediate left was a small, foldable table with matching chairs. On the walls around me were hundreds of pictures of Magical beings and a few Măgī Latīnī. "You must really get around. These beings are really rare and hard to find without them seeking you out."

He seemed puzzled by my remark. "How do you know that?"

"Easy, I've met a Flying Unicorn, a Flying Cuttlefish, which tried to eat my brother, a Nightmare of the Sea, an odd creature he was, and I've met a bunch of Latin Magicians." I smiled, and his jaw dropped.

"Are you a Magologist?" he inquired, his voice rising.

I laughed. "No, no. Besides, no one can be a true Magologist without being a Latin Magician and then only the highest of honored Latin Magicians are allowed to become Magologists. At least, that's what I got out of my experience."

"That's good to know!" Alyssa declared, as she walked into the room. "That means you can drop this silly nonsense and get a real job, a job where you can support a family."

Leo blushed and rubbed the back of his head. "Well… um… uh…I… Why did you have to bring that up?"

"Because," Aly responded, and an awkward silence pursued.

After a moment, I cleared my throat and said, "Well, I just *hate* to interrupt this extremely unpleasant moment, but do you happen to have some water available?"

The guy sighed, walked over to the kitchen, grabbed a water bottle from a cabinet, snatched a sandwich from the fridge, strode back to the doorway, and handed me the bottle and sandwich.

I took them gratefully and guzzled the water. The sandwich I looked over carefully to make sure there were no peanuts and, when I was satisfied that there were none, I wolfed it down.

Food had never tasted so good.

"Thanks, Leo," I said after I had finished.

He smiled. "You're welcome." Leo thoughtfully looked away, then, turning to me, said, "You seem familiar. Have I met you before?"

I shook my head. "I don't think so." However, when I looked closer, I noticed that he had dark brown hair and deep blue eyes. With those two features, he reminded me of... My eyes widened. "Does the name 'Frŏns' sound familiar?"

A hint of recognition flickered in his eyes but it quickly dimmed. "No, I don't think so."

I thought for a moment and then shook my head. "No, that can't be. I saw him, dead, with a wound that would never heal." I sighed and rubbed my neck.

He got the idea.

Intrigued, I pondered, *I wonder... no. He can't be Frŏns. He's dead. I buried him. Well, I guess he could be him if he was a zombie. No, there's no such thing as a zombie. Of course, then he would have had to have his head sewn back on like the Mad Hatter. So, no, it can't be him. And besides, he's too old to be him.*

"Just curious, who was this 'Frŏns' and what happened to him?" Leo asked.

A faint smile came to my lips as I said, "He was a good friend of mine. Like a brother to me. He would be seventeen now, maybe eighteen if I remember his birthday correctly. His younger brother was a Măgūs Lătīnūs. Both he and his Pătĕr, er, father were murdered maliciously by a couple of D-A-M-L agents. His brother, I think, is either captured or dead. I buried them. Frŏns' father was like a father to me when I had none. Well, enough about the past. I think I should be going. Time is of the utmost importance, and the driving done by Alyssa saved me days of walking, which I really appreciated." I began to walk out the door, but Leo caught my arm. "Wait," he said, and I turned around.

"What?" I asked, searching his eyes for any sign of his intent.

"I don't know why, but I want to help you," the man said, surprising me.

"But you don't even know me," I said, crossing my arms and cocking my head.

"Somehow, I think I do… I don't know. But there must be something I can do."

I thought for a moment then said, "Maybe you can help me get to my desired location, provide supplies, and possibly translate the native tongue into English since I have no clue how to speak Arabic. They say something, and I think that they're hacking up a hairball."

Leo let out a loud snort. "Yeah, I guess some of their syllables do sound like that. I just never really thought about it. But, yes, I think I could arrange that. And besides, I would like to get to know an actual Măgūs Lătīnūs." He winked at me, and I rolled my eyes.

"I may know a few Magical beings, but I'm no Latin Magician. I'm just associated with them. Here, I have proof…" I drew my knife from its scabbard, causing them to jump back with fright. "This is a knife which I am clearly holding, and because of a curse placed upon the Latin Magicians around four thousand years ago, they cannot hold weapons or make them. It is rather sad because if they touch a weapon, whatever part of them touched it would become numb and flaccid."

"Okay…" Leo replied with a sigh. "Alyssa, mind if you go to my truck and…"

"On my way!" She hurried out the door.

I knew it was just an excuse to get out of the hairy situation.

"So… where'd you get that toothpick?" he asked nervously.

I shrugged. "That's another mystery."

"Do you have anything else under that costume? To me you seem like some sort of Jedi from Star Wars with their cloaks and their Light-Sabers… you're not anything like that, are you?"

I was trying not to laugh. "Well, I guess you could compare me to them if you wanted to, but I don't think you would find much of a resemblance."

"Oh, well… do you fight for good?" he asked.

I had to think about it. *Think about it… that's not good!* "Well, um… truthfully, I don't know. I know there is a war going on, but I have my own problems that I have to deal with."

He shook his head. "You're a piece of work."

I chuckled softly. "Tell me about it."

CHAPTER 14

What Have I Become?

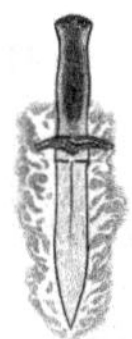

After about five hours, Leo had packed up and was ready to go. Apparently, his truck was a tan, crew-cab, 4x4 Tacoma; brand new; and was not a Chevy. I don't know why I like Chevys, and, if memory serves, it was a Chevy Camaro that my dad abandoned me in.

Anyways, when we were finally ready to go, Leo kissed his girlfriend goodbye, which severely grossed me out, and climbed in. I suppose I should explain why he was saying goodbye: what happened is that I freaked Alyssa out with my knife, and she refused to go near me. Leo didn't think that she could handle being within a foot of that knife for a few days. Wimp. Even my dad's girlfriend didn't scream when she saw the knife and swords and the rest. Though, I think that I scared her when I almost turned Mr. Ratty into rat stew.

We traveled on the road for days. It was so boring. I thought that I was going to die of nothing-to-do-ness, but at least there was Leo. It was like having Frŏns back! He was raised in the United States but moved to Saudi Arabia after sightings of weird creatures, or, as they turned out to be, Magical beings. He "discovered", since they were already discovered by Latin Magicians, a couple of new species of sea creatures. He also photographed a Nightmare of the Sea without knowing it, a Flying Cuttlefish, also without knowing it, and a weird creature I had never seen before. It had the head and tail of an iguana and the body of an octopus. On the end of each tentacle, it had a razor-sharp sickle. *Definitely a strange creature,* I thought to myself after seeing it.

Leo ended up doing most of the talking, which I appreciated since it was like listening to a radio or something to that effect. Finally, he asked me the question: "Why on earth are you going to the middle of the desert? Saudi Arabia, no less?"

I thought about it for a moment; I thought about my mission; I thought about the things I would have to do, which, until then, I had tried not to think about; I thought about all that had happened; and, finally, I thought, *Can I trust him?* I sighed and said, "I know you've told me a lot about yourself, but before I can tell you a wink about anything to do with why I'm going there, I need to know I can trust you."

He smirked. "What? My ramblings weren't enough to convince you?"

"It is the ramblings that might keep me from trusting you. Also, there is the possibility that you are working for the Damsels, and if that is so, I would be letting them know of my plan."

"So, how can I prove that I can be trusted?"

Leaning back in my seat, I thought, *Hmm… I wonder what he could do. Wait, I know! I'll read his mind! But… I don't know how to do that. I guess I could wing it. But that's not a good idea. What if he feels it? What if I accidentally erase his memories?* I tapped my chin and shrugged. *Eh, I think I'll take the chance. All right, here goes nothing!* I closed my eyes and focused. I played the little saying that my father used to say when I was a little girl, "Hocus Pocus, we need to focus!"

When I had let out any access thoughts, I, as weird as it sounds, felt around. I ended up feeling the warmth of a being that was close to me. It was Leo. I dove into the warmth and felt around until I found something cold. It was a door. *Puzzled much?* I thought to myself. Brushing off the confusion, I opened it and found myself in a giant room. There were thousands of doors on each wall of the room. I moved toward a door on my left, opened it, and stepped in. Looking around, I noticed that I was outside. There were birds chirping and rabbits bouncing every which way. I also heard a sound that sounded almost human. I moved toward the sound to find... Leo?

"Leo? Is that you?" I asked. He was, thankfully, wearing clothes. I say that because I didn't know what to expect in someone else's brain. He could've been wearing bellbottoms, a sparkly disco shirt, and an afro for all I knew.

He looked up, startled. "What are you doing in here? Wait, Alaĕna? What on earth are you doing in my head? Wait, you are a Latin Magician! I knew it! I just knew it!"

Well, that plan worked out well, I thought to myself. I had lots of practice hiding thoughts from the training I did with Vīta during the plane flights, so he wasn't able to hear them.

"I didn't know that Latin Magicians were able to communicate using telepathy! This is a breakthrough! Oh, George is not going to believe this!"

I shook my head with befuddlement. "Foremost: who's George?"

"A coworker of mine," he replied.

I nodded. "Okay, second: Latin Magicians do not communicate using telepathy. Third: you can't tell anybody anything because if I figure out that you told anybody, I will give you a bath in acid and watch you melt into a puddle of Leo soup. Understand?"

He gulped. "Yep."

I grinned. "Good."

"So, how come you can use telepathy?"

I shrugged. "One step at a time. First, I need to search your memories to figure out if you work for the Damsels or not. So, Vălĕ!" I walked back to the door hanging in the middle of the air, which was kind of weird, and he rushed in front of me to stop me.

"Please, I'll willingly show you all of my memories except the embarrassing ones, if you know what I mean by embarrassing." He smiled hopefully.

Shaking my head, I pushed him aside. "Nope, then that would give you the chance to hide your secrets. Sorry, chump." I slapped him on the back and walked through the door.

He was furious. "You can't just go around stealing everyone's most precious secrets; it's unconstitutional!"

I rolled my eyes. "It's not unconstitutional since there is no constitution here. So, how about you come with me, and whatever doors you don't want me to open, I'll most definitely open, understood?" I offered, and he loathingly agreed.

Within half an hour, I was able to search all of his memories. I chastised him for a few of the things he did in his past, and he ended up asking me why I hated relationships of any kind. I shook my head and before he could counter I exited.

As I opened my eyes, my only thought was *Hogwash! Huh, where does 'hogwash' come from, anyway? Maybe it was from the thought of washing a hog?*

Leo shook his head, and his eyes came back into focus. He looked at me and declared, "What was that? You were in my head! You were talking and walking and invading it like rats in a kitchen."

The only reply he received for that one was a glare. The only reason I didn't punch him was because I didn't want to crash.

"Come on, Alaĕna, you can't live in that secretive world you live in for the rest of your life. Sometimes you have to trust people."

"Well, you know what happens when you trust people, maybe even love them?" He was about to reply, but I said, "That was rhetorical." He nodded, and I continued, "They drop you on the side of the road to fend for yourself. Then, when things finally look bright again, and you end up putting the whole of your heart into trusting a few people, they get themselves killed or kidnapped, leaving you all alone again to fend for yourself for two years!"

He remained silent.

"This is the underworld most people don't know about. This is my life, and I fear it will one day be my death. You were clean, but I can't trust you with my secrets."

A mix of sadness and what looked like pity was on his face as he said, "I understand and I know you've been hurt in the past but…"

"No, you don't understand. You don't understand the emotions that went through my head, nor the Promise I made that day."

"What promise?"

I looked at him dead in the eye. "That I would kill their killers and their kind."

His face turned ashen white.

"I had the chance to slay a man that had been a curse to me since the day I was abandoned by my father, and I would've taken it if someone hadn't intervened. So, if you're still wondering what I'm doing here, I came to take back my family, and I don't have a problem removing any..." I thought for a moment for the right word, "*obstacles* that get in my way."

Leo shook his head angrily. "So, this is what your kind is like: vicious, blood-thirsty, and malicious. I'm sorry, but you'll have to walk the rest of the way." Pulling over to the side of the road, Leo unlocked the door as we stopped.

I opened my door, grabbed my bag, and jumped out. "We're not that different, you know."

"We are completely different!" He snapped.

I shook my head. "No, we're not. You're misunderstood, a reject to all, and so am I. Vălĕrĕ Iūbĕrĕ, one day we will meet again, that I am sure of." I shut the door, and Leo turned around, leaving in his dust. Sighing with contempt for the journey ahead, I began trekking the last few miles to my destination. It took nigh to five hours to reach the small Islamic town of... truthfully I didn't know what it was called since the only map I saw with it on it was in Arabic and I couldn't speak Arabic. Plus, my translator dude had been scared off. I really had to learn to hold my tongue. Oh well, he got the info he wanted to know. What I did know was that it was next to a pool of water which was scarce in that part of the country.

I walked around and looked for any sort of entrance to the base. After ten minutes, I was scrambling around sandy hills with various-sized rocks scattered everywhere. Eventually, I stumbled upon a house that was away from all the others. So, I walked over to it, knocked on the door, and waited. Once three minutes had passed without a peep from anyone that might be inside,

I touched the door and it swung inside. For some odd reason, it was unlocked and open. *This is a trap,* I thought as I stepped inside. A very familiar knot formed in my bosom. *Yep, it's a trap.*

I drew my sword and took off my Arab clothes since I wouldn't require those anymore, which exposed my knife, Căpĕrĕ Flămmaĕ, and my enchanted leather armor. I heard the creak of a floorboard and the sound of a sword being drawn. Raising my sword, I turned around and saw a Damsel. But this Damsel was different, and, as I studied him, I noticed that he was no older than Jacob.

"Who are you and what are you doing with that?" Strangely enough, he had a British accent. Looking down, he studied the sword in my hand. "Only an agent of the D-A-M-L carries a sword."

I made a figure-eight with my sword and declared, "Don't mess with me. I don't want to hurt you."

The boy did the same with his sword and replied, "And I don't want to hurt you. Now, tell me your name."

I shrugged. "Alaĕna."

His face twisted in recognition. "You! You killed General Thomson!"

"Killed who? Ooooh, so that's what his name is! Thomson, hmm, doesn't seem to fit him. Oh well. Anywho, I didn't kill him," I said as I cleaned the edge of my sword. "Though, I do wish I had, but, unfortunately, there are those who like to practice mercy. What I did to him was far worse. I gave him to an Ūnīcornīs Vōlătīcīs to be tried and possibly, no, most likely found guilty. That man, if you can call him that, will be forced to suffer for the rest of his life at the hooves of that wondrous breed of Magical being."

The Junior Damsel swung his sword once more. "You are the most wanted Măgūs Lătīnūs in history. Do you know what it will do to my job if I bring you in?"

"Do you know what will happen to you if you even try?" I grinned and twirled my sword in my hand.

His jaw set, and his gaze locked with mine.

"Come now, you must have been taught that I am not a very forgiving or merciful person. So, I would recommend skedaddling while you have the chance. Understood?"

The guy glanced behind me, nodded, lowered his sword, and sprinted out the door.

That was easy, a bit too easy. Wait, something's not quite... I raised my sword just in time to block the oncoming blade. I parried and twirled about to see an older-looking Damsel.

He had a light gray, scruffy beard and a heavily wrinkled face. Most likely, the Junior Damsel I had threatened was his grandson.

As I struggled to keep my cool, I said to Grandpa Damsel, "Listen, why don't you go get your grandson and let me do my job."

He shook his head and gritted his teeth. "You are the most wanted criminal in the entire world. You realize that?"

"Yes, but did you realize that you are the oldest Damsel in history?" I quipped.

He glowered at me and pushed me away from our gridlock.

I rested the tip of my sword on the ground and leaned on the hilt. "You know, old chap, this would've been a much nicer day if you had left me alone."

"No chance, girlie!" He swung his sword and within the moment.

I stood up straight, lifted my sword, and blocked. "Ha, so you're taking after Mr. Ratty, are you?" I laughed. "Oh wait, I mean General Thomson."

Grandpa Damsel grunted and tried his best to use his brute

strength to push me to the ground.

I allowed him to do his deed and, when he felt confident, he raised his sword above his head to execute me. I front kicked him with both legs in his private parts. He tried to scream, but I turned to my side and side-kicked him in the jaw, knocking him out. To my horror, his sword clanged on the ground, pommel first, and he fell upon the tip.

I turned my gaze away from him.

The Damsel was dead within the minute.

I kneeled and rested my forehead on the hilt of my sword.

After mourning the loss of life for a moment, I stood and looked around, lifting my sword in case there were other Damsels about. After a thorough search, I found a trap door under a rug. I lifted the hatch and peered inside. It was dank, but a perfect secret entrance. I jumped inside and fell twenty feet before landing. Thankfully, I landed in a large pile of sand, so I didn't hurt myself. Trust me, twenty feet might not seem very high, but it is!

As my eyes adjusted to the darkness, I noticed a passageway directly in front of me. The bad thing was that it was pitch black and anybody could sneak up on me. I thought for a moment and then commanded, "Sphaĕra Lūcīs Fŭlvīs, Vĕnī Ĕt Īnsĕquī Mē!" I looked around and saw an odd sphere of orange light floating in the air, following my every move. "Cool. It worked!" I beamed and trotted down the downward-sloped path.

Fetid smells of death and decay emanated from the tunnel walls, roots hung from the ceiling, screams echoed from the end of the tunnel, and, as the end of the tunnel was within sight, the hollers of pain stopped. Shivers ran up and down my spine and a knot formed in my stomach. When I finally reached the end of the tunnel, I was greeted by the most stomach-turning sight I had ever seen.

Thousands of kids, teens, and adults, assumingly Măgī Latīnī, their families, and their allies, were lying on the ground—dead. Some were skeletons, some were skinless, some were half melted, and some were in even worse shape than that.

I almost threw up at the stench, but then I realized that it wasn't the people that smelled. It was gas. I released my spell on the orb, causing it to disappear, and then, sprinting from shadow to shadow to avoid detection, I made my way to a door that was on the other side of the gigantic room.

As I looked back one final time before running down that tunnel, I put my free hand in a fist and decided that this sight strengthened my resolve to fulfill the promise I made those two long years ago.

This tunnel led to a small room with a bunch of computers and such on large tables. Computer Guy Damsels who were wearing full-body black suits were typing their little, stony hearts away on their black keyboards. I quietly made my way over to the door opposite me and ran down that tunnel. That time, I did so with more caution, since more people could be walking down the passageway.

After repeating that procedure about twenty more times, I came upon a long room with doors all along it. Some had a green light over the doorframe and others had red. I was assuming green meant someone was in there and red meant the opposite, although it might have been vice versa.

As I walked down the hallway-like room, I tried to feel for any sign of Dīcărě.

None.

I happened across an old, rusty door that looked as if it hadn't been opened in years and, as I got closer, I felt something. Taking a deep breath, I commanded, "Ŏstīūm, Pătĕfēcī!"

The door slid open, squealing with protest. A narrow passage led to a dark cage that was hanging in the air.

The yellow light peeking through from behind the door revealed a shadowy lump at the farthest corner of the iron crate.

"Hello?" I asked quietly. "Are you dead or alive or alive wishing you were dead?"

The lump stirred, and I saw one bony finger pointed up in the air.

I grinned. "Well, obviously you're not, since you held up a finger. Who are you?"

The lump turned, and its face was revealed.

My heart leaped within my chest. Feelings of anger, grief, and something else rushed through me, as a flood, for this tumor on the bottom of the metal coop was Dīcărĕ.

CHAPTER 15

The Heart

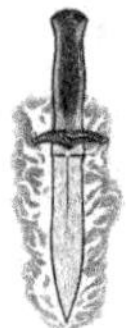

He was battered, bruised, bloody, and thin as a twig but still Dīcărĕ. Dīcărĕ squinted in the light and, as he focused, he no doubt saw my smiling face, for he hoarsely mumbled, "Alaĕna?"

I smiled broadly. "Sălvĕ, Dīcărĕ."

His still sapphire blue eyes lit up, and he tried to at least scoot over to me but his legs didn't move.

I looked around and noticed a control panel on the wall. There were three buttons: an *up*, a *down*, and an *open* button. So, I pressed the *down* button, and the cage was lowered to the ground. Then I pressed the *open* button, and the cage door opened. I shrugged. "Nifty."

As I sheathed my sword, the alarm wail echoed through the room and throughout the entire base. Adding to the chaos, a huge, red light flashed on the top of the wall.

"What's…" Dīcărĕ began, but I shushed him.

Swiftly, I ran into the cage, put his arm around my shoulders, put my arm around his waist, and lifted him. "Whatever ounce of strength you have left, use it now! I can't do this by myself!" I frantically whispered to him.

He weakly nodded and placed his feet on the ground.

As we reached the door, the silhouette of a person was blocking it.

Quickly, I set Dīcărě down and drew my sword. However, when I looked closer, I was able to see the person's face and asked, astonished, "Bart?"

"Alaĕna?" he asked, eyes wide.

Still holding my sword at the ready, I asked, "What on earth are you doing here?"

"I was going to say th…" He stopped as he looked at the lump of a boy on the floor. "Is he Dīcărě?"

I pursed my lips, and he understood the meaning. "I expect an explanation on the way. Now, help me with him!" I said, grabbing Dīcărě's right arm.

Bartholomew nodded and grabbed one of his arms. Together, we half-carried and half-dragged Dīcărě out the door.

"So, Bart, why are you here, and where are the others?" I asked as we entered a tunnel.

"What… others?" Dīcărě weakly asked.

"Your old buddies from Mulpa."

Looking distressed, he shook his head. "No, you went… to Mulpa? Did they hurt you?"

Bartholomew and I shared a look, and I inquired, "Why would they hurt me?"

Dīcărě just hung his head, for his strength was spent.

It was a good thing that my brother was there because if he hadn't… well; I didn't want to think about that. As we stumbled down the hallway, I wondered where the others were, so I said,

"Bart, the answer…"

"Oh, yeah," my brother grunted. "They are distracting the Damsels. That's why the alarms are blaring like an ambulance after Cheeky Monkey has been having too much fun."

I thought for a moment then chuckled. "Yeah, I guess they are." I paused a moment then queried, "Did you see…"

"Yes," he solemnly interrupted. "I didn't think that things like that could happen in the modern world."

I snorted. "Welcome to reality, little brother."

Twenty minutes later, we arrived back at the huge chamber. It was a war zone. Two teens, assumingly Isabella and Jacob, were turning Damsels into animals like crazy people. There were deer, rabbits, chipmunks, guinea pigs, moose, mice, rats, and… "What is that?" I asked my brother.

He shrugged. "I think they're echidnas."

"Echi-wha?"

Once more, he shrugged his shoulders. "I dunno. I just heard about it on my mom's TV once."

I sighed.

After just seconds, the Damsels saw us, and, when we were in the tunnel, Bartholomew made a signal for our comrades, who were battered and bleeding, to retreat to our position.

When she saw Dīcărĕ, Isabella gasped.

Dīcărĕ faintly smiled at her.

She was going to say something, but I cut her off. "Touching reunions can wait. First, we need to get out!"

She nodded.

Since it was still too dark to see, I commanded the orb to come again. It did, to the shock of everyone but Dīcărĕ.

"Where did you learn to do that?!" Jacob asked. "Vīr, that would've come in handy!"

I smirked. "I didn't learn it. I just did it."

Jacob shook his head as we ran down the clammy passageway.

Once we reached the end, we still had to get him up the ladder, which I had missed when I fell twenty feet down the hole.

"Now, what are we going to do?" Isabella inquired. "We can't get him up the ladder. He's too big! He's taller than Jacob!"

"Never say can't, Isabella, never." I focused, pulled out the amount of strength I had left, and commanded, "Lĕvă Pūĕr Ăd Sūmmūm Dĕ Scălă Ĕt Sĕrvă Ĕum Ībī!"

Isabella almost screamed as the surprised and terrified Dīcărĕ was lifted into the air.

I fell to a knee because of the rapid drop in energy. *No spell has taken any toll on me before. What's going on?* I asked myself. Shaking it off, I sheathed my sword and climbed up the ladder.

The others, still dazed by seeing a boy levitating in the air, followed close behind.

As I opened the trapdoor when I reached the top, I noticed that it was locked. *I don't have time for this. Damsels could start shooting at us any minute. And this spell holding up Dīcărĕ is taking a serious toll on my strength.* I drew my knife from its scabbard and commanded, "Căpĕrĕ Flămmaĕ, Ăccĕndī!"

The knife glowed like the flames of a bonfire, heat radiating from its core. I pulled back my arm and then drove it into the door, which quickly disintegrated under the heat.

Once the door was gone, I jumped out and drew my sword just in case, almost fainting with the motion, then lifted Dīcărĕ and set him on the ground next to the hole.

Jacob, my brother, and Isabella quickly followed.

After that, we picked up Dīcărĕ and ran to the door.

Isabella stopped, gazing at the dead Damsel, and asked with a quivering voice, "Did you do this, Alaĕna?"

"No, I didn't. He fell on his sword after I had battled him

and had won," I explained.

She stared at me a second longer than natural, but she joined the struggling group at the door.

I turned to the man one last time, sighed, and sprinted out the door into the Arabian Night.

When we were a safe distance away, which was about two miles, we flopped down on the ground and rested.

"Well… that was… exciting!" I panted.

Bartholomew ran his fingers through his hair as he faintly laughed. "Yeah, you could say that."

Grinning, I asked, "So, how on earth did you end up in that hole?"

He shrugged. "Well, all I remember is this: first, you ditched us, then we got on a couple more planes, and then a guy in a tan Tacoma gave us a lift here. He said something about a weird girl armed with a knife scaring the living daylights out of him and his girlfriend. Does he sound familiar?"

I nodded. "Yes, Leo. His girlfriend, Alyssa, gave me a lift to his place. He's a wannabe Magologist. It was weird. He looked and acted just like Frŏns. It felt like I had him around again. It was nice."

At this Dīcărĕ squinted and looked toward me, quietly asking, "You're sounding like Frŏns is dead. Is he?"

I looked him in the eye and said, "I'm sorry, but Frŏns and Pătĕr are dead. They were beheaded by those two Damsels." Placing a hand on his shoulder, I continued, "I buried them next to your mother. I'm really sorry. It feels like all of this is my fault: you getting kidnapped; your only family dying; and us being out here in the first place!" I pulled my knees in close to my chest and placed my head on them. "I wish we were all back home. I wish that everything was back to normal." I felt like such a lousy girlie girl wimp. I guess that Dīcărĕ was the last straw for me.

Dīcăr's lips quivered, and he covered his face.

Kneeling beside her friend, Isabella put a hand on Dīcărĕ's shoulder and squeezed it reassuringly. "We're here for you, Dīcărĕ." She turned to me and said, "I think everybody's ready to go home. First, we have to explain to Mr. Cĕtĕră what on earth we've been doing the last week or so."

"Yeah, I guess he'd be pretty distressed by now," I said.

Jacob thoughtfully looked up for a moment and then asked, "Where's the Ūnīcornīs Vōlătīcīs, Vīta?"

I shrugged. "I dunno. She left after the encounter with the Nightmare of the Sea. He foretold this Prophecy about the Queen of Magic."

Dīcărĕ immediately sat up. "What was the Nightmare of the Sea's name?"

Curious, I replied, "Cīnnabar, why do you ask?"

Dīcărĕ leaned over and shook his head. "Did he tell you the entire Prophecy?"

"Wow, you recovered fast."

"Did he tell you the entire Prophecy?!" he demanded.

"I don't know. He was pretty cryptic about it all."

"Does the man Măgīstĕr Ĕt Cĕtĕră sound familiar?"

Wagging my head up and down, I said, "Yeah, he used to be my teacher, but he ended up being a Mulpa agent."

"So, he gave himself up," Dīcărĕ mumbled. "Alaĕna, has he done anything strange when you knew him?"

I shrugged. "Nothing that I can think of. Though, as my dad—I'll explain later—explained to me that Bartholomew was my brother—again I'll explain later—he looked really angry. He was especially angry when they were arguing about my mom. Do you know why that is?"

He pursed his lips and looked away.

"Dīcărĕ, do you know?" I pressed.

"I hate him." The boy's nostrils flared, and a sudden violence came upon his countenance.

"What? Hate who?" I asked, trying to make sense of what he was saying.

"Do you want to know who made your mom leave and take Bartholomew with her? Do you want to know who made your dad abandon you to live on your own in the most dangerous city in the US? Do you want to know who told the Damsels where my family was? Do you want to know who?"

My breath stuttered.

"Măgīstĕr Ĕt Cĕtĕră! That's who!" he shouted. "That man is pure evil. He cares about nothing but the destruction of all of his kind. Us, Alaĕna, he wants us all dead along with his accursed boss. Because of that man, I can't use Magic!"

"What!" I exclaimed.

"That was the oath I took so that I could save your life, Alaĕna. I swore that I would never use Magic again," Dīcărĕ stated.

I glared at him as I inquired, "So, what would you have me do?"

With nothing but cold, bitter hatred in his eyes, he responded, "Kill him."

To my astonishment, my stomach didn't turn at the thought. Instead, there was a feeling of anticipation. *What's going on?* I inquired to myself.

"Are you crazy?" Jacob asked, distressed. "You know what Mr. Cĕtĕră means to all of us!"

"You don't know what he's going to do!" Dīcărĕ argued.

Standing, Isabella crossed her arms and asked, "Well, what is he going to do?"

"What he's going to do," answered Dīcărě, "is kill the girl from the Prophecy."

Jacob grunted. "You don't even know who she is." The look on his friend's face told him otherwise. "Do you?"

Dīcărě slowly nodded. "Yes, I have known ever since her Catēnūs told me."

"Catēnūs? Bonded One? I thought there could only ever be one, and that's yours," Jacob stated.

"What?" Dīcărě looked confused.

Jacob clamped his mouth shut and mumbled, "Oops."

"Vīta Lyrārūm," I explained.

Dīcărě nodded with recognition. "Well, the girl's Catēnūs is Născī Flămmărūm. If you ask him, he might just tell you, or he'll say it's not the right time. He does that a lot."

"You sound like you know him well," Isabella said.

He nodded. "Ever since my mom was murdered. He told me who the girl was and that I needed to protect her and guide her through her hardest times. Unfortunately, with me being kidnapped, I left her in her greatest need. I only know this because of a man who came to visit me every day to give me food and water. I didn't realize he was telling the truth until I saw you, Alaĕna. I could tell just by the look in your eyes that I had failed."

I laughed, making everyone jump with surprise.

"What's so funny?" Bartholomew asked.

"The fact that Dīcărě is secretly implying that I am bonded to Născī Flămmărūm and that I am the girl from the Prophecy. Of course, it's all preposterous but funny. And how on earth could you tell something like that from a look in someone's eyes?"

Dīcărě glared at me as he whispered to me, "You've done well hiding what you really are from the world, but I can see past it all. I'm not blind to your many faults like they are."

My smile turned into a frown. "What's your problem?"

"I spent years trying to deny the person you were destined to become but, now I know who you are: a murderer. I guess my feelings for you blinded me."

My face turned ashen white while the others, save Isabella, laughed.

"Are you kidding? That cage did a number on you. Alaĕna couldn't murder a person even if she wanted to. I know she has a lot, and I mean a *lot*, of issues, but she cannot murder someone." Bartholomew laughed, but then he looked at my face. "What's wrong?"

"Excuse me." I quickly stood and sprinted away, sealing the answer of that allegation in stone.

Bartholomew glared at Dīcărĕ as he got to his feet to follow me and snapped, "There's no way she could ever be that or do anything like that! What is your problem? I mean, who would do that to the girl who just rescued your sorry hide? Maybe we should've let you rot in that cage." He stormed off, calling after me.

I heard him coming up behind me, but I ignored him. All there was around me was sand and a few thorny bushes. The sky was clear, and the moon was full and bright. It made me think of Vīta.

"Alaĕna! Alaĕna, wait!" my brother called.

Finally, after he had called me thirty-two times, I had enough of it. So, I turned around and said, "Listen, Bart, I need some alone time right now. Please, just leave me in peace!" I stormed off into the night, leaving him to head back to the camp reluctantly.

This was supposed to be happy, I thought to myself, *like some sort of reunion. But this is just plain awful. I guess this is what you get with a kid who was locked up in the dark for two years of his life. Maybe he'll be better if I talk to him alone. Maybe…* I rolled my eyes and shook my head. *What am I? Some sort of drama-loving buffoon? No, I don't think so! Besides, all he's going to do is just accuse me more of being… that. But I guess I do need to face my demons at one time or another. Time to Cowgirl Up and deal with 'em.*

Reluctantly, I turned on my heel and marched back to the camp where everyone appeared very surprised, especially as I put out the fire that they had just lit.

"Come on. We need to get moving so those blood-thirsty Damsels don't catch us." There was a sharp, angry tone in my voice that seemed to scare them a bit, and, when they just sat there, I commanded, "Don't just sit there. *Get up!*"

Wide-eyed, they quickly packed up and followed me out into the desert. *So much for Cowgirl-ing Up.* I sighed.

Once we were about a mile away from our previous en-campment, Bartholomew asked me, "First, it's Dīcărĕ who's acting weird. Now, it's you. One minute you're as happy as a dog with tickets to the National Cat Show, then you're as sad as the cats at the National Cat Show, and now you're as mad as the dog after he was scratched up by the cats at the National Cat Show. What's going on?"

I shook my head and walked faster.

"You're becoming your old self again!" Bartholomew called after.

Abruptly, I stopped, turned around, and faced him. "You haven't met my old self, Bartholomew. You would be scared stiff if you knew what my old self was like. I just put on a good face for you. I always saw you as family, and I didn't want you to know the things that I've seen, done, will do." I shook my head and quietly mumbled, "So much…" As the last words left me, I walked off, leaving Bartholomew to ponder what I had said.

After ten minutes of walking around like a mad man—er, girl—I ended up resting against the trunk of a tall, thorny tree which was green from the roots to the leaves. Thoughts ran through my head, creating a nauseating mesh of emotions and memories. *Oh, why couldn't I have procrastinated a little bit longer? Why did I have to rush to save him? Why did I have to make the Promise?*

Soon, I heard rapid footsteps behind me and the sound of Bartholomew calling my name over and over again. I didn't even look at him when he came next to me, asking me hundreds of questions. All I did was look solemnly at the full moon overhead. *I just want to go home.* I broke down crying. I had reached my breaking point and, by then, I had forgotten about Bartholomew standing next to me.

His voice came back into focus, and I could hear him as he questioned, "Hey, hey, it's okay. Don't cry. What's wrong?"

This time, I looked at him as I said, "Nothing you could understand, Bartholomew, nothing." I stood and continued walking.

He grabbed my arm and turned me around.

I glared viciously at him.

"Alaĕna, why do you do this? You shut everyone out: your friends, your family, everyone! Why do you do this every time you have a problem? Is it because we are too 'good' to under-stand? Is it because we are too old or too young? Or what?"

I stayed silent.

He shook me by the shoulders and commanded, "What!"

Pulling away from his sturdy grasp, I said, "I have been alone for all of my life. I may have had Pătĕr, Frŏns, and Dīcărĕ, but it wasn't the same."

"The same as what?" he demanded.

"A family!"

He looked down, ashamed.

"You had your mother. I had no one! Because of who I am and what I can do, my father had to abandon me! And do you know who offered to become my family first? Guys like Banana Bear, Cheeky Monkey, and Breaker; drug dealers, murderers, and gangsters. They showed me things you have never even heard of. I don't tell you these things so that I can protect you from these horrible things. I've seen people shot, strangled, cut, smashed in the head, run over, die of suicide… I've seen just about all of it! And I can't take much more because if I learn or see anything else I *will* become like them and that is *not* a person you would like to come across."

My brother closed his eyes and shook his head. "No, you'd never become like that."

A small, evil glint came to my eyes. "You'd be surprised, brother." It disappeared with a quick blink and shake of the head.

The horror was evident on his face. "Something isn't right. The way you look… it's different."

"I guess your feelings for me as your sister blinded you as well." The ire in my voice surprised me.

"Are you saying that Dīcărĕ was right?" He stepped backward, away from me.

I looked him in the eye and replied, "Yes."

A tear fell from his widened eyes. "No, please tell me it wasn't on purpose!"

"Yes." My voice cracked with grief and guilt as I said this. A single tear of disappointment that was falling down Bartholomew's cheek quickly turned into a river as I continued. "Some would say it was in self-defense, but I knew deep down that I could have spared him or that I could have knocked him unconscious or that I could have done something else. But no,

I did it. Sliced his neck! And you know what? Deep down, I enjoyed it. Not for the revenge of all the deaths that he caused, but for the thrill of the power I felt. I've fought it for so long, but no more!"

My brother trembled with anger and grief. "You were my hero! You had always refused to become what was around you! And now, I know that everything you say is a lie. Now, tell me the Promise!" I hesitated, and he yelled, "If you have one ounce of truthfulness left in you, then tell me what that the Promise is!"

My face hardened as I recited by heart the Promise. "I will rescue Dīcărĕ Cōr from the clutches of the evil D-A-M-L and, when I am done, I will not rest until every single one of those Damsels is dead!"

Anger boiled in his eyes, but then a flicker of hope. "You can break your Promise. Y-you can still avoid this. You can still prove Dīcărĕ wrong!"

"No, a promise taken in Latin cannot be broken under penalty of death." I clenched my hands into fists, turned around, and marched back to the group lagging.

"What are you going to do now?" he asked bitterly.

Looking back, I solemnly replied, "I will first escort you as far as the city of Almuwaylih."

"And then what?" Bartholomew halfheartedly asked.

"I fulfill my Promise."

Chapter 16

The Death of the Light

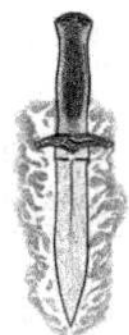

Bartholomew didn't speak to me for the entire time we walked, which was approximately two weeks. That meant that I couldn't tell him the entire story of the man, not that it mattered with what I said. Whenever I thought of that day, the image of that man haunted me. I tried to brush it off, but I never managed it.

In the sands of the largest desert in Saudi Arabia, I felt everything. It was a sense of honesty I felt with myself. I had lied to my father, my brother, my friends, my Heart… everyone. I knew that one day my secret would be revealed, but little did I know how badly it would be taken.

Bartholomew didn't tell anyone else about what he had learned. He didn't speak to anyone. I think it was his punishment to me, since his constant chattering was rather enjoyable, although I never showed it. It felt as though I was being shunned, but I supposed, no, I knew that I deserved it.

All but Dīcărĕ could figure out why on earth the usually talkative Bartholomew was now as silent as a dead beetle—my apologies to those who love bugs, again.

"Frăter! Bartholomew James Healdton, listen to me!" After reaching the seashore, exactly where Vīta had abandoned me, I had finally had enough of his dead cockroach impersonation— oh, if you love bugs enough to find this traumatic, then you've got issues. Find a new creature to adore, such as the Īnsŏmnīūm Mărīs.

He turned around to face me and asked, "Why don't you just go home?!"

"Because without you, I don't have a home! You were always there to brighten up the world I was forced to live in. Don't you see that? You are my brother, Bartholomew. You're the only true family I have. I don't count dad because he abandoned me. I don't count mom because I have never met her, and so that leaves you and you alone."

My brother sneered. "Well, then, it's *not* mutual." He stormed away and turned around to say, "At least you have Dīcărĕ!"

I reddened as I turned to Dīcărĕ, who had recovered to the brink of normal. "This is all your fault!"

"Me? Who murdered someone?!" he accused.

"He was a Damsel, he had come after me, he had me cornered, and I injured him then ran away. He followed. I took a wrong turn. He attacked. I defended. I had my knife at his throat, and he lunged forward. I took the final slice, and he died. I didn't really want him to die, at least the sane part of me! I saved your life and to repay me you made me lose the only family I have in this accursed world!"

"Trust me when I say that it was for the best," Dīcărĕ replied.

"Quōmōdō Īn Tĕrră Īllud Prō Ŏptīmūm Ĕst? Hōc Nŏn Possĕ Prō Ŏptīmūm! Nŭnquăm, Dīcărĕ, Nŭnquăm!" His face was expressionless as I finished.

"Scīĕntīă Tūă Latīnī Crĕvī Pōstquăm Ultīmūs Tĕmpūs Vīdō Tĕ," Dīcărĕ stated.

"Ītă, Dīcărĕ. Īăm Ūt…" Because there is so much Latin in this conversation, I will translate the rest into English. "…Now that we understand each other, I want to know why you told them."

"Simple: so that you can fulfill the Promise," he replied.

My eyes widened with surprise. "How did you know about the Promise? And why would you want me to fulfill it?"

"Because it is your destiny. Your purpose."

"My purpose is to fulfill that accursed Promise? Because of that dumb Promise, my brother hates me! I wish I didn't have to fulfill that Promise. I wish I could just walk away, but I can't because…" I turned my gaze to the sand underneath me which was almost twenty feet deep since, while I was talking to Dīcărĕ, we had absentmindedly walked on top of a huge dune, and shook my head.

"Because you'd die?" he finished.

I nodded.

"I guess you have a choice, then." He held up one finger as he said, "One: kill all of the murderers and become a murderer yourself, but live." He held up a second finger. "Or two: break your Promise by taking another oath that you would not fulfill your Promise and die, saving the lives of all those murderers and dying with a clear conscious. Seems easy enough to me." He shrugged and walked back down the dune to rejoin the others down below.

I groaned and thought about it. *If I do fulfill my Promise, I'll lose my brother forever. If I don't, then I'll die, but Bartholomew will think of me better and might forgive me.* I sighed and slid down the dune, spraying sand everywhere. Once I reached the bottom, I tried to shake the hot sand out of my clothes, but to no avail. So, I gritted my teeth and continued on my way. For the rest of the day, I thought about what to do, and when we had set up camp for the night, I looked at the people in front of me.

Bartholomew was trying to keep a straight face while listening to Dīcărĕ and Jacob, who were making jokes.

Isabella chuckled time and again.

I faintly smiled.

Bartholomew's eyes were shining with a joy that I hadn't seen in a very long time, Dīcărĕ was laughing and jesting around like his old self, Jacob was virtually bouncing with jubilancy, and Isabella seemed to just be glad to see Dīcărĕ safe and sound.

They were my friends and my family, and I didn't want to disappoint them. So, I walked away from the boisterous group of kids—minus Isabella, who was an adult—and sat down by the seashore. I took a deep breath and said shakily in Latin as a tear rolled down my cheek, "Prōmĭttō Nŏn Prōmīssiō Mĕă Prīmă Cŏnfĕcĕrĕ!" *I promise not to fulfill my first promise!* Although the pain that immediately followed was unbearable, I didn't cry out but simply collapsed. My heartbeat slowed, my breath became labored and shallow, my hearing flickered, my vision blurred, and my thoughts became muddled until all I could do was watch the black waves lap against the golden sand in front of me. And, as my last breath escaped from me, and death was just a second away, the voice of Născī Flămmărūm echoed through my mind. *Well done, dear one.*

Epilogue

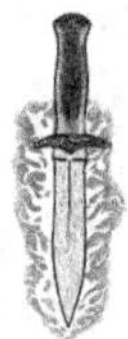

Bartholomew looked around for his sister, but she was nowhere to be found. After scanning the area for a few more minutes, he hushed the others, who were merrily laughing. "Where's Alaĕna?" he asked.

Jacob shook his head with confusion and Isabella shrugged her shoulders, but Dīcărĕ looked down while squeezing his eyes shut as a silent tear fell from his cheek.

"Dīcărĕ, do you know where she is?" Bartholomew inquired.

Dīcărĕ remained silent.

"Dīcărĕ tell me!" Bartholomew demanded.

Looking up, Dīcărĕ simply replied, "She's dead."

Bartholomew shook his head. "How could that be?"

Gulping down his rising emotions, Dīcărĕ answered, "Because, when Alaĕna made her Promise, she said it in Latin and a Promise taken in Latin must be fulfilled under penalty of death. She knew that you would never forgive her if she fulfilled her Promise, so she took another oath in Latin that contradicted the original."

The boy placed his head in his hands and rocked back and forth for a while. Once he got over the initial shock, he stood and said, "Let's go find her. If she is dead, then I want to bury her. If she's not, then I want to know why you would jump to such hasty solutions, which I'll still want to know." He marched off toward the beach, leaving Jacob and Isabella to scramble to catch up with him. After what seemed like hours, Bartholomew fell to his knees, put his head in his hands, and wept, his tears mixing with the salt water splashing against his pants. "She's gone. I can't believe she's gone!"

Isabella put a sympathetic hand on his shoulder. "I'm sorry, Bartholomew."

"Don't be sorry, be glad." They jumped at the voice. Looking around, they saw Dīcărĕ standing not three feet away.

Something inside Bartholomew snapped and his old self fell into a deep, dark canyon, never again to see the light. He stood, trembling with emotion, and roared, "This is all your fault! My sister would never have had to die if you had stayed in your cell!"

Dīcărĕ was about to respond when a gurgling roar came from the sea.

The group looked into the black abyss and, with widened eyes, saw two white eyes hovering fifteen feet above the waves.

"Cīnnabar," Dīcărĕ muttered incredulously.

The Light is dead, Dīcărĕ, and her body is gone, Cīnnabar said to Dīcărĕ. The time of ignorant peace is over and begun the time of war. Prepare yourself for both men and beast alike will hunt you until every single one of you is dead. If they succeed, the Light will become

Darkness. If they fail, then the Light will glow brighter than ever before. Train Bartholomew as you did Alaĕna for he will be a valuable ally in the years to come. So, I say, prepare yourself for war, for glory, and for honor! Păx Ăd Tĕrrăm Per Măgōs Latīnōs Ĕt Ūnīcornĕs Vōlătīcĕs! His eyes disappeared into the dark depths of the sea.

Dīcărĕ looked down and squeezed hands into fists. "Let's go."

Bartholomew glared at Dīcărĕ. "What? You're not even going to look for Alaĕna's body at least?"

The young man shook his head. "No, there's nothing left to find."

"What do you mean? How do you know?" the boy disbelievingly queried.

"Cīnnabar, the white eyes you saw, told me," Dīcărĕ enlightened.

"Why didn't he tell me?"

"Because I am her guardian and protector, I am to fight by her side the coming war, and I am to train you as I did Alaĕna. So, come on, Bartholomew, let's get back to the States. There's nothing more for us here." Dīcărĕ grabbed Bartholomew's arm and began dragging him back toward camp.

The boy dug his heels in the sand and jerked back. "I'm not going anywhere with you. I'm going home to my mom, the only true family that I have left, and I don't ever want to see you again!" He ripped his arm from Dīcărĕ's grasp and stormed off.

Dīcărĕ's eyes narrowed as he rushed in front of Bartholomew. "Listen here, punk," Dīcărĕ spat as he jabbed the boy in the chest. "You are coming with me whether you like it or not. I miss my family, too, but I know what's coming. The war ahead is not going to be pretty. All of the Măgī Latīnī and their families and friends, especially you and your remaining family, are going to be hunted and slaughtered like animals.

Blood will flow like rivers and none will survive if there is no one to defend them. The Măgī Latīnī are completely defenseless, and, one of these days, an ML will accidentally turn a Damsel into a great Predator seeking the flesh of only the Măgī Latīnī. So, you better come with me or I will kill you where you stand because it would make it a whole lot better for me."

Bartholomew matched Dīcărě's vicious glare. "Fine, but I warn you that I'm not who I used to be. My hero, the one person I could look up to, turned out to be a murderer. I can't be who I was. Are you sure you want that?"

Dīcărě was surprised by Bartholomew's sudden change of heart but showed no sign of it when he said, "Yes."

Bartholomew held out his hand for Dīcărě to shake, and his new mentor shook his hand firmly.

Panting, Jacob stopped right before Isabella, who had been sadly watching the interaction. "What's going on?" he asked, confused.

Isabella shook her head sadly. "Alaĕna's gone for good, and so is Bartholomew."

"What do you mean?" Jacob inquired.

"I mean that the old Bartholomew has died, and a new, more evil Bartholomew has taken his place. I'll miss that funny little boy always messing around with his sister like a little boy should."

Jacob frowned. "Now what's going to happen since both Alaĕna and Bartholomew are gone?"

Isabella pursed her lips and sadly replied, "We prepare for war, I suppose, because Cīnnabar, the Vătĕs Fūtūrōrūm, has spoken to Dīcărě and said that a war is coming, one that many, if not all, the Măgī Latīnī and their allies will not survive."

Jacob sighed despairingly. "I wanted Dīcărě back so badly. No, I wanted my best friend back so badly. But I guess he's gone too. Is anyone still around?"

Isabella nodded and placed a hand on his shoulder. "I am."

Jacob faintly smiled. "Yeah, and so am I. I won't change who I am. Not even if it means my life."

"Well, with what Dīcărě's saying, I think it just might be the price of remaining true to who you are."

"Then so be it," Jacob said solemnly. "Let the war come, the guns fire, and the swords swing. I will be good, no matter the price."

"So will I," Isabella agreed, looking at the two boys getting ready to become soldiers for a war like none have seen before nor will see again until the world comes to an end. Thinking of the battles and tragedies to come, she mumbled once more, "Yes, so will I."

My story will continue in Bombyx Biographies: Book 2.
Farewell, my ever faithful readers, for now…

The Language of the Latin Magician

Latin Word	Meaning
Alaĕna Ĕx Bombyx	The full name is Vĕnī Ă Ălaĕ Ĕx Bombyx, which means 'Came from Wings of Silk.'
Amīca Catēnī	Friend of my Bonded One
Bōnūs	Good
Căpĕrĕ Flămmaĕ	To Contain the Flames
Căpĕrĕ Flămmaĕ, Ăccĕndī!	To Contain the Flames, Ignite!
Căpĕrĕ Flămmaĕ, Exstīngūī!	To Contain the Flames, Extinguish!
Catēnī	Bonded One's (male)
Catēnūs	Technically this means "bonded" but for my book, I use it so that it means "Bonded One". "Catēnūs" is the masculine (male) version of the word.
Cīnnabar	Dragon's Blood
Cōr	Heart
Cŏxī Hīc Cībĕ Ăd Pĕrfĕctīo!	Cook this food to perfection!
Dīcărĕ Ădservō Cōr	Dīlūcĕsĕrĕ Cărĕ Ădservō Cōr (which is Dīcărĕ's real name) means 'Grow Light at Great Sacrifice and Save the Life of a Person'
Dīĕ Bōnă Abu Kharim, Kharim.	Good day Abu Kharim, Kharim.
Drăcōmūscă	Dragonfly

Dūx	Duke
Ĕs Grătūs, Vīta Lyrārum.	You are welcome, Life of Songs.
Ĕs Sĕrpĕns!	You are a snake!
Ēvēnī Ŏvă Tūă, Lībĕrī Cīnnabarī, Ēvēnī Ĕt Vīdĕ Lūcăm! Ēvēnī Ŏvă Tūă, Lībĕrī Cīnnabarī, Ĕt Cŏntīnŏ Pătūm Tūūm Ĕt Mătūm Tūūm! Ēvēnī Ĕt Cŏntīnŏ Tĕrrăm!	Come out of your eggs, children of Cīnnabar, and see the light! Come out of your eggs, children of Cīnnabar, and meet your father and your mother! Come out and meet the world!
Ĕxīstō Mŭrĕs, Ētĕnĭm Qūŏd Ĕst Qūĭd Tū Ĕs!	Become rats, for that is what you are!
Filīa	Daughter
Filīūs	Son
Frăter	Brother
Frŏns	Foliage; Frons
Īmmanīs Lacĕrta/ Īmmanīs Lacĕrtīs	Monstrous Lizard/Monstrous Lizards
Īncĕndīūm Fĕrŏx	Wild Conflagration
Fŭrōr	Rage
Gărrūlītăs Pīxīs	Chatter Box
Germăna	Sister
Germăna Mĕa, Nĕ Dĕrĕlīnqūăs Mĕ. Qūaĕsō Sōrōr Nŏn Mōrī, Sīs!	My sister, do not forsake me. Sister, I ask you not to die, please!
Gūbĕrnătŏr Ăssistĕntĕs	Pilot Assistant
Hă! Sī Īllūd Ĕst Optīmūs Tūūs, Qūăm Ĕs Dēdēcūs Ăd Spēcīĕ Tūŏ!	Ha! If that is your best, then you are a disgrace to your species!

Hĕūs! Măssă Măgnă Cībă Mărīs, Vīdĕ Hīc!	Hey! Huge lump of sea-food, look here!
Īnsŏmnīum Mărīs	Nightmare of the Sea
Ītă, Dīcărĕ. Īăm Ūt...	Yes, Dīcărĕ. Now that...
Ītă, Tū Grătīă.	Yes, thank you.
Ītă.	Yes.
Lĕvă Pūĕr Ăd Sūmmūm Dĕ Scălă Ĕt Sĕrvă Ĕum Ībī!	Lift up the boy to the top of the ladder and keep him there!
Lībĕrī	Children
Lībĕrī Cīnnabarī, Spīră!	Children of Cīnnabar, Breathe!
Lūctūs Bōnūs!	Good Grief!
Ălă Lūnă	Moon Wing
Lūx, Splĕndĕ Īn Ŏvă!	Light, shine into the eggs!
Măgīstĕr Ĕt Cĕtĕră	Teacher and the Rest
Măgūs Lătīnūs/Măgī Latīnī	Latin Magician/Latin Magicians
Manībūs Ŭngūībūs/Manībī Ŭngūībī	Claw Hand/Claw Hands
Mănūs Ăcĕr	Sharp Hand
Măter	Mother
Mŭrĕs, Dīgrĕdī Ĕt Vīrī Qūī Fūĕrūnt Mūtăvĕrūnt Īn Mŭrĕm, Mūtă Īn Sĕ Sūōs Prīmōs Hūmănōs! Praĕtĕr Prō Mŭrĕm Cūm Ŏcūlōs Mălōs Părvōs Rūbĕrōs.	Rats leave and men who were turned into rats turn into their former human themselves (or selves)! Except for the rat with evil, little eyes.

Mūs Mălūs Cūm Ŏcŭlī Rŭbĕrī, Mūtă In Vīr Impurī Fŭīstī, Sĕd Dīcăs Mē Rēspŏnsă Ăd Hŏc Īntĕrrŏgătă: Ūbī Dīcărĕ Ĕst?!	Evil rat with red eyes, transform into the filthy man you were, but you must tell me where Dīcărĕ is!
Născī Flămmărūm	To Be Born of Flames
Nŏctă Bōnă, Alaĕna!	Good night Alaĕna!
O Ūnă Vulnerătă, Ămō Tĕ. Ūnă Vulnerătă, Vīvă Ĕt Spīră! Aŭdī Ăd Vōcĕm Mĕăm! Aŭdī Ăd Cŏncōrdīăm Mĕăm! Aŭdī Ĕt Sănă! Aŭdī Ăd Cărmĕn Mĕūm! Aŭdī, Ūnă Vulnerătă, Ŏb Ămō Tĕ, Lūcĕm!	O wounded one, I love you. Live and breathe! Listen to my voice! Listen to my harmony! Listen and heal! Listen to my song! Listen, for I love you, Light!
Ŏstīūm, Pătĕfĕcī!	Door, open! *Or* Open Door!
Pătĕr	Father
Păx Ăd Tĕrrăm Per Măgōs Latīnōs Ĕt Ūnīcornĕs Vōlătīcĕs.	Peace to the world through the Latin Magicians and Flying Unicorns.
Prō Īăm	For now
Prōmīttō Nŏn Prōmīssīō Mĕă Prīmă Cŏnfĕcĕrĕ!	I promise not to fulfill my first promise!
Pūĕr/Pūĕrī	Boy/boys
Quīd In Tĕrră Īllud Ĕst?	What in the world is that?
Quĭd In Tĕrră?	What in the world?
Quōmōdō In Tĕrră Īllud Pro Optimum Ĕst? Hōc Nŏn Possĕ Prō Ŏptīmum! Nŭnquăm, Dīcărĕ, Nŭnquăm!	How in the world is that for the best? This cannot be for the best! Never, Dīcărĕ, Never!

Rĕdĕ Īn Vīrūm!	Turn back into a man!
Rĕdĕ Vīrĕ!	Return, man!
Sălvĕ Amīca Parvă Mĕa!	Hello my small friend!
Sălvĕ/Sălvĕtĕ	The first is the singular version of *Hello* the second is the plural version of *Hello*
Sălvĕtĕ, Bartholomew Ĕt Jacob	Hello, Bartholomew and Jacob
Scĭĕntĭă Tūă Latīnī Crĕvī Pōstquăm Ultīmūs Tĕmpūs Vīdō Tĕ.	Your knowledge of Latin grew since the last time I saw you.
Sĕpīa Vōlătīcă	Flying Cuttlefish
Sīs, Sīstă Plŭī!	Please, stop raining!
Sīstă!	Stop!
Sphaĕra Lūcīs Fŭlvīs, Vĕnī Ĕt Īnsĕquī Mē!	Orb of auburn light, come and follow me!
Stătīs Ībī Ĕt Spĕctătīs Ăpŭd Mē, Cŭr?	You are standing there and staring at me, why?
Stlăttărīa	Sea-Born
Tĕrră	Land or Earth
Tĕrră Sīlvărum Ĕt Flūvĭŏrūm Dīvīsī Īn Bōnūm Ĕt Mălūm.	Land of the forests and of the rivers divided into good and evil.
Ūnīcornīs Vōlătīcīs	Flying Unicorn
Vălĕ, Frătĕr Mĕūs, Nōs Cōnvĕnīrĕm Rĕrsūs, Ūtinăm, Sĕd Prōmīttō Rĕddĕrĕ Ăd Tĕ, Ūtinăm Pŏssūm.	Goodbye, my brother, we will meet again, if only, but I promise to return to you.

Vălĕ, Germăna Mĕa!	Goodbye, my sister!
Vălĕ/Vălĕtĕ	Goodbye (singular)/ Goodbye (plural)
Vălĕrĕ Īubĕrĕ	To bid farewell or Farewell
Vătĕs Fūtūrōrūm	Seer (or Prophet) of the Future
Vīta Lyrārūm	Life of Songs
Vīvūm!	Man Alive!
Vŏx	Voice

Key to the Symbols

The symbol "˘" is properly called a Breve.

A Breve is an upward-faced, rounded "V" that shortens a vowel. It is commonly used in Latin, Greek, as well as many modern day languages.

I used the Breve above the letters "A", "E", "I", "O".

The symbol "¯" is properly called a Macron.

A Macron is a short line placed above a letter. It lengthens a vowel. It is commonly used in Latin, Greek, as well as many modern languages.

END